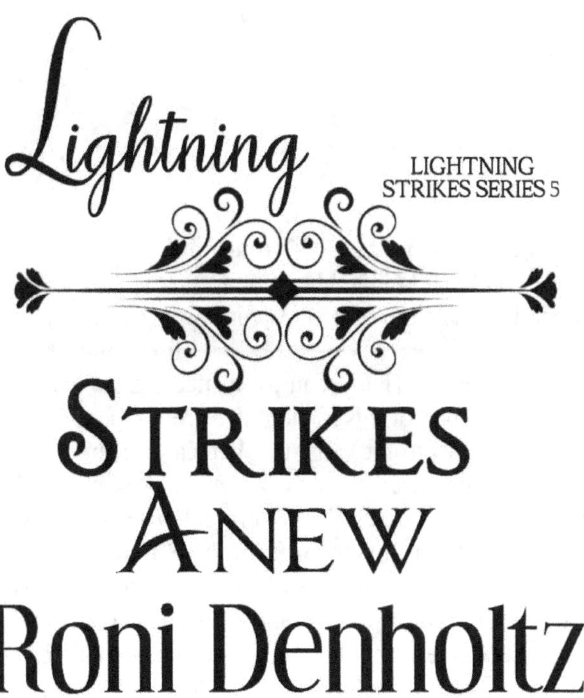

Lightning

LIGHTNING
STRIKES SERIES 5

Strikes Anew

Roni Denholtz

Lindsay wondered if she was developing the ability to read people's thoughts, an ability which her boss had after he and his twin had been struck by lightning at a young age. It would be exciting if she was developing *any* ability! And so satisfying.

She looked around again. Everyone appeared immersed in their work. Perhaps someone in another room had thought of her? It would be wonderful if she'd zeroed in on their thoughts!

She refocused on her laptop. She was just going to switch the screen to her work email when she felt that sensation shoot through her again, then heard footsteps near her.

The steps paused, near her cubicle. She looked up.
"Hello, Lindsay."
Brian Clarkson, her first love, stood there.

DEDICATION

For My Wonderful Friend and Critique Partner

Elizabeth John

With Heartfelt Love and Thanks for Our Years of
Friendship, Support

And sharing our Writing Journeys!

ACKNOWLEDGMENTS

Many thanks
to my insightful critique partners
Elizabeth John and Mia Lansford
And
My editor extraordinaire
Judi Fennell
And
Thank you to my niece
Tracy L. Denholtz
For advice on the workings of the NJ legal system
Any mistakes are purely my own.

CHAPTER I

I should have expected this. I should have known.

Lindsay Hughes stared at the list in front of her as an electrical charge swept through her body. Every molecule within her went to high alert.

Brian Clarkson. His name had alarm bells ringing—and a compelling awareness—inside her. Brian Clarkson—her first love. And he was coming here, today.

She should have guessed he would end up as a client here.

Brian Clarkson was coming to The Lightning Center today—her place of employment------and the chances were high she would run into him at some point.

She couldn't stop the unwanted tingling all over.

Lindsay swallowed. It shouldn't shock her that he would be a client of The Lightning Center. It was the premier center for testing and research on people who had been struck by lightning and developed abilities like ESP, precognitive dreams, and more. She knew very well that Brian had been struck by lightning when he was a teenager; and subsequently developed the ability to see ghosts. The spirits of the dead who were hanging around or looking out for their loved ones. He was not the first to see those entities.

The Lightning Center had opened about five years ago, so it hadn't existed when he'd been struck by lightning. But it was here now, and he must have found out about their research.

When she'd gotten the job here—to her delight— she should have expected to someday see her old boyfriend. After all, it wasn't as if there were a lot of facilities doing this kind of research—and definitely not in New Jersey.

She looked up and saw her coworkers gathering around the oval table in the conference and break room. Some, like her, were reviewing the list of today's clients; others were pouring themselves cups of coffee or grabbing a bagel or muffin.

She focused again on her iPad. *Brian Clarkson.*

Okay, so she'd probably run into her old boyfriend. She'd just have to deal with it. She sat up straighter. She was a professional; she could handle this awkward situation. What was the worst that could happen?

Parker Costigan—their staff neurologist, director, and the inspiration behind The Lightning Center—called the meeting to order. They started every morning by reviewing the information gathered from the previous day, then the plans for today.

"We have a busy day," he said, glancing around. He quickly reviewed highlights of yesterday's sessions and exams, and ended with "…and Mrs. Fisher's basic ESP evaluation was much higher than normal."

"We have to put her at ease," his twin, Dr. Pamela Costigan Lassiter, who was the main psychiatrist at The Lightning Center, said from beside him. She glanced at the other employees seated around the table. "She's having anxiety about her new-found ability--precognitive dreams."

"Since you have the same ability, I'm positive you can help her," Parker said to Pam.

People nodded. They all knew Pam was a wonderful psychiatrist and great with people.

After everyone had spoken about the testing or meetings with clients from the day before, they went on to do a quick summary of today's activities.

"My father will be doing the usual general assessment of our new patients' health," Parker stated, with a glance at his dad, Dr. Edward Costigan, who was a general practitioner. All patients had a basic health assessment by him or by Larry Weissman, their other GP. Both of them were semi-retired and worked part time at the Center.

Afterwards, their new patients would meet with Parker, their neurologist; plus Meredith Costigan Belton, their social worker; and one of their psychiatrists, either Dr. Pamela or her husband, Dr. Evan Lassiter. Then the patient would be tested over the next few weeks for ESP, and for their specific ability, by one of the research team members, like herself.

"Doreen Danvers has experienced extra sensory perception episodes since she was struck by lightning four years ago. She comes from Easton, Pennsylvania and recently learned about our studies here.

"Brian Clarkson was struck quite a few years ago," Parker continued. "He heard about us through Evan," he angled his head towards his colleague and brother-in-law.

Evan took up the conversation. "He went to my high school, and we were both on the swim team, and in the national honor society. We grew up in the same neighborhood but hung out mostly with different friends, since he's a couple of years younger than me. He saw an article on line about me working for The Lightning Center and got in touch with me. I recommended he come in."

"That's interesting," Sabrina Costigan, their dark-haired reference librarian who was married to Parker, said. "I'll add that to our notes about how all these people are finding us in case we want to do a more complete study on that, since we don't advertise."

So far they hadn't needed to, Lindsay knew. Most of their patients came from word-of-mouth, doctor referrals, or research recommendations from other institutions and universities. Their clients and studies here were rapidly expanding, which is why new staff members like herself had been hired recently.

Once the initial interviews and assessments were completed, their new patients would be assigned to one of the psychic testers here, like herself.

She definitely didn't want Brian to be assigned to her!

Rather than bringing that up at the general meeting, she planned to speak to her boss Parker or to his older sister Meredith, whom Lindsay knew best on the staff, about the fact that she and Brian had a history. It would be better if he was tested by someone else--someone more objective. She was certain they'd agree with her assessment.

Parker had moved on to reviewing the other patients being tested today, and who was testing them. She refocused on what he was saying.

"Mrs. Smith will be tested by Courtney, and Lindsay, you're assigned to test Mrs. Kearns and Mr. Parillo today."

"I'd also like to speak to Lindsay about a recent study I found out of a university in North Carolina on people who've seen ghosts. Since she did grad work on that subject. I think she'll want to hear about this research." Sabrina looked directly at Lindsay. "Will you have time between your testing subjects?"

"I'll make the time," Lindsay answered. "Between three and four would be best."

"Okay, please come to the library then." Sabrina, a former reference librarian, ran their extensive research library, which was used not only by their staff, but by interested students and patients. She spear-headed much of their research.

"Great." Lindsay made a note to herself on her iPad.

"And Ashish, I'm assigning Mrs. Pepper to you for her annual evaluation. You tested her last year. That's it for today. Any questions?" Parker asked.

No one had a question, so Parker dismissed everyone. "Have a great day."

As soon as people got up, and began to leave the room, Lindsay moved over to Meredith. "Can I speak to you? Whenever it's convenient," she said in a low voice.

"Sure." Meredith gave her sunny smile. "I have some time now before I have to meet my first client."

"It's kind of personal," Lindsay whispered. "But I have a few minutes now."

"Come to my office," Meredith whispered back.

Lindsay followed the redhead back to her office nearby, on the first floor. When they were inside, Meredith shut the door and waved at the chair beside her desk and Lindsay dropped into it.

When Lindsay had become serious in college about pursuing a career in psychic research, she'd learned about The Lightning Center starting up and their unusual mission: to study those struck by lightning who'd developed different psychic abilities. She'd written to TLC and developed a correspondence with Meredith Costigan— now Meredith Belton. who had her doctorate in social work and was one of the few staff members at TLC who didn't have an innate psychic ability herself, either from being born with one or from being struck by lightning and developing one afterwards. However, Meredith had proven one of the Lightning Center's theories: that with practice, you could learn to develop or improve your ESP skills. Meredith had done this. Lindsay and Meredith had kept in touch via email and when Lindsay was finishing her doctorate, Meredith had urged her to apply for one of the job openings here, since they were expanding their staff. Meredith had supported her application, as had Evan Lassiter, who remembered her from high school, despite being several years ahead of her.

"What's on your mind?" Meredith asked softly.

Lindsay swallowed. "I would prefer if you could assign Brian Clarkson to another psychic tester other than me, each time he's tested."

Meredith's eyes widened. "You don't want to work with him? Why—oh," she sat back and gazed at Lindsay. "Is he the one who got you interested in psychic phenomena, then broke off your relationship?"

"Yes," Lindsay admitted. "We were dating in high school when I was a sophomore, and he was a senior." And they'd gotten serious very quickly. "We were constantly together." She'd told Meredith the basic story, once before, but she wanted to be sure she understood all the implications. "He was struck by lightning that April and developed the ability to sometimes see the spirits of those who had passed on, hanging around their loved ones."

Meredith nodded. "That's what sparked your interest in psychic abilities." She toyed with her wedding band. Meredith was married to Richard Belton, a meteorologist who was known for his expertise on lightning. It had been her job to convince him to come work for TLC.

"I was so fascinated I made psychic research my life's work," Lindsay said. "But after two years of being involved, Brian broke up with me, and it broke my heart." And he'd scoffed when she told him of her plans to study parapsychology.

That day was still vivid in her mind. She'd wanted to shrivel up and die. She'd truly loved Brian, even though they were young, and she'd been convinced that he loved her too. "Plus, my mother was sick. It made everything worse. I felt that the world was coming to an end."

Meredith got up and laid a hand on Lindsay's shoulder. Lindsay sent her friend a wan smile. She appreciated her kindness. Meredith sat back down and waited for her to continue.

Lindsay's voice came out in a choked whisper. "I truly loved him. He didn't comprehend that. He thought that I only cared for him the way you would care for a lab specimen, that I was more interested in research than anything else. Just because I kept asking him questions! And he felt—stifled, he said. Like I wouldn't give him space."

Meredith nodded. "I can understand how hurt you were."

"I became more determined than ever to show him, and prove to everyone—and myself—that I was serious about my studies." She didn't try to mask the anger now tinging her voice.

"Try to remember you were both young when that happened," Meredith said. "Young people sometimes do hurtful or stupid things."

"Yes, but I still believe I really loved Brian. I'd rather keep any contact with him to a minimum." She knew it could be awkward, at best, to interact with him.

She'd run into Brian a couple of times in the town

where they'd grown up. Their interactions had been uncomfortable.

"Yes, you're right.," Meredith said. "But Lindsay, you might run into him here."

"I can handle superficial interactions," Lindsay stated. "I don't want to have any influence on his test results." Since she'd had such an intense reaction to seeing his name, she knew it could be difficult to remain neutral around her first love. But she'd deal with it.

"I'll definitely discuss it with Parker and Pam." The three siblings were the brains behind the Center.

"Thank you so much." Lindsay said. She stood up, sending Meredith a brief smile.

As she left the office, she could almost feel Meredith staring after her.

Meredith sent an email to her brother and sister asking to speak to them during the afternoon, and they agreed.

"What did you want to discuss?" Pam asked, sitting beside Meredith.

"Lindsay Hughes. She asked that she not be the one to test Brian Clarkson, when he's ready for psychic testing."

"Did she give you a reason?" Parker, a studious man, appeared curious.

But Pamela, his twin sister, frowned.

"She said they had a prior relationship in high school that ended badly," Meredith said.

"She did mention the relationship to me after she started working here," Pam said. "But not the guy's name. Just that she was in love with a guy who thought she only cared about his psychic ability, not him as a person."

"You got it," Meredith said.

Parker leaned forward. "That guy was Brian?"

"Yes, but let's keep this to ourselves," Meredith said.

"Evan probably knows their history." Pam also leaned forward. "He was on the swim team with Brian and they grew up in the same neighborhood in Monroe Township. He knew Lindsay only slightly in high school, since she was younger—but you know in high school, everyone knows the status of everyone else."

Parker nodded. "Of course we can honor her request. We have plenty of researchers and testers on our staff. We'll keep this private. And their emotions might interfere with test results."

"Not so fast," Pam interjected. "She needs to interact with him sometimes."

Her brother and sister turned to look at her, their mouths open.

"Why?" Meredith asked.

"Because I believe they could end up together." Pam gripped the arms of her chair. "I had a very vivid dream just last night about them in each other's arms."

Everyone knew Pam's especially realistic dreams were precognitive dreams that usually came true. She had even dreamed about ending up with her husband Evan when they were still enemies.

"How do you know it was Brian?" Meredith asked.

"I met him when he came in for his general check up with dad."

"I see." Parker picked up a pen and tapped it on his desk, a thoughtful expression on his face.

Meredith smiled at her younger sister. "I love your romantic dreams."

Pam had dreamed about Parker falling in love with Sabrina long before he'd met her. The siblings had been amazed when Sabrina came to TLC seeking help with her astral projections.

"Ok, so suppose she doesn't test him? He's going to be here on architectural matters," Parker reminded them. "They could run into each other by chance as he's working and drawing up his plans."

Evan had recommended Brian for redesigning the office space for their research and testing staff, which was growing rapidly. He knew a psychiatric group who had used Brian last year. The Lightning Center presently used the cubicles that originally came with their office building for the psychic research team; but he, Pam and Meredith and the staff wanted something more aesthetic and functional. And then if they were happy with the job Brian did, they were going to approach him about designing the dog day care center and a child day care center they wanted to build in the back acreage they owned behind the Center.

Pam nodded now. "I guess that could work. Leave it up to fate."

Meredith added, "I agree with Parker. If Lindsay tests him, and gives off negative vibes, it may affect the test results."

"True." But Pam still frowned. "But trust me, guys. It's my instinct that they are meant to be together. They'll need to interact sometimes."

Back at her desk, Lindsay checked the time. Mr. Parillo would be here in forty minutes. Since this was the first time she was testing him, she was giving him the standard ESP test today. Later she or others would repeat the tests, then test him for his specific ability, the ability he'd shown to predict earthquakes, something they hadn't seen often at the Center.

She expected that like most of their subjects, he would test higher than the average person on the ESP test.

She was getting the cards she'd use ready when she felt a strange sensation go through her head. A kind of tingling. It wasn't anything that she'd felt before. Glancing around, she noted her coworkers appeared busy with their own tasks in their cubicles. Why was she getting this odd feeling? Was someone else thinking about her, and she'd somehow caught their thoughts? She bit her lip.

Lindsay had been practicing for years to increase her ESP abilities from average to something better. Meredith, who had successfully worked on improving her own ESP, had been her mentor and told Lindsay which exercises she'd practiced herself over the years.

Lindsay wondered if she was developing the ability to read people's thoughts, an ability which Parker had after he and his twin Pamela had been struck by lightning at a young age. It would be exciting if she was developing *any* ability! And so satisfying.

She looked around again. Everyone appeared immersed in their work. Perhaps someone in another room had thought of her, like Meredith? It would be wonderful if she'd zeroed in on their thoughts!

She refocused on her laptop. Her schedule for the day was pulled up on her monitor. After Mr. Parillo, her late afternoon appointment, she could leave. She was just going to switch the screen to her work email when she felt that sensation shoot through her again, then heard footsteps near her.

The steps paused, near her cubicle. She looked up.
"Hello, Lindsay."
Brian Clarkson stood there.

CHAPTER II

A tremor swept through her, and Lindsay tried not to stare at Brian.

He was here? But he wasn't scheduled for testing today. Just his doctor appointments.

Then she took in his clipboard and the measuring instrument in his hand. Belatedly she remembered that last week Parker had mentioned that a commercial architect would be visiting TLC in preparation for making some changes to the research and testing area of their office building. The area she worked in.

"Hi." Her shaky voice reverberated

He was studying her, so she took the opportunity to gaze at him. A crisp, clean, masculine scent wafted to her—different than the strong aftershave and bodywash he used to use. She liked it.

Brian was an attractive man, and in the years since she'd last seen him, he not only looked older and more mature,, but his demeanor was now that of a confident, professional man. Not merely the cute college guy whom she'd loved. Brian's face was handsome, and his blue-gray eyes were fringed with thick lashes. She'd always been jealous that he had better lashes than her. His hair was dark brown, and still wavy.

She swallowed and strove to control her tone. "How

are you, Brian?" Glancing around, she saw several of her coworkers looking at them. Had those people who had ESP caught her swirling emotions?

She stood up. Her heart rate accelerated, and her mouth dried. "You look well."

"So do you." He smiled.

They stood awkwardly. Did he want to talk? She indicated the door. "Everyone's busy working. Come in to one of our testing rooms," she invited, her voice pitched low so they wouldn't disturb those who were concentrating.

She led the way on legs that trembled slightly, cursing herself for such a strong physical reaction to seeing her first love. Why couldn't she feel nothing at all? Why did she have to have such an intense reaction? Her nerves radiated a tension she wasn't happy about feeling.

Brian, on the other hand, looked unperturbed. He wore a neutral expression.

He had sought her out! Why? She wondered.

She walked ahead to the first testing room, an amazing alertness sweeping through her

The walls of the room were a stark white and plain, without photos or pictures, allowing for no distractions that might impede psychic tests. The mini-blinds were down and pulled tight. Little light and noise could enter the space.

She sat in the chair usually occupied by the researcher, and waved him into the chair on the other side of the table for subjects.

Facing him, she tried to assume a simply curious expression despite her thudding heart. "How are you doing, Brian?"

"Fine. How about you?"

They sounded like the most casual of acquaintances, she thought, not former lovers.

He wasn't going to make this easy, she thought. "How are your parents? Do they still live in the same house?" He'd grown up in a neighborhood not far from hers, with larger homes on bigger lots. He'd lived just down the street from Evan Lassiter's family, in Monroe.

"They're fine, healthy and still living in the same house." He hesitated. "My father had a heart procedure last year, but he's been healthy since then."

"And you live there?" Her heart continued to beat more rapidly than usual. She willed it to slow down, without success.

"No, I moved to a place in Morris Township. A condo. Kind of a standard condo, but it's spacious and near my office."

"Nice." Her tone remained neutral, but she was still sitting tensely. "You're here to make changes in our research and testing area?"

"Yes. Right now I need to see how it's being used currently. Then I can figure out improvements." He smiled.

"You always wanted to be an architect."

"Yes." He nodded.

She studied him. "Well, I don't want to keep you from your work."

"I'll see you around," he said, and smiled again.

After he left, Lindsay sat for a moment, then let out a relieved breath and tried to relax her muscles. That hadn't been so terrible. If she ran into him again—and she would--she could handle it. She had just proved that to herself.

Except she'd had such a strong physical reaction to her old boyfriend.

Would it have been different if their relationship hadn't ended badly?

She stood, intending to go back to her desk. Instead, she walked over to the ladies' room. Once there she dampened a paper towel and touched it to her neck, attempting to cool off.

Of all the architects there must be in the area, why did her first boyfriend end up with this job?

But she could guess the answer.

Brian Clarkson had been struck by lightning and developed the ability to see departed spirits, as they liked to say. So he was also here for testing and guidance in adjusting to his ability, which he had felt conflicted about in the past. Plus, he could enhance their studies and help TLC's research.

And perhaps learn to better cope with his strange gift, and the repercussions.

"C'mon in," Evan invited, and Brian sat in the chair in front of his friend's desk later that afternoon.

"Parker said you asked to speak with me," Evan added as he too sat down.

"Yes. When Parker told me every client here speaks to a psychiatrist, I told him I'd like to speak to you." Brian leaned back. He'd just finished studying The Lightning Center's office space for the second time—his first visit, with Parker Costigan, had been when they were closed on Sunday—and today he'd checked his measurements and refined his ideas, now that he'd had a quick chance to observe how the people worked in those spaces. He'd need to study them at work again soon,

He'd already had his general check-up with Edward

Costigan this morning, followed by a neurologic work up by Parker Costigan. He'd figured if he could see Evan this afternoon after doing some of his architectural work, he would make good use of his time and wouldn't have to return immediately. Thus avoiding seeing the woman who had been his first love and his strong reaction to seeing her earlier. Nostalgia—regret—caring—guilt--all the confusing emotions had hit him when he ran into Lindsay Hughes.

"Tell me about the day you were struck by lightning," Evan said, also leaning back in his chair.

"I was a high school senior—like you—and it was a warm day in April. I'd been walking home from the bus stop, looking forward to the day I'd get my own car—which would be in a few weeks-- and be able to drive. Usually my friend Kyle dropped me off, but that day he had a club meeting so I took the bus. It was partly sunny, partly cloudy. Then out of the blue I felt a zap in my back, like something burning." He could almost feel the sensation as he spoke.

"Did you fall down, or collapse?"

"I fell to my knees-- it hurt! I wasn't even sure what had happened, but the kid walking behind me shouted was I okay? and said he saw lightning hit me." Brian grimaced. He could still recall that sudden, sharp pain. "I got up and stumbled home, and called my mother. My parents were at work. My older brother was away at college. My mom said she'd be home in ten minutes. She made it in eight. She called an ambulance when she saw the mark on my back."

"How were you feeling?"

"It still hurt—though not as bad—and I felt scared."

"What happened after that?" Evan asked.

Brian looked at him. "The ER couldn't find anything wrong, even after they checked my vitals and did a Cat-scan. So they discharged me. Everything seemed normal for a couple of weeks.

"Then I saw my father's mother's ghost hanging around him one night. She had died about four years before."

"And your reaction?"

"I thought I was daydreaming or imagining it or something. But then I saw her again a few days later, and told my parents. My father--he's a lawyer and is very logical and almost scientific—found it hard to believe, until I described her clothes. Then my mother—she's a lawyer too-- said she remembered that outfit. My mom had an easier time believing me. She's always been interested in the occult, as she put it."

Evan nodded. "My own parents were both surprised at the research we're doing here, and that I chose to get involved when Pamela and I got back together. But after their initial surprise, they were supportive. So I understand what you went through."

"Yeah, well, after I saw more souls or whatever you want to call them, my dad came around too."

"That's fortunate." Evan leaned back in his chair, and Brian found himself relaxing as well. "Not all parents are so understanding," Evan continued.

"This went on for a few months. But then I had a kind of bad experience." Brian paused.

"I had a girlfriend in high school, and I was head over heels for her." He frowned, remembering details of his relationship with Lindsay. "You probably remember that."

Lindsay Hughes had always been a cute girl, and she

had pursued him once he gave her a little encouragement. He'd been a senior and she'd been a sophomore, but they'd fallen in love after they'd been dating for several months.

"I thought she loved me too—and it got serious fast." Enough for them to get intimate when she'd turned sixteen that summer and he'd been eighteen. "It was about twelve years ago. She was my first love--and first lover," he admitted.

"Lindsay told us about your--relationship." Evan put it delicately. "She wanted to be up front with us about her past experiences with the paranormal when we hired her. Because we ask all our employees how they became interested in psychic abilities. She didn't use specific names, but I realized you were the guy she spoke about. I remembered how you guys had been constantly together back in high school although I didn't know then you'd been struck by lightning."

Brian shifted in his seat, suddenly bombarded with memories. Lindsay had been both sweet and passionate— making him a very happy guy. He could recall her soft breasts, her silky skin—he had to stop thinking like this, and concentrate on speaking with Evan.

When he'd seen Lindsay earlier he was affected much more than he'd let on. Lindsay was absolutely stunning now. She'd developed from a slim teen to a still slim and gorgeous woman with curves in all the right places,. Her dark hair was shiny and thick, making him itch to run his fingers through the satiny strands. Her lips looked even more kissable than years ago. And her breasts were more lush-looking in the bright green sweater she was wearing today than when she'd been young. "Yes, well…" he shifted in his chair. "I never forgot her. But she hurt my feelings., and it caused me to break up with her."

"Can you talk about that? I'd like to hear," Evan encouraged him.

Brian nodded. He'd first contacted Evan after reading an article on-line about his old friend and swim teammate. Brian had been fascinated learning about the research The Lightning Center was doing. He had hoped to contribute to their studies, and also to better understand what he'd been through, and come to terms with his ability. When he first met them, Evan and Parker had reassured him that everything that went on here was kept confidential as far as names were concerned. And he'd discovered that their research was ground-breaking.

"After I was struck by lightning, she asked me tons of questions and seemed to always be studying me and anything I said or did. I started to feel like I was nothing but a lab specimen to her," Brian said. "She was fascinated by my experiences, and started reading and researching psychic abilities. She wanted to spend most of our time together talking about that. She was actually proud the day that she told me her ambition was to go into psychic research as a career! I admit I put her down. I didn't realize it was a real area of research at that time. I started to feel that had become mostly the basis for our relationship. I ended up resenting her.

"Not only that," Brian rushed on, "but she was becoming very clingy—wanting to be constantly with me everywhere I went, after school and on weekends. I felt stifled by her so many times." He frowned. "Looking back, I believe maybe I should have been more understanding. It was about that time that her mother's cancer came back and she was going downhill. But I felt like I couldn't do anything without Lindsay, go anywhere by myself, or with my friends--and I resented it."

Evan nodded, his expression sympathetic. He laced his fingers together.

"One day I couldn't take it anymore, and I suggested we needed some time apart. She reacted badly, crying and saying I'd broken her heart. Maybe—maybe I had." His words came out starkly.

"Both of you were still teenagers," Evan pointed out. "It's not surprising that your relationship didn't last."

"I felt so guilty—I still do," Brian added.

"That's understandable. We can work on that," Evan said. "But there's no reason for a person to continue in a relationship that is uncomfortable for them."

Brian sighed. "I should have been more understanding."

"Again, you were young. Perhaps she should have been more understanding too," Evan suggested.

He hadn't thought of that. "I did run into her a couple of times, in town," Brian said. "I tried to be nice, say hello. Maybe I thought there was a chance we could start over. She was the most caring girlfriend I ever had. But she was so cold to me each time I saw her. I think she was still hurt," he admitted. "I went to the wake with my parents, when Lindsay's mother died; but she was so distraught I don't think she even noticed."

"Maybe she was simply acting out of hurt feelings. As far as the wake—people often are overwhelmed with all the people going through," Evan said, smiling kindly.

"I realized a couple of years later, when I thought back on that time, that maybe I should have been more understanding," Brian repeated. "And more supportive of her career choice. After all, I had healthy parents who cared about each other. She didn't. Her parents were divorced by the time we started going out."

"But you were a young man—very young—and you can't be expected to solve everyone else's problems," Evan pointed out, tapping a pen on his desk blotter. "Teens tend to be immature until they reach a certain level of adulthood, and you were dealing with suddenly acquiring this new and strange ability. Let's discuss that further."

"Yes, I did feel like I was a freak sometimes. But I should have been more understanding," Brian said, reverting back to the earlier topic and shaking his head.

"We'll work on your feeling better about your decisions," Evan promised. "And handling your special 'talent'."

As they continued speaking about Brian's conflicting emotions, he told Evan how he'd been both excited and afraid of his new-found talent. Evan's soothing voice helped Brian to relax. A little

But he still felt guilt weaving through him every time his thoughts flew back to Lindsay.

Would Lindsay forgive him for ignoring her feelings? Did he even want her to? Would it make him feel better if she did forgive him?

He discussed his mixed emotions, both towards Lindsay and about his ability to see spirits. He continued speaking with Evan, and they finished up his session. He scheduled his next one, and gathered his architectural notes. But he had a sneaking suspicion those thoughts about his first love would haunt him tonight, when he was home.

CHAPTER III

Well, *that was awkward,* Lindsay thought as she packed up her tote at the end of the day. Since it was Wednesday she wasn't working tonight, so she could go home and relax. She wanted to mull over the brief but strained encounter with Brian and she wanted to discuss it with one of her friends.

She shoved the last of her notes and her iPad inside the tote. She could tell her younger sister Jessica what had occurred. But Jessica hated the fact that Brian had hurt Lindsay badly and would not understand her impulse to be nice to him. Lindsay barely understood it herself. Plus, Jessica's view of men had been decidedly negative for years. She hardly spoke to their father since the incident that tore their family apart. And just last year Jessica had had a bad break up with the guy she was seeing.

Lindsay knew enough to recognize that Jessica's pattern of dating different guys, then splitting with them when things got too serious, had roots in their family's history. While she, Lindsay, had had the opposite reaction, clinging to relationships which had already deteriorated because she wanted to maintain the status quo. She sighed at her introspective thoughts.

Once back at her apartment, which was only five minutes from the office, she trudged inside and up the stairs, dropped her purse and tote beside the living room couch, and kicked off her shoes. She washed up and changed to yoga pants and a long-sleeved T shirt, then took a can of diet cola from the fridge and plopped down on the sofa to think.

She wanted to call someone. Maybe not her sister, but someone. Her best friend Carolyn, who she'd known since third grade, lived and worked about an hour south of northwest New Jersey, the location of The Lightning Center, or as they affectionately referred to it as, TLC.. But Carolyn was busy on Wednesday nights with a grad school course. Carolyn was a teacher who was studying part time for her master's degree.

She thought about her other close high school friends, Jade and Krista. She wasn't as close with them and she'd be meeting them and Carolyn for lunch in a couple of weeks, so they'd have plenty of time to talk then.

She decided to call Danielle, her best friend from college. When Lindsay got voicemail she just left a message saying hello. Lindsay knew Danielle was pretty busy with her fiancé right now, choosing things like the wedding venue and music.

So she lounged by herself on the couch. She couldn't help going over the scene with Brian in her mind. Why had she had such a strong reaction to him? He was definitely attractive, and she'd always thought he looked hot in a kind of nerdy, cute scientific way. Was it the simple attraction of a woman to a good-looking guy that she was experiencing? Or was she experiencing emotions because of their shared past?

Her mind drifted back to days long gone, when she'd run into him between high school classes, or he'd stolen a kiss in back of the building after school. And then there were the times they'd made out in the basement rec room in his house when his parents weren't home, or in her house when Jessica was out with her own friends and her mother was out with hers.

Thinking about those times alone with him, remembering how he'd gently held her during the times she cried when her mother was getting worse, or the times their kisses had turned passionate and they'd made sweet love, she heard a sound and realized a sob had escaped her. And tears were sliding down her face.

Angry at herself, she grabbed a tissue and wiped her face. But the tears continued to trickle down. She'd loved him so much, and had wanted to spend forever with him!

But Brian had walked away, leaving her heart shattered. And she'd been so terribly alone.

As Brian drove home, he thought about his session with Evan. About his desire to break up with Lindsay years ago, and the guilt that had never quite left him.

Was Evan right, and some of this was ordinary teenage angst? What if they had stayed together? Would one of them have broken it off later? He had done what he wanted, and split up with her. He'd done what was best for *him*.

He'd been mostly okay feeling that way for years. But seeing her again, being near enough to touch her silky hair, smell her feminine perfume, he wasn't so sure he'd done the right thing. She'd needed him, needed his support when they were both young and she was especially vulnerable. And he hadn't been there for her.

Evan had promised him they would work together

on his mixed emotions. Like any psychiatrist, Evan wanted him to feel better.

But no one could tell him how to feel right now.

And at this instant he was thinking about another chance for him and Lindsay.

Was he crazy to be thinking of that at this point in his life? They'd both moved on.

Maybe…

Thursdays were their busiest days at The Lightning Center with "all hands on deck." Every employee was there for the total 12 hours they were open, in case one needed to consult with another.

They began the morning with their standard meeting, going over quick summaries of the patients seen yesterday, and plans for those who were being seen today. Parker did report that architect Brian Clarkson would be around over the weekend to see him, Meredith and Pamela to discuss his ideas for renovating the psychic research and testing area before submitting his final drawings. Lindsay wasn't surprised that he'd be having another discussion with the siblings.

Fortunately, every other Saturday the staff worked only a half day and the other Saturdays they were off. Lindsay vowed to herself she'd steer clear of Brian until she had a better handle on her emotions. Yesterday had proved she still had feelings for him, buried deeply.

Evan's report on his session with Brian was brief. Brian had talked about his mixed emotions about having an ability after being struck by lightning. Many of their patients reported the exact same confusion.

After the meeting concluded, Lindsay's morning

started with giving a young woman the standard ESP test all their new patients received. Sarah, had been struck by lightning six months ago and now saw ghosts on occasion—just like Brian.

As they finished, Sarah asked her, "Can I tell you something?" in a nervous voice.

"Sure."

"There is a—a spirit near you. I think—it's your mother."

Her mother?

Lindsay stared at Sarah.

"My-my mom?" she squeaked out.

Sarah nodded. "I think that's what she's indicating. She does look a little like you. She appears to be watching over you."

After her mother had died, Lindsay had prayed for weeks for a sign from her that she was at peace in the afterlife. Or perhaps that Brian, with his ability to sometimes see ghosts, would see her. And maybe she'd give him a message like "make up with Lindsay." Her teenage self had yearned for that so badly.

But if Brian had ever seen her mother after she passed, or gotten a message from Deena Hughes, he had never spoken about it. And gradually those heartfelt prayers had stopped. She went on with her life, coping as best she could with the devastating loss; trying to be a good big sister to Jessica as well.

Oh, she had certainly dreamt about her mother in the ensuing years. And she comforted herself that the dreams might have been signs that her mother was happy and now healthy, in Heaven. She had even discussed it with their minister, a kind woman who also agreed that God had sent her a sign that her mother was in Heaven watching over her.

She hadn't discussed it with her father. He had already divorced her mother and married his new wife, Kaycee, by the time Deena died. Lindsay had tried talking to her sister Jessica but Jessica had retorted angrily that she didn't believe in anything. Lindsay knew she'd taken their mother's illness, the divorce and Deena's subsequent death even harder than Lindsay had, and Jessica, who hadn't been as optimistic a child as Lindsay had been, had turned bitter about everything afterwards.

When she first began working at The Lightning Center, Lindsay had been introduced to Lorna, a volunteer on their staff. Lorna saw spirits and Lindsay had hoped she would tell her she saw Lindsay's mom. But it had never happened, much to her disappointment.

Now she stared at Sarah, her mouth open.

No patient had ever seen her mother before.

She shut her mouth. "Thank you for telling me." Lindsay's voice was hushed.

Sarah nodded. "She's fading now."

Lindsay had to force herself to concentrate on giving Sarah the ESP test and not think about Sarah's sighting of her mother. Still, when she escorted Sarah out, she felt a delayed shakiness.

Her mother was around.

Lindsay drew a sharp breath.

"Are you alright?" their receptionist asked Lindsay.

"I'm—fine." Lindsay abruptly turned and headed to get a cup of coffee.

Stirring her sweetener and milk into her mug, Lindsay thought about Sarah's seeing her mother, and that Sarah had a lot in common with Brian. He was an architect, and Sarah was an engineer. Lindsay knew Brian had had to take engineering courses as part of his education. Plus they both saw spirits. He might even meet her by accident at TLC.

She shook off the thought.

She had a few minutes before her next client, so she wandered into the library to speak with Sabrina, needing to do a normal activity.

"I'm wondering if you have those books I requested the other day?" she asked Sabrina.

"Of course, right here." Sabrina moved to a shelf where two books lay with a sticky note on the top one which read "For Lindsay." Handing them to her, she said, "I just ordered a new book of case studies of people who've seen ghosts, written by a professor in Denver. It sounds interesting."

"Let me know when it comes in!" Lindsay said.

"Of course." Sabrina smiled.

Their reference librarian was brilliant at ferreting out useful information and keeping up with a variety of paranormal studies. Lindsay knew having her as a staff member was invaluable.

As she strode down the hall, she saw a tall figure emerge from the stairwell.

Lindsay slowed.

Wait… Brian couldn't be here again so soon, could he? He was supposed to be here on Saturday afternoon, when only Parker and his sisters would be around!

Her heart started to hammer as Brian moved to turn, then froze in place. His eyes met hers.

A tingling sensation moved through her.

CHAPTER IV

 rian stared at Lindsay.

It had been no shock to see her yesterday. He'd heard from friends in town that she worked here, and Evan had mentioned it as well. When he'd seen her yesterday he'd been surprised by her cool demeanor. She had changed from the cute, enthusiastic, and intense girl he remembered.

It had been a spur of the moment decision to come back again today. He wasn't sure he'd gotten the correct dimensions of the storage closet and that could mess up his architectural plans for the second floor research and testing area. He knew he could have waited until tomorrow to obtain the measurements. Still, he had a sneaking suspicion that his visit today had less to do with his compulsion to get everything right before talking to the Costigans, than it did to do with his desire to see Lindsay Hughes again.

She tilted her head up to look at him now, and he noticed her fingers tightened on the books she held.

"What are you doing here?" she asked, her voice a little gruff.

He pasted on a smile. "I need to check my measurements up here." He indicated with his hand the area he was going to renovate.

"Oh." She sounded stiff.

He studied her. She was as beautiful as she'd always been, darky wavy hair and wide brown eyes in a classically pretty face. She wore a gray pantsuit and a dark blue blouse. As he recalled her many attributes, he felt himself twitch.

He swallowed, and impulsively asked, "want to have a cup of coffee?"

"I have a client coming in a few minutes. Sorry." The words sounded clipped.

"Maybe another time." He tried to sound merely friendly.

"Maybe." She gave a brief smile, then walked away, towards the area she shared with her coworkers.

He stared after her. She was still as desirable as ever. He sucked in a breath.

She spun around suddenly. "Maybe another time." As she repeated his words, her voice sounded more friendly this time. Had she rethought his invitation?

"Okay." He smiled.

Walking slowly, he approached the storage closet, wondering at her change in attitude. And why he cared whether or not they met for coffee.

Ten minutes later Lindsay met her next client downstairs in their reception area, and brought him up to testing room #3. It looked like all the testing rooms were booked for this hour, as she saw Laura and Courtney leading their subjects just ahead of her up the stairs.

Her heart was still hammering. Why did a simple brush with Brian make her heart pound like this? She hated that she was having this strong physical reaction.

"Today I have the second set of ESP tests, right?" her client asked

"Yes," Lindsay replied. "We test everyone for ESP twice when they first come in." She had explained that in their last session, but she sensed he was a little uneasy again. "Then, on your next two visits, we will do testing geared to your ability." She smiled at him, trying to reassure him.

"Okay." As they entered the small, starkly white room, he took a long, noisy breath. He seemed like a nervous type, although the tests today was standard. Pam had told them that he was a rather uneasy man, who had a generally negative outlook. Lindsay tried to put him at ease. "How you do isn't something you get a grade on," she stated. "We just have to get an idea of your general ability." She smiled, hoping her kind tone would reassure him.

Lindsay indicated the seat for him and sat across the table. She shuffled the large cards, each one marked with a shape.

"I'm sure you remember how this works from last time," Lindsay said, trying to calm the the man's worries. "Triangle, circle, square, wavy lines or a star is printed on each card."

"Yes," He took the test, and he did slightly above average—the same as on the first test she'd administered.

When he left, Lindsay had a break. Instead of studying one of the books from Sabrina, she sat and thought about what Sarah had seen, and about her encounter with Brian.

Should she meet him for coffee in the future? It really wasn't a pressing matter.

She knew that some members of the Lightning Center had dated, and later married, other staff members—like Meredith and Richard,

But had anyone dated a patient?

Yes, she reminded herself, she'd heard that Parker had gone out with Sabrina—when she was no longer a patient. Then she'd become a subject again, but by then they'd fallen in love.

What if she was to see Brian? Would that be a violation of policy?

But they weren't dating. Surely having a cup of coffee with their architect who was someone she *wasn't* seeing would not be a problem.

She made a mental note to find out. She wanted to be thorough and completely professional.

So why was she still feeling contrary emotions?

CHAPTER V

Although Lindsay loved her job, Thursdays were such busy days that she was tired by the time she got home. She trudged up her stairs, dropped her tote and purse in the living room and proceeded to the bedroom where she shed her clothes, took out her comfy old flannel PJs and got into the shower. Once she was clean, she donned her pjs and settled on the couch to relax with the weather channel and some popcorn.

They were predicting cloudy skies for tomorrow and rain at night. Not unusual for late March, but this week had been a bit chilly and it looked like it wouldn't warm up til next week.

She found herself mulling over her time spent with Sarah. As they often found at TLC, their clients did better than average on the standard ESP tests; and Sarah was no exception. Lindsay wanted to practice her own ESP but there'd been no time today, between patients and meetings with some of the other staff.

Lindsay knew Meredith had practiced until she began to show better than average ESP ability, and in corresponding with her, Lindsay had determined she'd do the same. Now that they worked together, Meredith sometimes helped her practice and retake the tests.

The statement from Sarah that she saw Lindsay's

mom had come as a complete surprise. But a welcome one! Lindsay felt comforted, knowing her mom was looking out for her. But also, a little spooked, if she were to admit the truth. She sighed, reached over to her purse, and removed her cellphone.

Looked like she had missed a call while she was in the shower. She quickly called her favorite aunt back.

"Hi Lindsay," Aunt Jane said. "I just wanted to check that we're still on for lunch on Saturday. It's still good for your cousin Erica and I."

"Yes. And I will double check with Jessica," Lindsay promised. Aunt Jane was her mother's older sister, and a very sweet woman.

They chatted for a few minutes, and Lindsay told her about the incident with her patient seeing Deena.

"Wow," Aunt Jane said. "I feel sometimes like Deena is around me, but I've never seen anything. It's good to know she's still looking out for us."

Lindsay agreed.

After a few minutes, they hung up and Lindsay impulsively dialed her sister.

"Hi Lindsay," Jessica greeted her. "What's up?"

Lindsay told her about Sarah seeing their mom.

"I find it hard to believe," Jessica scoffed.

Lindsay sighed. Jessica had always been skeptical about abilities like ESP or mental telepathy. Ever since their mom got sick and their parents got divorced, she was a confirmed skeptic about *everything*. She'd been against Lindsay's studying paranormal psychology, and had tried many times to convince her to go into some other kind of work, even after Aunt Jane and Uncle Bill had supported Lindsay's ambition. Jessica had dropped out of college, where she had started to major in psychology, and after trying a few different careers, had become an assistant manager at a large florist in the area where they'd grown up. Lindsay was glad she'd finally found something she liked.

She changed the subject from ghosts to how she'd run into Brian, and Jessica listened, interrupting once.

"Why are you talking to Brian? He broke your heart!"

"I have to be professional," Lindsay asserted. "He's a client. Plus he's designing some renovations in our space, so I'm going to run into him in the future. Although I did speak to Meredith about having someone else test him."

"That's good," Jessica said.

Lindsay reminded her about their lunch this weekend and then asked her sister what else she had planned for the weekend.

"I'm working both a half day Saturday and all day Sunday. We have funerals scheduled both days, and I have to coordinate the deliveries of the flowers," Jessica said. "I have Monday and Tuesday off, and a half day next Saturday. How about you?"

They chatted for a few minutes, and then hung up. Lindsay frowned at her cellphone. She didn't feel any better after the discussion. She was glad she and Carolyn had scheduled a shopping soon. She'd be glad to talk to her best friend about what was happening in her life and her conflicted emotions regarding Brian. How could she be so affected by the man who'd broken her heart?

She stared at the TV and sighed.

CHAPTER VI

The morning started as a damp and dreary day with a definite chill in the air. *Typical March weather*, Lindsay thought as she pulled into the back parking lot at The Lightning Center which the employees used. Getting out of the car, the wind buffeted her and she pulled the hood of her coat up. It felt like snow, which was not unusual for this northwestern area of New Jersey even in the spring. She had watched the weather channel which said light snow squalls were very possible later today

Last night had been a rough one. She'd tossed and turned for at least an hour before falling asleep. Thoughts of Brian and their past had kept her awake for too long. Should she see him again, even for coffee?

Now she reached into her car and removed her tote and purse, walking towards the building. Ashish, another researcher on their team, joined her and they greeted each other.

"Do you have any plans this weekend?" she asked him.

"Just to go home with my brother and visit my parents," he replied. He made a face. "I always want to see them, but they're trying to set us both up with women from our hometown."

She recalled he'd been brought up in Edison, about

an hour away. And he rented a house with his brother now, who worked close by.

"It's difficult when parents do that," she agreed. "My aunt tried to match my sister and me a couple of times but she wasn't successful. So she leaves us alone now."

He grinned. "Many Indian parents make successful matches for their children; so mine keep trying."

"I'm lucky my aunt gave up," Lindsay said as they entered the building and headed towards the conference/break room. "It was annoying."

Once inside, she dropped her purse and tote on a chair, shrugged off her coat and went to take a cup of coffee. She greeted her coworkers who were in the room already, and Meredith, who entered after her, took the seat next to her.

They went over the basic info gleaned from yesterday's tests and patients, and research. Then they scattered to go to their various offices, and Lindsay began her day's work. She had a new client to test. Vince was a young man in his late twenties who had been struck by lightning last year and had developed pre-cognitive dreams, like about when a relative was diagnosed with cancer or a friend was going to move. And he didn't like his new ability. After Lindsay found he was scoring higher than average in the standard ESP test—not a surprise as many of their clients did—he confided that he kept dreaming of a beautiful woman whom he fell in love with.

"I'm looking for her," he admitted. "I don't know if I should be." He wore an anxious expression.

"I hope you find her soon," Lindsay said lightly. "Perhaps you can talk to Dr. Lassiter about your feelings."

"I have an appointment to see him next week," Vince said, preparing to leave.

Lindsay's next subject was a business woman in her

fifties who had climbed the corporate ladder. She'd been struck by lightning two years prior, and had developed the ability to often know what her co-workers were thinking. She was not able to do that with her family, though. According to Pam's notes, the woman was closer to her fellow employees than she was to her siblings, so Pam concluded that was not unusual for her.

Since Fridays were half days at TLC, Lindsay was glad to pack up and leave with other staff members after their eleven o'clock to twelve appointments were finished. She was tired from her disturbed sleep.

But she found herself restless too, and so on impulse she stopped at the nearby shopping center and went into a home furnishings and accessories store. She'd only been in her apartment for a few months, since getting her job offer to work full time as a researcher; and she could use some more decorative items in her apartment. She selected a frame for a picture of her with her sister and cousin from last summer, and some throw pillows for her new couch. She'd replaced a lot of the hand-me-down and mismatched furniture she'd collected in grad school to furnish her small apartment there and wanted her new place to feel more stylish and cozy..

Once home, she changed to a pink sweatshirt and matching yoga pants, then curled up on her couch.

She started to watch the weather channel, something she did everyday. But then, restless again, she began flipping channels. There was nothing she was interested in. Finally she shut the TV off and slouching on the couch, she closed her eyes for a few minutes. She'd get up soon, she told herself, and read her email. That decided, she intended to merely rest for a few minutes.

She woke up with a start when the downstair neighbor's door slammed shut. She struggled to sit up.

She could see out the window at the darkening sky. She must have fallen asleep for several hours. No wonder, she'd been fatigued from lack of sleep. Stretching, she went to get a bottle of water from the fridge. That's when she noticed that her phone said there was a text. She must have been sleeping soundly if she didn't hear it.

Checking it, she read *I know your secret.*

Her secret? That sounded ominous. She stared at the message.

She didn't have any secrets. She had shared just about everything with her friends, her sister and her cousin. What secret were they talking about?

She looked to see the number and it said Unknown.

She sat down abruptly, frowning.

The only person she knew well who had some secrets was her younger sister Jessica. Jessica had had a run-in with the law at one point. Could this message be for Jessica and not herself?

Or could it be just some scam to get you to click on something and pay money? There were plenty of scams going around.

She went back to the kitchen. Instead of cold water, this time she reached for her tea kettle. She needed something warm to thaw her suddenly freezing hands.

Lindsay texted her sister saying she wanted to talk to her after their lunch with Aunt Jane and their cousin Erica, and Jessica agreed.

She enjoyed the lunch and was able to relax. When they all parted, Lindsay stopped by Jessica's car and shared the text she'd gotten yesterday. Jessica looked surprised, then puzzled.

"I have no idea what they're talking about—unless it was that time when I got into trouble." She focused on Lindsay. "Why do you think you were sent this message?"

Lindsay shook her head. "I don't know. It could be a scam. Like, they want me to click on a link or something. And the trouble you had—that was ten years ago."

She thought about the text while she drove back home. She had to pass The Lightning Center, and acting on impulse, she pulled into the back parking lot. A glance at the clock in her car showed it was nearly three. She knew Brian had that meeting with the partners. Was he still there? The meeting was probably over by now.

Rounding the building, she saw only two cars were in the lot: Neil Wu's new dark green Mitsubishi, and a blue jeep she didn't recognize.

Before she could consider further, she parked near Neal's car and slid out of hers. Her boss often worked extra hours on the weekend, and many times so did Alicia, his second-in-command in the testing and research area. But she didn't see Alicia's tan Chevrolet.

She walked rapidly to the building, unlocked the door, and locked it again, proceeding to the stairway. Her heart started hammering. Would she see Brian?

All was quiet on the second floor. Light spilled from the doorway of Neal's office, and as she approached the shared office area where she worked with others, Neal called "hello?"

She had tried to walk quietly, but obviously he'd heard her footsteps in the carpeted area of the hall, or perhaps on the stairs.

"Hello," she answered her boss. Feeling the need to explain why she was here on a Saturday after hours, she walked up to his doorway. He was at his desk, his computer screen showing what looked like a research paper,

"I forgot something," she said hastily. "I'm just in for a minute."

"Okay," he said. "I'm checking out some research I didn't have a chance to review during the week."

Lindsay knew he could have done that in his own home, but she also knew he preferred to put in extra hours at TLC. She wasn't sure whether it was to impress the Costigans; to set an example for the others, or to compete with Alicia. They seemed to have a competitive relationship plus something more. A sexual attraction?

Although Alicia wasn't here today. Whose car was the blue jeep?

"Anyone else here?" she asked Neal casually.

"Brian's around." He waved his hand. "Somewhere up here. He's checking something. I'll lock up when he's ready to leave."

"Okay," Lindsay said, her heart increasing its rhythm. "I'm just here for a minute. Have a good weekend."

"You too." Neal went back to concentrating on his work.

Lindsay walked over to the large area she shared with the others. It appeared empty. To confirm her reason for supposedly being here, Lindsay went over to her cubicle, opened the top desk drawer, waited a moment, took out a large paper clip, then shut the drawer with a thwack. She opened her purse and dropped the clip in, continuing to make noise so if Neal happened to be listening, it sounded like she really had come in for something.

"Acting like Nancy Drew" her Aunt Jane would have called it.

She heard a sound and whirling around, she found Brian standing a few yards away.

"Hi, Lindsay." He stared at her.

"I, uh, forgot something," she stammered.

She took a step back, her heart rate zooming up. Damn it. She'd wanted to catch a glimpse of him—like the lovesick teenager she'd once been. But she hadn't anticipated his actually seeing her or being stuck in the room with him in close proximity! *This is so embarrassing,* she thought.

"Hi." She added a brief smile. She had only herself to blame for this run-in. She'd been the one to impulsively stop in here.

He stepped closer. His hand reached towards her—then dropped by his side.

"Hi. Are you here to work? I don't want to disturb anyone."

"No. Just forgot something." Her words came out hastily. She realized she was repeating herself. Had he seen that the only thing she'd taken from the drawer was a large paper clip? She could feel herself flushing. "What about you?' she switched the focus to him.

"I refined some of my ideas, after talking to Parker, Pam, Meredith and Neal. I'm trying to draw them now."

"I see." They were silent for a moment, and then she said, "Well, I better get going. I'll see you."

"Wait." He smiled. "Do you want to go out for a cup of coffee or something?"

She stared at him. Now? For the longest time she'd hoped for that, years ago. Now she wanted to avoid him. *Maybe.* She wished her heart wasn't suddenly beating harder. No, she didn't want to spend time with him.

Yes, she did.

Why did her traitorous heart make her so confused?

Well, why not? She could find out how he was, what was going on in his life. Then maybe she could feel more like a casual acquaintances than his ex-lover.

"Okay," she agreed.

She saw his posture relax, and he grinned.

"Where do you want to go?" he asked.

"There's a Panera five minutes away," she suggested.

"I know where it is."

"I can meet you there in fifteen minutes." She wanted to go spruce up, look her best. She refused to consider why.

"Ok, perfect. That will give me time to wrap up what I'm doing."

They parted, and she went to the lady's room, where she freshened up, brushed her hair, and applied lipstick. She had dressed nicely but casually for lunch, in black slacks, a teal T shirt and gray sweater. She frowned, wondering what Brian saw when he looked at her. She'd been quite thin in high school, but now she'd put on a few pounds and although she'd remained slim, she knew she appeared curvier than she used to be.

His car was still in the parking lot when she left TLC.

It was a quick drive to the Panera. Brian arrived shortly after she got there.

They went to the order area and Lindsay ordered a coffee, then added a scone to go with it.

Brian ordered a coffee with a scone also. "I've got this."

She started to protest, but he shook his head. "My treat. I'm the one who suggested having a snack."

She let him pay, and they proceeded with their scones, to fill their coffee cups.

"So," he said once they settled in a booth, "how have you been, Lindsay?"

She clamped down on the desire to snap " *fine, just fine. No thanks to you.*" Instead, she replied in a business-like manner, "I'm fine. And you?" She needed to keep it professional, casually friendly, she reminded herself.

His dark eyes met hers, as if searching for her secrets. "I'm fine. I work for an architectural firm in Morristown. We specialize in commercial architecture, although I've done some other kinds of designs. We have seven architects plus support staff, and some of the other people do residential and renovations."

"Just like you always planned to do," she said wistfully. She could still remember him sharing his dreams of being an architect, designing office buildings and spaces. He'd wanted to do that despite his parents both being lawyers, and his older brother wanting to follow in their footsteps. Brian had had his own dream.

"It seems like you followed your dreams too," he observed. He blew on his coffee. A warm sensation moved up her spine. She remembered his blowing into her ear once upon a time, and how that would cause a tremor in her. She thrust away the memory. *Not now*, she told herself. *Don't start reminiscing now.* Bending her head, she inhaled the robust aroma of the coffee.

"Yes. I studied parapsychology and then got my doctorate in the subject. I was fascinated by the research The Lightning Center has been doing."

"Because of me." It was a statement, unemotional. He sipped his coffee.

"Yes. Because of you," she admitted, sighing. "Maybe I should thank you?" She felt a painful twist when she said it, but voiced it as a question so it wouldn't sound sarcastic. He'd accused her of viewing him as a scientific oddity, an experimental subject. But it wasn't true! He had never been a scientific specimen to her. He'd been so much more. Her throat grew tight.

"Well." He hesitated. "So we both achieved our goals."

"Are you trying to make me feel bad?" she asked. *This whole sharing coffee had been a mistake. She should not have agreed to come.* This whole conversation was becoming emotional.

"No, not at all." A flash of guilt crossed his face. "I'm saying we followed our dreams."

"Separately." She heard the caustic note in her voice.

He stared at her, calmly sipping his coffee. She shifted in her seat.

"I'm glad you were able to follow your dreams," he said a minute later, his voice neutral.

She shifted the subject, trying to relax into her seat despite the memory of his being doubtful about her career choice. "Yes, well… how is your family?"

"As I mentioned, my dad had a heart procedure last year, to remove a blockage in his artery. He gave us quite a scare. Since then, he and my mom have tried to ease up on their schedules, and delegate more to my brother. Andrew's been doing more and more closings."

She recalled they were real estate attorneys. Andrew must be over thirty now. "And how is Andrew?"

"He's doing well. He just got engaged. Nice woman. You know, he keeps in touch with your boss Evan's sister. Kristen became an attorney too."

"I know that. She graduated, I think, a year behind us," Lindsay said.

"How about you? Are you still close to your friend Carolyn, and the other two you used to hang out with?"

"Yes, I'm close to Carolyn, Krista and Jade. Especially Carolyn. We were all bridesmaids for Krista last year." She paused. "I see them often. What about you? Still friendly with Jon?"

"Yes, although he moved to Massachusetts when we graduated college." He paused too. "How is your sister? And… what about your father?"

She made a face. "Jessica barely talks to him. I speak to him occasionally. He and Sharona just had their third child." Sharona, who wasn't much older than Lindsay. She grimaced at the thought. Had she ever told Brian that?" She added, "My father's new wife is only five years older than me."

He gave her a sympathetic look. "Does your dad see you often?"

"No. The last time was around Christmas."

"That's a shame. He should appreciate you more."

You didn't, she thought.

But that was kind of harsh. He was looking at her with sympathy now.

I wish I had appreciated you.

She sat up. *She'd just heard Brian's voice in her head!*

The words had been clear as a bell. Yet she was absolutely sure Brian hadn't spoken them aloud. Had she somehow received his thoughts? ESP? She knew it was possible. Like Meredith, she'd practiced, hoping it would happen to her. Had all her practice sessions been successful?

"Are you okay?" Brian raised his eyebrows.

"Y-yes." She swallowed, then bent her head and sipped her coffee. The warm liquid slid down her throat.

If she had read his thoughts, she didn't want him to know that.

Did he truly wish he'd appreciated her more?

She hoped so! It would make her feel better. A wave of hope surged through her.

She had wanted to be appreciated a long time ago. Did he now realize he hadn't? And was he sorry at this point?

If she'd read his thoughts, he did wish that.

She didn't hear his voice ringing in her head again, though she found herself straining to hear it. *Darn. Nothing more came through.*

"Linds?" Brian asked.

She snapped back to the present. She had no idea how he felt… except maybe she had caught his thoughts, and he was sorry he hadn't appreciated her. She tried to get back to the conversation. "I, um, resent my father for what he's done, but I realized years ago he won't change. He has a new life, a new family."

"And you and Jessica were left high and dry."

"Not exactly. We have my Aunt Jane, and Uncle Bill."

"That's good." He nodded.

She looked down at her coffee, puzzling over the words she'd heard in her mind. If she had begun to hear people's thoughts—or, Brian's, anyway--that was a big reason to celebrate.

Or was the experience because she and Brian had once known each other well? Had once had a strong connection?

But that connection didn't exist now… or did it?

She did feel a pull towards him every time they encountered each other.

"I'm glad you have other family members you can count on," he said. "I realize I'm lucky. My parents did have other aspirations for me—a law career-- but when they realized I was determined to be an architect, they cheered me on."

She stirred her coffee, just to have something to do.

"What do you like best about your job?" he asked.

That was easy. "Learning about the fascinating abilities that people have." She met his eyes. "There are some I never even was aware of when I was younger. Like, we have a patient who was struck by lightning and can now sense earthquakes a day or two before they happen—even some fairly far from here."

"Wow," he said.

"And I meet all kinds of people," she added. "What about you? What do you like best about your job?"

"I like bringing people's dreams to life." He waved a hand. "Designing what they are dreaming of for their careers. Or taking a vague idea and helping bring it to fruition."

"Sounds very satisfying," she remarked.

"Do you like your career as much as you thought you would?"

His expression looked eager.

"More than I expected. Your getting struck by lightning was fate, yet it opened up a whole new world for me. Seeing ghosts, ESP, so many other psychic abilities. I'd barely been aware of them before."

He raised his eyebrows.

She stared at him for a minute, stirring her coffee. She recalled his words the day he'd broken up with her. He'd said she regarded him as a lab specimen.

She'd protested against his belief, but had been unable to change his mind.

They'd argued. Broken-hearted, she'd finally parted from him, and the few times she'd run into him in town had been uncomfortable.

Until now. Now she felt… not exactly comfortable, but… a certain degree of acceptance? *Approval? Tolerance? Some kind of link?*

She met his eyes, hoping to catch his thoughts again. But though she leaned forward and strained, she couldn't hear any inner dialogue.

He didn't say a word, just touched her hand, stopping her nervous stirring.

"I'm glad we had a few minutes to talk today," he said.

A spark zoomed from her hand, up her arm, and warmed her entire body

"Me--too." Her words sounded choppy to her ears.

They stared at each other. Her hand still tingled. Hastily she wrapped it around her cup. Bending her head, she drank more coffee, which had cooled.

She still was shaken by the fact that she'd heard his thoughts.

And by the connection she was feeling towards him.

She glanced at him, seeing him sit back and stare at his own cup of coffee.

She decided to try a more neutral topic. "Do you have any idea what your plans for The Lightning Center changes are?"

"Yes, I have a pretty good idea." He met her eyes. "I can show them to you next time I'm there. I'd like your opinion."

He wanted her opinion. Intrigued, she said, "Okay."

He finished off his coffee, and set the cup aside. "I'll be there at least one day next week."

She nodded.

"I should get going." He said the words slowly, as if he was reluctant.

"Me too. The weather predictions are for storms later."

She wiped the crumbs from her fingers, and scooped up her trash. He did the same, and soon they were walking out together in companionable silence. Almost like old friends.

The gray afternoon had a damp feel now, and the wind had kicked up. Lindsay's dark hair blew around her shoulders.

"Thanks for joining me for coffee," Brian said, standing on the sidewalk.

"Thanks for asking," she responded, smiled and walked to her car.

Once inside, she watched Brian get into his. He really was a good-looking guy, she observed.

She drove away, back towards her home. She noticed Brian's car going the opposite way. Towards his home in Morristown, she assumed.

She couldn't help the excitement that brewed inside her as she drove home.

She was almost certain she'd heard his thoughts— obviously some form of extra-sensory perception! Maybe her practicing was starting to pay off. Or perhaps it was because of the strange yet intense connection she'd felt to Brian—a connection that must still exist on some subterranean level. A connection she hadn't wanted to feel with the guy who'd hurt her, yet there it was…

She sighed. She was both disturbed and intrigued by the spontaneous hour she'd spent with him.

Either way, that was good news for her. Her ability must have awakened! Everyone at The Lightning Center believed that *every* person had some innate extra abilities. Some people had it stronger than others, of course. And some peoples' increased under certain circumstances, like her coworker, Evan; or with practice, like Meredith. And many people developed an ability or increased strength of an ability after being struck by lightning. Those were the people it was TLC's mission to study. Their staff was contributing greatly to research on paranormal abilities.

She unlocked the door to her apartment, walked through, then shut and locked it again, and dashed up the stairs. She grabbed the box of cards used to do the simplest ESP test. Then she gave herself the test.

Thirty minutes later she scored it and smiled. She had gotten two more right than her previous test, meaning her ESP had improved very slightly. Of course, there was a measure of chance, since it wasn't significantly higher; but she was still pleased by the result. She was moving in the right direction!

She opened up her computer file and added the results to the excel work sheet she'd created just for her own use. Studying it, she could see steady improvement in her performance. It was by small increments, but it was there!

She left it open on her computer screen so she could glance back at it. Then she went to Amazon and ordered a new book about improving your psychic abilities. She knew Sabrina had already ordered it for TLC's library, but she wanted her own copy, to peruse and highlight.

Satisfied, she was ready to fully relax. It was dinner time, but the full lunch and snack she'd had earlier had filled her up.

Saturday night with nothing special to do. Sometimes she loved that time alone to read or watch a movie; other times, she was restless and would shop or call a friend at the last minute. Sometimes one of her coworkers like Alicia or Laura, who were both single, would go to the movies or dinner with her.

But tonight, after such a busy and satisfying day, she settled on her couch with the newest Nora Roberts novel she'd saved for the weekend.

Before she opened the book she found herself thinking about Brian. Why had he wanted to spend time with her? Was it a mistake to see him? Despite everything in their past, she'd enjoyed the hour they'd been together, had even been able to push aside her negative feelings for a while.

And she may have read his mind!

She'd have to talk to Parker about his mental telepathy and talk to Evan about his experience when he'd first heard Pam's thoughts.

Wind rattled the windows. Lindsay glanced up. They were probably the cheapest the builder of the apartments could put in, because she could feel the draft. She got up and walked over to pull the blinds down. As she did, rain began to ping against the window.

She went back to the couch. Contentedly she scooched into the cushions and opened her book.

<hr>

Brian thought about Lindsay the entire way home. He mulled over their break-up years ago.. She'd been so clingy, and to his teenage self that was more than annoying. He'd felt smothered, used. Plus he'd felt like a lab specimen she was studying. She was constantly asking about his paranormal experiences and observing him. Not asking about his swim team achievements, his honor society accomplishments or plans to study architecture. No, it was all about seeing ghosts and ESP.

But now he could see the woman she'd become. And how gorgeous she was. And he felt compelled to spend time with her. Why not get to know her all over again?

Of course, she seemed to resent him. It was understandable. He'd hurt her badly. And worse yet, it had been at a time when she needed support—had needed him.

He felt a pang in his gut. *Guilt.*

Well, he asked himself, what was he going to do about it now?

Maybe try to make up for his callous behavior? Is that what he wanted? Some kind of second chance?

He drummed his fingers on the steering wheel as Mick Jagger sang about wanting satisfaction. The clock on his dashboard said it was getting near to dinnertime. He'd agreed to meet his friend Tony later for a drink at a sports bar and to watch a basketball game being broadcast on TV. He suddenly wished he had asked Lindsay to eat dinner with him.

Is that what he really wanted? To spend time with her?

He'd been looking forward to seeing Tony, a college friend who lived nearby, but who had been traveling for work. They hadn't gotten together for at least two months.

He'd have time during the next few days to ponder seeing Lindsay again, and whether it was a good idea or not.

Should he attempt to get a second chance at a relationship with the woman who'd he once loved? Who had once loved him? He just didn't know.

Sunday afternoon Lindsay was at the laundromat and reading her new novel when her phone pinged.

Like before, the text read *I know your secret.*

She almost laughed sarcastically. Her secret? She had no secrets.

She tucked her phone back in her pocket. This was getting annoying. She had looked online once, but saw nothing about this being a new scam. Undoubtedly, if she replied "what secret?" or "who is this?" the person from the *Unknown* phone number would probably try to get money. Maybe they were hoping a certain percentage of people did have secrets and would fall for that scheme.

She hadn't found anyone talking about this kind of spam, so she mentally shrugged and went back to her laundry. If it got really annoying, she would ask Parker if his friend Matt had heard of it. Matt was in charge of security for The Lightning Center and owned a top-notch firm. She knew that last fall when Courtney and her fiancé Ben had been threatened, Matt had increased security at the Center.

She shoved it to the back of her mind, thinking about her upcoming week's clients and research. It should be a stimulating week.

And who knew how many times she might run into Brian?

CHAPTER VII

Lindsay ping-ponged between teenage-like eagerness to see Brian again and the wish to avoid him.

The logical part of her brain warned her that he was too desirable—handsome, confident, intelligent and successful. It would be too easy to fall into the trap of caring again for her first love. She didn't want to get hurt again!

By the morning, she had concluded that avoidance was the safer bet.

She tried to start Monday in a positive way by thinking about her ESP experience. She arrived early for their staff meeting. Getting up for the job she loved was rarely a problem. Once at TLC, she dropped her tote upstairs at her desk and brought her iPad downstairs to their meeting and break room, where she joined the others at the oval table.

She sent a quick text to Evan, asking if she could chat with him later about his first ESP experience. Then she took a seat beside Courtney.

Evan and Pam walked in two minutes later, and Evan gave her a brief nod.

As she sipped her coffee, he texted her. "I am solidly booked all morning. I have lunch 12-1. Are you available then?"

She replied, "Yes, I have lunch the same time. I can stop in your office first."

He sent her a thumbs up emoji.

Two minutes later, Parker called the meeting to order. They summarized clients they'd seen Friday and Saturday and testing results. Sabrina reported on a couple of new, interesting books she'd added to the library. Then Parker went over the clients being seen or tested today. There were some questions about a new client who'd displayed the ability to move objects, or telekinesis, an ability that Neal shared but the staff didn't see often.

Then Parker announced that Friday he wanted to put aside some time at their morning meeting to briefly discuss the special projects that people were choosing to spearhead. Right now there was one big project that the entire staff was committed to: studying how people with paranormal abilities appeared to have their abilities boosted when around others with abilities, even if the talent was a different kind. TLC had been conducting studies in this area since its inception.

When the meeting broke up, she followed Courtney upstairs and prepared for her first client, a nurse from Long Island who had been struck by lightning last year and developed the ability to see auras, like Richard and several of their clients.

When it was her lunch time she trotted down to Evan's office.

As one of their psychiatrists, Evan had a nice office on the first floor, near Pam's. He was a handsome and tall man, always nicely dressed; with blond hair and blue eyes. He was always professional in all his interactions.

"What's on your mind?" he asked, indicating the chair by his desk. She sat there as he settled in the one behind his desk.

"I wanted to ask you about your first, spontaneous ESP experience. Pam told me a little, about how when she was in danger over a year ago you could hear her thoughts."

His face took on a far-away expression. "Yes, it was my first ESP experience. Before that I was skeptical. But I never doubted the existence of ESP after that."

He gazed out the window, as if viewing what had happened on that day. "I'd had a fight with Pam, and we weren't speaking," he admitted. "And then I realized I was wrong, and really loved her, and didn't want to lose her. While I was driving up to see her here at The Lightning Center, I could suddenly hear her voice in my head, calling out to me. She needed help!" He re-focused on Lindsay.

"So I drove as fast as I could and got here in time to help rescue her." He smiled.

"And she was alright."

"I was so happy, so relieved she was okay, that I proposed to her on the spot." His grin grew wider.

A tap sounded on the door.

"Pam?" Evan asked.

His wife peeked around the door. "Are you ready for lunch? I brought yesterday's salad for both of us, remember." Pamela looked polished as always as she slid into the room, clad in a black pantsuit with a bright green shell.

"I was telling Lindsay about my first ESP experience," Evan said.

Pam perched on the desk and faced Lindsay. "It was an emotional one for Evan, since I was in danger." Studying Lindsay, she asked suddenly, "did you have an ESP experience?"

"I think so." Lindsay hastily described the time

she'd spent talking with Brian, and how she thought she'd heard his thoughts.

Both Pam and Evan nodded as they listened.

"What do you think?" she asked, sliding forward on her seat.

The couple glanced at each other, and then Pam said, "It sounds like you *did* read Brian's thoughts."

"I agree," Evan added. "I'd be interested to hear if it happens again."

"I'll definitely let you both know," she replied. She stood up and smiled at them. "Thanks. I'm excited at the thought. I've been practicing with the ESP cards, like Meredith did. I'm going to tell her."

The three of them left Evan's office to eat lunch. Lindsay determined she'd see Meredith at some time during the afternoon.

The afternoon flew by, and Lindsay didn't have a chance to speak to Meredith until after she finished with her last client.

Meredith was excited to hear about Lindsay's experience. "Keep practicing!" she said to her. "It does make a difference. I still practice myself."

Lindsay was feeling pretty good when she drove home later. She wasn't scheduled to work tonight, so she ate a quick dinner and then relaxed with the book she was reading. She was interrupted with thoughts of Brian a few times, but by the time she went to sleep she felt content.

At their morning meeting the following day, Lindsay saw Brian's name on the list to be tested. He'd been assigned to Ashish.

"Like so many of our clients, Brian sometimes is happy about his ability; sometimes angry," Evan said, reviewing Brian's record..

Evan addressed the room, not looking at anyone in particular. But Meredith met Lindsay's eyes. "He has some guilt issues about the way he behaved after being struck." Evan added.

Guilty? *Really?* Lindsay hadn't known that. Of course, as part of their staff, she was used to hearing confidential information. But this was also personal for her. These important issues had to be shared with the staff. She pondered Brian's feelings, while Evan went on to say he'd be meeting Brian again next week to work on accepting his ability and coming to terms with the repercussions.

Guilty. Maybe he should feel that way. Lindsay looked down at her iPad. Brian's feelings should satisfy her. He'd hurt her terribly. And at a time when she'd been young, and vulnerable because her mom was so ill. Yet the feeling of satisfaction she expected to rush through her wasn't there. Instead, she felt a little surprise.

Maybe she had accepted the past—better than he had.

Her fingers tightened on her tablet as she thought that. It sounded like she felt superior. Did she? She resented him, certainly. For breaking her heart. But, she knew he had been young and vulnerable too, not sure of his new ability, and feeling a lot of conflicting emotions about it.

Maybe it was time she put the happenings of ten years ago firmly in the past where they belonged. She could understand them better now that she was an adult.

They went on to speak about the next patient, being tested by Laura, and Lindsay made a few notes as the staff talked. At almost ten o'clock, Parker ended the meeting telling them to have a good day.

Lindsay got busy testing a man who was in for an annual visit. His ability was having precognitive dreams, and when she gave him the standard ESP test, he did even better than last year, when he was first tested. It seemed, from chatting with him, that his ability was improving. When Lindsay asked him if he felt that was so, he confided that he was having his dreams more often. He wanted to discuss that with one of the psychiatrists. So they went to make an appointment for him in with Pam, whom he'd seen last year.

After he left, Lindsay went on to greet her next client, a woman who had a few telekinesis episodes when she got angry, and like the former client, she was in for her annual tests. She had been coming for several years. Her ESP test results remained the same as last year.

It wasn't until after lunch that Brian was scheduled to arrive, and so Lindsay didn't dwell on thoughts of him.

After testing the woman, she got up to search out Sabrina and tell her about the book she had ordered and started reading.

She had just left the room she shared with the other researchers, when she heard footsteps on the stairs. Glancing over to the staircase, she saw Brian.

She couldn't help the sizzling energy that shot through her as she regarded him.

"Hi, Lindsay," he greeted her with a wide smile. He was dressed in a nice pale blue shirt, striped darker blue tie and khaki pants.

She steeled herself against the instant appeal she felt. She didn't want to feel this way, she reminded herself.

"Hi," she said in her most casual voice.

He took a breath. "I was thinking… do you want to get together sometime over the next weekend?"

She gave him what she hoped was a distant smile. "I'm working. And besides, it might not be a good idea."

He drew closer. "Why?"

She paused. "Because. Well, our past history wasn't great. I don't want it to interfere with our research here." That idea for not seeing him had popped into her mind just now.

He raised his brows. "Interfere? I know that plenty of people here have formed relationships that started at the Center. Parker was telling me about him and Sabrina."

"You want some kind of relationship?" Surprise made her voice come out sharper than she'd intended.

"I don't know, Lindsay." The way he said her name sounded intimate, somehow.

"Maybe," he added cautiously. "Maybe I just want to see…"

"See what?"

"How we'd get along now. I'm not talking anything more than getting to know each other again." His voice was persuasive. "I want to get to know you, the adult Lindsay. The one who's achieving her dreams of success."

"The dreams you didn't believe in." The sharp words sprang out of her before she could stop them, as if they'd jumped straight from her brain.

He stepped back, a startled look on his face. Then his expression changed and he looked regretful, his face sagging. "I guess you're right. I didn't encourage your dreams of doing psychic research."

"Thank you for admitting that." She sighed, knowing that was big of him. But she needed to escape. Their interaction had become too emotional, too much for her to handle at the moment. She had to leave. Being so near him was causing her blood to simmer and her emotions to overwhelm her. "I'll—I'll think about seeing you again. See you later. I have to meet Sabrina." She dashed off, not looking back.

He could have sworn that last weekend Lindsay was feeling the same curiosity and friendliness he'd felt towards her. But today she was more guarded, and cooler towards him. She looked and acted business-like and not like the warm girl she'd been before.

Had she changed her mind about getting to see him and knowing him better? Or maybe he'd misread her. Maybe she'd never felt that way.

Or maybe his impression of her was wrong. Maybe she was no longer the warm and caring girl she'd been before. Maybe she had turned more aloof and distant.

A pang of disappointment reverberated inside him as he stared at the spot where she'd stood.

Brian's image kept interrupting Lindsay's thoughts all afternoon.

When she tested her next subject, his visage flashed in her mind often during that next hour. She had to force herself to concentrate on the client.

On her coffee break, she met up with Tanya and Laura, who were in the conference room. Tanya said the bridal shower gift the female staff members had selected for Courtney had arrived at her house and she and Madison were going to wrap it and bring it to the shower a week from Saturday. The women were all chipping in for a luxurious comforter and matching sheet set.

All the employees of the Center had been invited to Courtney's wedding in June. It would be huge—over 300 people—since both had big families, lots of friends and Courtney's fiancé Ben was a billionaire who happened to be an investor in The Lightning Center. He also had been struck by lightning and had an unusual ability, clair-audience--the ability to hear, but not see, spirits. Lindsay was looking forward to the happy event. She had been invited with a "plus one" but had no date to bring.

The shower, the Saturday after this coming one, would be a fun one with her co-workers. Pamela, Meredith and Sabrina were among Courtney's bridesmaids along with some other friends, her sisters and some cousins.

As they spoke about the upcoming wedding Lindsay found out that one was bringing her boyfriend. Others, like Laura, were considering bringing a "plus one."

Lindsay hadn't given the subject much thought, but now she did. Laura said she thought it might be more fun to bring someone but was hesitant to bring a casual date.

Lindsay mulled it over as she left the room. Would it be more fun? And who would she bring? She wasn't seeing anyone. She couldn't bring Brian-- she certainly didn't consider him boyfriend. She was unsure about seeing him again.

The conversation had her thinking about Courtney, who had a very unusual ability—the ability to see past lives, especially important ones, in other people.

She had never asked Courtney about her own past lives. But perhaps she should. Sometimes there was a connection to the present. Maybe it would shed some light on the situation she was in now, with Brian.

Courtney was a very dedicated worker, and when

Lindsay returned to their research area, she glanced at Courtney's station. It was empty. She must be testing a client.

Lindsay sat at her desk and sent Courtney an email, asking if she could meet with her during the next few days. She typed that it was something personal. Then she got back to her own work, reading a paper that Neal recommended that everyone read.

Courtney emailed back later that she was working tonight but could speak to her when they both finished. Lindsay checked the schedule. Lindsay's last appointment was at seven, which would last until 7:45. Courtney had an 8:00 appointment, but had no seven o'clock appointment. They agreed to meet when Lindsay finished with Ms. Albert.

When Lindsay was finished, she met Courtney in one of the testing rooms.

"What can I help you with?" Courtney asked. Courtney, a beautiful woman with brownish-auburn hair, was dressed in a simple teal blouse and dressy black pants. A fruity perfume clung to her.

Lindsay sat down at the table across from her. "There are some things going on in my life, and I was hoping you could tell me about a past life that might shed some light on my circumstances now."

The woman across from her furrowed her brow. "I can sense several past lives in you." She closed her eyes. "Yes, there's one that definitely stands out." She hesitated, then opened her eyes, focusing on Lindsay. "You were—you were some kind of disciple for the Oracle at Delphi. In Greece."

Lindsay stared at her, swallowing. "A—disciple?"

"You left there, where you had served the Oracle.

They were sad to see you go, but they understood. You had fallen in love with a man who was visiting from a nearby Greek island."

Courtney's eyes widened. "He was—he was that architect, the one who's been coming around!"

Lindsay's whole body tensed. "Brian? I fell in love with Brian?"

"Yes." Courtney studied her. "It's his soul, his essence. I believe you had a very happy life together." She closed her eyes for another moment, then opened them. "I see you surrounded by some children in front of a home."

Lindsay sat back. "Well." She said the word loudly. "That may explain some things in my life. Like, I've always had a strong desire to visit Greece." In fact, she'd started a savings account to save for the trip. If she put a little money in it every month, she reasoned, she'd get there… eventually. "I don't have family there but I want to visit badly." She thought rapidly. "If Brian and I once had an important life together, that also explains why I am still so—drawn to him. In spite of the fact that we were dating as teenagers, then broke up."

Courtney nodded her head vigorously. "Yes. A part of your soul remembers how happy you were in that life."

"And now I'm forced to see him here, in this life."

"Yes, and it sounds like part of you wants to be together again." Courtney smiled, adding "do you know my story?"

"Something about it," Lindsay said. She didn't know details.

"I was regressed by a therapist—not Pam-- who really didn't know what she was doing," Courtney began. "I was brought back to a traumatic incident, where I witnessed my lover in Venice, during the Renaissance, bring murdered." She shuddered. "I searched for him for years and met Ben at Pam and Evan's wedding. He was a friend of Pam and Parker's in high school. They all stayed close, and he became an anonymous donor to The Lightning Center; although everyone here knows about it now. Anyway, I recognized Ben right away when we met last year. He didn't recognize me; in fact he didn't know much about past lives and reincarnation. But we fell in love after the wedding."

"Oh, how romantic!" Lindsay declared.

Courtney smiled wider. "Yes. And now we're getting married in June. I hope you can come to the wedding."

Lindsay couldn't help the twinge of envy that curled inside her. Lucky Courtney. She was only slightly older than Lindsay, and she was marrying her soulmate.

She fervently wished the same thing would happen to her. It had happened to other women here—Sabrina, and Meredith, and Pamela. Why not her? Could she meet her soulmate here, at The Lightning Center?

An image of Brian flashed in her mind.

Could Brian be her soulmate? Her true love? The one she'd always secretly hoped for?

"Well." Lindsay considered the idea. "Maybe I need to give this—relationship with Brian—a chance."

"I believe there is a reason you were brought together in this life. For a second time."

Lindsay considered the idea. Was it possible? Should she see what developed between her and Brian?

Could she take the risk?

CHAPTERVIII

It had been a busy day and evening, with Lindsay's schedule pretty booked up. She didn't get a chance to think much about Courtney's advice until she got home.

As usual, she showered and got into her comfy pjs before reaching for her phone to call her sister and tell her about today's events.

Jessica's advice was succinct. "Don't try to get back with him."

"Why?" Lindsay asked, figuring she could guess her sister's opinion from her negative outlook.

"The bastard broke your heart! Why would you want him back?"

Lindsay sighed. "Because maybe we are meant to be together. Maybe it would work if we try again."

"Bull."

"We're both adults now, Jess. We're different, more mature. I admit I was very needy back then."

"And you think things will be different now? He didn't believe you would succeed in your chosen career, either. If he wasn't willing to help when you needed him—and he didn't support you—"

Lindsay knew where this was going. Her sister had broken up with a lot of boyfriends.

"Everyone makes mistakes," Lindsay said firmly.

"Linds, you remember when I dated Sam?"

"Yes. And you broke up with him after a year, but then you got back together."

"And he started asking me for money just like he did the first time. That's when I knew he just wanted me for my money, wanted *things*—like a bigger TV."

Lindsay did remember Sam. He was a mechanic who lived above his means, always wanting the latest phones and other items. "Yes, and he spent every penny he earned and then some," Lindsay pointed out.

"When I realized he was just using me, I broke up with him."

"Which you had every right to do."

"What if Brian's just using you? I know you make good money at The Lightning Center."

"He doesn't need my money," Lindsay said. "He seems quite comfortable. He's an architect with, I'm sure, a good salary. Plus his parents always had money," she added. "I'm sure he doesn't need mine."

"Maybe so, but I wouldn't trust him," Jessica argued. "He may have ulterior motives. Or he may not give you the support you need."

Remembering how he'd hurt her, how he'd negated her wants and her dreams, Lindsay sat up straight.

"If I start seeing him again, I'll be very cautious," she promised.

"Just don't trust him."

The rest of the week sped by, and Brian consumed a lot of time in her thoughts. More time than she was comfortable with. She waffled between wanting to see him again, and being afraid to spend time with him. She feared she couldn't trust him not to walk away again.

But she *did* want to see him. Yearned to. Should she give this thing a chance to grow and flourish? she questioned herself for the thousandth time.

By Friday she hadn't seen or spoken to Brian again, but Parker mentioned at the end of their daily meeting they would see him working at TLC later.

Courtney stopped by Lindsay's desk right afterwards and asked in a low voice what she had decided to do regarding Brian.

"I'm still not sure," Lindsay admitted. "I'm very conflicted."

"Well, I think you should let him back into your life," her friend advised. "He was important to you once; and he could be again."

Lindsay stared at her. "Maybe I'll take a chance…"

She had to concentrate on her next client, a woman who saw auras and was in for her annual testing. But afterwards, while waiting for her next appointment, her thoughts drifted to Brian again.

She tested Mr. Vogel, a new client, and made an appointment for his second test. She escorted him to the door. Returning upstairs so she could get things ready to leave for the day, she spotted Brian coming out of one of the testing rooms.

In that moment, looking at him, she experienced the familiar pull towards him. Like an invisible rope tugging her closer.

She *wanted* to see him again. Maybe she needed to.

"Hi Brian," she said, her voice breathless.

He hesitated, studying her. "Hi." His voice was cool.

She didn't blame him. Earlier in the week she'd kind of given him the brush-off.

She drew closer. "I'm sorry I was so short with you

the other day." She lowered her voice and went on. "I was tired and having a bad day." She followed that statement with what she hoped was a regretful look.

She saw his body visibly relax. "How is your day going today?"

"Much better. I—" she plunged on as she noted Felipe rounding a corner. "Do you want to meet for lunch?"

"That works," he agreed. "Where should we meet?"

There's a really good diner less than a mile from here on the highway."

He flashed a smile. "I love diners. You can get anything there." Glancing at his watch, he added, "I can meet you about twelve thirty, I'll be done with my work then, and I know the office closes early on Fridays. Does that work?"

"Perfect." She smiled back, and then went to her desk to make some final notes on today's tests.

She was glad she was seeing Brian again. She looked forward to lunch.

He'd been expecting another cool reception when he'd run into Lindsay.

But she'd surprised him, and had acted warmer. He wondered just what had changed her attitude. But hc didn't mind. He wanted to see her again and spend time with her.

He finished the work he needed to do, refining a few ideas. He knew he could have worked on them in his office or even at home. But he'd had the strong urge to see Lindsay again.

He got to the diner a few minutes early, snagged a

booth toward the front, and sat facing the door so she'd see him when she entered.

Lindsay entered a few minutes later, looking smart and attractive in her back pants, white t shirt and red sweater, her hair brushed to a neat shine. It curled softly by her shoulders.

She spotted him at once and worked her way over to his booth.

"What are you getting?" she asked as she slid in opposite him.

"I figured I'd order a cheeseburger."

"They're burgers are good."

They both glanced at the menus the waitress gave them. When she returned he ordered a cheeseburger deluxe and a coke while Lindsay ordered a turkey club sandwich and diet cola.

Then, when the waitress left with their order, they sat awkwardly staring at each other.

"So, are you working on any special projects?" Brian asked after sipping from his soda.

"The usual testing and research… plus, we have a few group projects."

"Are you at liberty to tell me about them?"

"Yes, in general terms. I can tell you," she added, "I personally am working with Meredith on one project about people who practice to improve their ESP. That's public knowledge. The results so far are promising."

"How do you practice to improve a skill like ESP?" he asked.

"You keep taking the standard test, the one where you predict shapes like wiggly lines, stars and triangles. That has helped many people. Including," she finished, "me."

He raised his eyebrows. "That's interesting."

"Yes, it is. We've already documented Meredith's improvement. Of course, she's been practicing for a longer time than I have."

"Has it helped you?" He leaned back in his seat.

"It seems to be helping." She sipped her drink. The clatter of dishes being stacked up nearby and the calls of hello from a booth behind them were familiar sounds.

"Evan told me he didn't think he had any ability; didn't even believe in ESP until recently," Brian stated.

"True. It proved itself with his connection to Pam. He knew when she was in danger."

"That's extraordinary," he said. "How do you think you're doing?"

"It's too early to tell, but I'm cautiously optimistic," she answered. "I seem to be slowly improving."

Again, they stared at each other. Then Lindsay asked how his own work was going.

"It's going well. I had to refine a few ideas at Parker's request, but I think they'll turn out better than before."

"Someone said you might do some other work for TLC," she said.

"Yes." He smiled. "They want to put a doggy daycare center and eventually, a child daycare center in the back, where most of the acreage is empty except for Richard's lightning equipment at the far end."

Lindsay smiled. "I know some of the married couples would like to have children in the future, and many of the employees want to get dogs but don't want to leave them alone for long periods. That would be a huge perk for us, including, someday, me. I can't have pets in my apartment, and right now my hours are long, so this would help in the future." She beamed at him.

"I have a few ideas, but like you said, that's for the future," he said.

She asked about a couple of his high school friends, what they were doing and where they lived. He was describing them when their meals arrived.

The cheeseburger and crispy fries were perfect. He munched contentedly.

Their discussion turned to some of her friends and family, and they had polished off their lunch by the time they were caught up.

"This has been a nice lunch," Lindsay said, a note of surprise in her voice.

"I've enjoyed it. Can we get together again? Say, tomorrow?" he asked. He didn't have plans. But she might have a date, he thought, and steeled himself for disappointment if she did.

"This is the Saturday I'm working," she said.

"All day?"

"Well, no."

"So how about going out to dinner? Are you free then?"

She seemed to hesitate for a second, then relented. "Okay."

"I know there's a steak place nearby," he said, wondering why she still seemed hesitant.

"It gets very crowded on weekends. We'd have to go early."

"That's okay with me. I can pick you up at five if that's alright."

"Yes, that will work," she said lightly, with a quick smile. She gave him her address and he put it in his phone. He recognized it as a large apartment complex that was close by.

He insisted on paying. She insisted on leaving the tip. "But Saturday it's my treat," he told her as they left the diner, wanting to be sure she knew it was a date.

He touched her shoulder lightly. Instantly he felt warmth flow through him, Surprised, he followed her outside. It had been years since he touched her, but it seemed like he still felt a charge when he did.

When they parted by their cars, he was tempted to hug her, but resisted. He sensed she wasn't ready for that.

"See you tomorrow," he said, and opened his car door.

"See you then." She walked toward her own car.

As he drove away, he glanced back. She was standing and watching him depart.

Maybe she had felt that jolt of awareness too?

The day had grown warmer. Lindsay sighed as she tossed her red sweater into the hamper, leaving just her T shirt on, and proceeded to change from her black pants to jeans. Or maybe she felt warm because she'd been in Brian's company?

She hoped she wasn't making a big mistake by spending time with him this weekend. She knew her sister thought it would be. She wanted to discuss it with Carolyn, but Carolyn would still be at work. Maybe she could call her on her way home since the teachers left the building earlier on Fridays.

She left her friend a voicemail message suggesting that, then took the book she was reading off her nightstand and sat down on her couch to read.

But she didn't open it to the page where she'd left the bookmark. Instead, she found herself gazing into space, thinking about Brian.

And what Courtney had revealed about their past lives.

She sat like that for a while. She thought of Pam, who had reunited with Evan. Maybe she should talk to her. She had been in this very same situation with the man who had been her first love.

She decided that was a good idea. She'd speak to Carolyn, and maybe tomorrow, to Pamela.

That decided, she opened up her book.

The following morning, she still had mixed feelings. Carolyn had had reservations when they spoke yesterday, advising that Lindsay try going out a couple of times with Brian to see how she felt; but to proceed with caution. She's also suggested that Lindsay be careful and not ask too many questions about his ability in a social situation.

"You don't want him to think you consider him a 'lab rat,' as he accused you at the time," her best friend declared.

Deciding Caroln knew her and the situation well and that the advice was sound, Lindsay planned to follow it.

She got to work on the early side and texted Pam that she wanted to chat with her. When Pam and Evan arrived, Pam approached her.

"I'm booked up solid til noon," Pam said. Can you come to my office after twelve?"

"Sure," Lindsay agreed.

When her appointments were done just before noon, Lindsay packed up her tote, then went downstairs to meet Pam.

Pam was escorting her client out. She returned to her office and shut the door. Facing Lindsay, she asked, "What's up? Is it Brian?"

"Yes," Lindsay said, dropping into the chair in front of Pam's desk. "I'm conflicted." She described her feelings to Pam.

Pam sat behind her desk and listened to Lindsay. When Lindsay finished, she said, "I understand completely. I was in the same position a couple of years ago. I ran into Evan at a conference, and then he came here to visit The Lightning Center. He had opposed our research for reasons I won't go into now, but we were still attracted to each other. Finally, I gave him a chance, and we started seeing each other after another conference he attended where TLC was giving a presentation. We almost broke up until he had his own ESP experience when I was in danger, and, as they say--the rest is history." She glanced at her gorgeous, sparkling, pear-shaped diamond ring, and smiled

She focused on Lindsay again. "I would advise you to do what I did. Go out a few times at a pace that's comfortable for you, and see how you feel. Otherwise, you could have regrets later."

"I could do that," Lindsay said. She studied Pam, and an idea popped into her mind. "Pam, are you having dreams about me and Brian?"

Pam's mouth dropped open. "You must have read my thoughts."

"You are, aren't you?" she pressed on. "Having precognitive dreams."

Pam sighed. "Yes, I had one a few weeks ago. And another one just last night."

"Please tell me about them."

"In the first one, you were walking down the aisle in a bridal gown. At the end Brian was waiting for you."

"And the second?"

"You were a couple. You were cooking together in a spacious kitchen, and Brian was tasting something you made."

"Oh." Lindsay sat back. Well, that sounded conclusive. They all knew about Pam's precognitive dreams. They were always more vivid and realistic than her regular run-of-the-mill dreams. So many had come true.

She smiled at her friend. "Thanks for telling me."

"I was going to wait before telling you. I didn't want to influence you one way or another. But you asked."

"Yes, I did." Lindsay stood up, gathering her purse and tote.

"And Lindsay?" Pam stood too.

"Yes?"

"I meant what I said. You picked up on my thoughts."

Gladness flowed through Lindsay.

Brian spent the morning at the Y's indoor pool, doing laps and then swimming at a more leisurely pace. Years of swim team practice were imprinted on him and he wanted to keep in shape. Plus he'd always enjoyed the water.

Afterwards he showered, went back to his condo to do some tidying up and laundry. He had a cleaning service which caane every other week so he didn't have to spend time doing that. After checking his email, he went to meet a friend from work for lunch.

But through the morning and afterwards, Lindsay lingered in his thoughts. He even discussed her, briefly, with Jake, his friend, who was two years older than him.

"Sounds like you want to pick up with her again,"

Jake had said. "But be careful, man. She may have changed."

"She still seems the same," Brian said. "Maybe a little more cautious, but I don't blame her for that. I know I hurt her feelings badly"

"Still, you don't want yourself getting hurt this time. Or her, if you decide it wouldn't work. Which could happen again."

"I know." The thought of them hurting each other bothered him more than he'd expected.

When he returned home. he listened to music but considered what Jake had said.

He didn't want Lindsay getting hurt again—or himself either. He better move ultra cautiously.

Lindsay spent extra time on her hair and make-up. She'd decided, after the discussions with Carolyn and Pam, to keep the evening casual and friendly, but no more. No acting like she had more than a light interest in Brian. No acting too cozy or romantic.

And she had better not treat him like a "lab rat" as he had accused her years ago. She intended to take Carolyn's advice.

She dressed in nice black pants, and a sapphire blue top. She wore low-heeled short black boots. Nothing too dressy.

She was just sitting on her couch listening to music when she heard the outer door to the vestibule open, and he rang the bell.

She took the stairs at a medium pace—not too fast—as if she wasn't eager. Opening the door, she found him in khakis, a white and blue striped shirt with the sleeves partially rolled up, and a navy blue vest.

"Hi!" she said brightly. "I'm ready."

He led her to his dark blue jeep. Once they were belted in, he drove to the nearby steak restaurant, while the radio played some old rock music.

"My mother used to listen to this music all the time," Lindsay said, thinking about coming home to hear her mother with her CDs playing. "She especially loved Fleetwood Mac."

"My parents still listen to that music too," he said, stopping at a red light.

It only took a few minutes to get to the restaurant, which was crowded despite the early dinner hour. The hostess showed them to a booth and left them with menus.

As she opened the menu, her cellphone pinged.

"Do you mind if I get that?' Lindsay asked Brian. She couldn't imagine who was texting her on a Saturday evening.

"Go ahead." He opened his menu and began looking at it.

She drew her phone out of her purse. There it was again: the same annoying message. *I know your secret.*

She frowned. This was getting ridiculous.

"I hope it's not bad news," he said, watching her.

"No. It's a message I've gotten twice before. I think it's some kind of spam. They're hoping I'll click on something, and they can part me from my money, probably." She showed him her phone.

He took it from her, frowning. "Probably," he agreed. "Although I haven't heard of this particular scheme." He lifted his eyes to meet hers. "You should talk to Parker and Matt, his security friend, about it."

"I think I will. I have no idea how they got my number." She took her phone back and dropped it in her shoulder bag. "I'm not going to check my phone again," she said, not wanting to be glued to her phone. She wanted to enjoy Brian's company. "Now, let's see what to order."

They both gazed at the menus.

When their waitress arrived, Brian ordered an apple martini and a large steak with a loaded baked potato. Lindsay chose the steak and crabmeat special of the day with a glass of red wine.

Once their waitress departed, Brian reached for the crusty bread. "Do you mind working at TLC on weekends?"

She shook her head. "Not at all. It's only a half day every other Saturday. And we get half days on Fridays. Plus the Costigans are generous with the vacations they give everyone. We even get a break between Christmas and New Year's. like the schools".

"That's good. I have to work some weekends, too," Brian said, "but I can make up my own schedule for the most part."

"How many people work there?"

"Counting some office staff, about fifteen. I interviewed for a large, well-known firm in Trenton when I got out of college, but I preferred the smaller firm. I read about The Lightning Center on line before contacting Evan. I see they've really grown." He buttered his bread.

"Yes." Lindsay reached for her own slice, inhaling the comforting fresh-baked scent. "They started with immediate family and a few researchers, and we've grown a lot in the last 6 or 7 years. Now Parker and some of the senior staff have been invited to do workshops all over." She smiled proudly.

"I think your goal, to research the effect of lightning

strikes and the resulting psychic abilities in people, is very unique."

"True. No one else is doing this exact type of research."

"Parker and Evan were telling me they've found some people with extraordinary abilities that haven't been documented or researched elsewhere."

"That's true," she said, warming to the subject. "It's no secret that Courtney, one of our researchers, has the ability to see important past lives; and we have two clients who can predict earthquakes twenty-four hours in advance. And some, have had their abilities to an extraordinary degree not seen elsewhere."

"Sabrina, Parker's wife? I met her last week and she told me about her ability."

"Yes. There are some individuals who can astral project; but she's by far the best of whom we've encountered. She even helped find the child of a New Jersey politician who'd been kidnapped."

The waitress brought over their drinks.

"Cheers." Brian saluted her.

She clinked her glass with his. "Cheers."

"That's impressive, that Sabrina could do that," he continued. "What's the ability that interests you the most?"

"We just had a woman who came in with the ability to quickly pick up other languages. We haven't seen that talent before; and Sabrina can't find anyone else who has it, in all her research. Sabrina's a reference librarian."

"Wow. That is fascinating. Don't worry. Parker already talked to me about confidentiality. I don't want to know names. What I really needed to know was the kind of research and testing you are doing so I can help maximize spaces."

"I won't tell you any names except for the abilities that are public knowledge, like Sabrina's. She used to get teased and made fun of. Can you imagine? It's a rare gift she should be proud of!"

"Agreed," he said.

They were interrupted by the waitress bringing their side salads. When she left, Brian continued. "That ability with languages is interesting. That's the first I ever heard of it."

"Yes," she agreed enthusiastically. "We're testing her now."

She took a forkful of her salad as he dug into his. "We also have several new clients who have unusual talents I never saw before."

"Parker tells me he can read someone's thoughts—"

"True," she said.

"Brian?" The exclamation by a tall, slim blond woman with startling green eyes interrupted them. The blond focused on Brian.

"How are you?" the woman practically gushed, as though she hadn't seen him for a long time.

He looked up at her. "I'm fine, Sharona." He turned back to Lindsay. "Lindsay, this is Sharona Jones. Sharona, Lindsay Hughes."

"And this—" she waved at the man behind her—"is Todd Cooper."

He was a rather stocky but masculine man, with a small beard and attractive face. Lindsay glanced at him, then back at Sharona.

"It's so good to see you again!" Sharona declared.

"Nice to see you too." Brian sounded neutral. His mouth settled into a straight line.

Lindsay got the feeling he didn't think it was so nice, and felt glad. The blond, Sharona, seemed pushy.

"What are you doing with yourself these days?" Sharona pressed on.

"Still working at the same architectural firm."

"I changed jobs," Sharona said, "and I'm now working for a large corporation near here." She tossed her hair back. "Doing advertising, of course."

Brian looked unimpressed.

Lindsay suspected he had no desire to get into a long conversation. The waitress came over with their meals. "Here you are!" she said brightly, squeezing past Sharona.

"C'mon. Tess." Todd, the man with her, frowned and tugged her elbow. "Our table is ready."

"Bye!" she said brightly to Brian before turning and letting Ryan lead her away. "It's nice to see you again!" she called back over her shoulder.

"Nice to meet you," Lindsay added, while Brian said, "Bye."

Sharona bent towards Ryan and whispered something, an angry expression on her face.

Lindsay sprinkled salt and pepper on her buttered, steaming baked potato. "I think she wanted to be invited to join our table."

"No way." Brian dug into his steak. "I don't want to spend time with her."

Her insides warmed. "Is she an old girlfriend?"

"Kind of. I only dated her for around two months," he said. "I broke it off when I realized she was self-centered." He shrugged.

Lindsay smiled. "She does seem rather--pushy. Did you date her recently?"

"It has to be over two years ago," he said. "Let's talk about something else besides old relationships."

That was fine with her. Years ago Brian had claimed

Lindsay was "smothering" him, and she guessed Sharona had been just like that.

Lindsay dropped the subject. *Sharona's annoying.* She thought she heard Brian's thoughts.

ESP again? She tucked that thought away. She didn't feel jealous now. There was no need. He obviously wasn't impressed by his old girlfriend.

"Do you believe you can increase or foster ESP in yourself?" she asked, curious.

He paused in the middle of cutting a piece of steak, focusing on her. "I never thought about it. I know Evan said you guys are working on the theory that with practice, you can improve whatever ability you have."

She nodded enthusiastically. "Meredith is proof of that. She tells everyone that she originally tested as average in the ESP tests, but practiced ESP skills for years and now tests above average—and had some true experiences."

He nodded and smiled.

She might as well see what he thought. "I've been practicing, too,"

"Really?'

"Yes, really. And recently, my skills seem to be improving." She hesitated, then plunged in. "For example, you were thinking that Sharona is annoying, weren't you?"

He stared at her. "Yes, I was. But maybe you figured that out from my body language."

Had she been wrong? She felt like a deflated balloon. "I don't think so. I can't see your whole body."

He gave her a brief smile. "Let's not talk about her. Let's talk about you. Have you done any traveling in the last few years?"

She shook her head. "I really couldn't afford to. When I finished grad school, I was dying to take a trip, but I had little money saved. So Carolyn and I ended up going to Boston for a few days. I'm still hoping to go to Greece in a couple of years." She didn't say anything about the past life Courtney had seen. She wasn't ready to broach that subject yet. She gave him a brief smile. "What about you?"

"I went to Italy last summer with Jason, a friend from grad school. It's beautiful, and the architecture is amazing." He described some of the churches he'd visited, like the Sistine Chapel,

"Of course you would want to see those sites. I'd like to someday." She said the last wistfully.

"I'm sure you will," he encouraged her.

The nearby table burst into "Happy Birthday!" as servers brought over slices of cake. The singing was centered on an older guy and ended with "Happy Birthday dear Tom, Happy Birthday to you!" finishing with raucous applause as other tables joined in.

Lindsay smiled and clapped at what looked like family and friends surrounding the man. She wished her mother was here to be celebrated in the same way. She voiced her thought.

"I understand that," Brian said. "It must still hurt that she's missing these moments in life."

He sounded like he'd become more sympathetic over the years, she thought.

Switching the topic, she and Brian discussed places they hoped to see eventually while they finished their meal, and ended with coffee. Lindsay was too full for dessert, but Brian ordered a piece of apple pie and offered her some. She took a taste.

"It's yummy," she said, noticing him studying her. Self-conscious, she asked "What?"

"Just wondering about something." He didn't elaborate.

She dabbed at her mouth with a napkin. Why was he staring at her mouth? Did he want to kiss her?

She asked to get the topic off of her, "What was your favorite city in Italy? Rome?:

"No, Florence. The art and the architecture were inspiring."

"I've seen photos. It looks beautiful."

They left the restaurant a few minutes later. Passing Sharona's table, Lindsay couldn't help hearing their raised voices.

Brian grimaced. Maybe he'd been in the same position as Sharona's boyfriend in the past?

At that moment Todd said in a hard voice, "I said no!"

Sharona stood up and stormed off towards the rest rooms.

Lindsay moved away from the scene.

Once outside, Brian led her to his car. They spoke little on the way back to her apartment. At a red light, Brian turned to glance at her. "I've been thinking about those texts you're getting," he said in a somber voice.

"What about them?"

"I really think you should talk to Parker's friend, Matt. The security guy." Brian's voice sounded concerned.

She sighed. "I didn't want to make a big deal of it, but at this point I agree. I intend to talk to him on Monday." She had met Matt a few times when he was checking the security cameras or other things at the Center.

"Good." Brian nodded.

When they reached her apartment building, Brian parked and walked her up to the door.

She was very tempted to ask him to come in for a drink, but resisted. After all, at this point they were only friends, she reminded herself. Instead she smiled and said, "Thanks for a lovely evening."

"I'd like to see you again."

Before she could stop herself, she asked, "Why?"

"Because, Lindsay, I like you. I want to get to know the adult Lindsay better." He met her eyes. "Maybe… give this thing a chance."

This thing?

She shook her head. "I don't know if that's a good idea," she said slowly, considering. Even now, after a pleasant dinner, she felt a hole in her stomach. What if she came to care for him again—really care? And got hurt when he changed his mind?

Or what if she found she didn't like the more mature Brian, for any reason? He could get hurt too.

But isn't that the chance you take with any relationship? Her mind seemed to shout the words at her.

They had reached her door. He opened it and they stepped into the vestibule. Turning to face him, she repeated, "I just don't know."

"I want to try. He touched her face lightly. "Can I see you again next weekend?"

She shook her head. "Next Saturday is the bridal shower for my friend Courtney Wallenberg. You know, the researcher at TLC. You've probably met her at some point."

"Yes. All day?"

"It's in New York City. All the female employees are going and we're chipping in for a limo. It's going to be a fun Girls Day. I have no idea when I'll be home." She knew she sounded like she was babbling, but it was all true. She had been looking forward to it for weeks. She smiled to take the sting out of declining his offer. She slid her key into the lock.

"Can I see you Sunday instead?"

Part of her jumped at the idea of seeing him again. "I usually do errands and chores, but I guess so." Part of her was reluctant, on the other hand. To avoid hurting his feelings, she added in a lighter tone, "Why don't you come over and I'll make dinner?"

She hoped she wasn't making a mistake.

His whole face lit up. "That sounds perfect."

"I guess you bachelors can't resist a home-cooked meal," she teased.

"I can't resist spending time with *you.*" His low, intimate tone sent a shiver down her spine. Despite her conflicted feelings, she suddenly felt glad she'd invited him.

"Why don't we confirm a definite time during the week? Probably around six.," she suggested.

"I'll be there," he declared. "I'll touch base with you about the exact time on Thursday. I'll be at the Center going over my final plans with Parker, Meredith and Pam and their parents, and Neal Wu. I'll stop by your office."

"You'll be done then?" She couldn't help the disappointment that tinged her voice.

"Only temporarily. Once the Costigans give me the go-ahead on my designs, I'll have to submit them to the township for approval. My remodels require extra electrical wiring," he elaborated.

"I see." So she would probably see less of him after that. She sighed.

He leaned over, and kissed her lightly on the lips.

"Okay," she whispered, unlocking her door. "Bye, Brian, and… thanks for dinner."

"Goodnight, Lindsay." He turned and left.

She went inside and automatically locked her door. After climbing up the stairs, she went to her front window.

She caught a glimpse of him striding down the walkway before he rounded the corner of her building to walk to the parking lot.

Once he did, she backed away from the window,

He wanted to see her again. And despite her misgivings, she wanted to see him again, enough to invite him over for dinner.

She sat on her couch and shut her eyes as memories bombarded her.

Her. And Brian. She recalled how she'd enjoyed every moment of his company. And how his touch would fill her with the sweetest longing, and then satisfaction. The memories reverberated through her brain.

When she met Parker during her lunch break, Lindsay told him about the text messages. He expressed concern at the three messages she'd received and offered at once to call Matt.

"Yes, I'd like to talk to him," Lindsay agreed.

They made arrangements for the following day.

As she sat down on Tuesday afternoon with the security expert, and Parker, who said he wanted to participate because he was concerned, she said, "I may be making too big a deal of this, but it's making me uncomfortable. The person who texted hasn't asked for money or anything. Is this a scam going around?"

"I haven't heard of this particular message going around." Matt raised his eyes from her cellphone to regard Lindsay. "It could be the prelude to asking for bribe money or something like that. It appears that he or she doesn't even know your name."

She bit her lip. "Should I be worried?"

"Not at this point," he reassured her. "But let's be cautious. Have any of your friends or relatives been getting the same message? Maybe someone with a grudge is trying to get at a group of you."

"I can ask the rest of the staff at TLC," Parker volunteered.

"That will help," Matt said, nodding.

"I've already discussed it with one of my friends," Lindsay said, thinking of Carolyn.

"Make up a list of those closest to you, and ask them," Matt suggested. "Include your close family members. And when you're done, please give me a copy with their phone numbers. Meanwhile, I will try to track down this particular number." He wrote some notes on an iPad. "If the person is clever, it could be a burner phone."

"Okay," Lindsay agreed, feeling relief already. "Thank you."

Once she was back at her desk, she prepared to test one of their new clients, a woman in her sixties who was an empath who picked up on others' emotions. It was not an unusual ability, but since this woman had been struck by lightning last year, she was now experiencing an enhanced ability. And was having trouble dealing with it. Lindsay studied her record and saw that she was being counseled by Pam, who recommended more sessions.

Mrs. Caselli did better than average on the basic test that Lindsay administered, and they made an appointment in two weeks for the next one, when she'd be tested by Felipe. Lindsay felt satisfaction as the woman bid her goodbye and left.

Lindsay paused to peer out the window after her client left. The day had been another one so far that was warmer than the ones last week, heralding spring. But the partly sunny skies had now turned gray, with thick clouds hovering overhead. They'd have rain by this evening.

She had a few minutes before her next appointment. Her thoughts turned to Brian, and their dinner a few days ago.

She was already looking forward to seeing him on the weekend. Maybe too much.

That caused her stomach to clench with uneasiness. How could she still want to see the man who'd broken her heart? Why was she giving him another chance?

Because it's what you want, her mind whispered.

A vibration from her silenced cellphone had her glancing at it.

Her next patient was here.

She hurried downstairs to greet Mr. Toohey, forcing herself to thrust aside thoughts about her personal problems.

"Brian, do you have the final plans for your Lightning Center client?" Brian's boss Todd Logan, founding partner of Logan, O'Hare and Prescott Architectural Firm, one of the finest in the area, appeared in the doorway of Brian's office.

"I have them right here," he told Todd. "I meet with them Thursday night to get the final go-ahead from the owners of the firm."

"Great, that's great," Todd, a tall and lean man in his late forties, said enthusiastically. "I'd like to go over them with you and see what they are looking for."

"Sure. Now?"

Todd Logan glanced at his watch " How about at four o'clock?"

"That works." It was almost three now, so that would give Brian time to anticipate his boss' questions and prepare answers.

"Okay. I'll meet you in conference room A," Todd said, and walked down the hall.

Brian worked on the preliminary ideas he was sketching out for a dentist who was opening a new office, then took out the Lightning Center plans and quickly reviewed them. He guessed which questions Todd might ask him.

He'd had a little trouble today keeping his mind on his work. Lindsay kept interrupting his thoughts, floating through his mind periodically. Her beautiful face. Her smile. The subtle perfume she wore. Seeing her again had reawakened something in him, and he kept having these guilty pangs over the way he'd broken her heart years ago. He hadn't wanted to be tied down at the age of eighteen—which he'd been reassured by Evan was a normal feeling—but he now recognized that's what Lindsay had desperately needed when her mother was dying and her father had abandoned the family. He hadn't been considerate about her feelings of love for him. He had crushed those feelings and her spirit at a time when she'd been completely vulnerable.

Evan had confided in him, when they'd shared a cup of coffee, that he'd had a very similar experience with Pam, showing her little sympathy when a patient had committed suicide during her residency. Evan hadn't realized til much later just how devastated she had been. On top of that he'd been very skeptical about the whole idea of the Lightning Center. Of course it took years until The Lightning Center was up and running and working on their mission. It wasn't until other circumstances had brought Pam and Evan back together that they had realized they could have a second chance to reignite their love.

Now Brian mulled over the idea: was it possible for the same to happen to him and Lindsay? Did he want it to?

Yes, he did.

He had an appointment for a counseling session with Evan next week. He was eager to discuss the idea with him.

In the meantime, he would spend time on Sunday with his old girlfriend…

Thursday morning Parker let Lindsay know that he'd arranged for her to have a break just after dinner so he and Matt could speak to her.

She hoped the security expert had learned something, so she was eager for the meeting.

When she joined them in a small conference room on the second floor, she looked at Matt expectantly.

"Did you find out anything?" she questioned him, sitting across from the two men.

"Yes," Matt answered. "Does the name Norman Brown mean anything to you?"

"Norman Brown?" She started to shake her head, then, recalling the short form of that name, she asked

"Norm Brown?" Surprise flooded through her. "He was my sister's boyfriend... before the last one, Sam. But she broke up with him--three or four years ago, I think."

Matt held out his iPad with a photo that looked like a high school yearbook picture. "Norman "Norm" Brown, known well for being our star soccer goalie..." she didn't read the rest.

"He didn't even use a burner phone," Matt told them, placing the iPad down on the table.

"Why would he send these messages to me?" Lindsay asked.

"I'm not sure. Right now he's working a decent construction job for a large company, and he lives in an apartment in Old Bridge. I had one of my security people down in that area make some inquiries. Norman's a loner, and not currently going with anyone. Do you know if he's trying to get back with your sister?"

Lindsey shook her head. "I'm pretty sure Jessica's not dating anyone now, not since she ended things with Sam back in November." Meeting Parker's, then Matt's eyes, she said, "it's no secret that she dates guys for a while, and when those guys get too serious, she has a history of breaking things off."

"I'd like to talk to your sister," Matt said. "Is there a chance we can call her now and get her on a conference call? Maybe she could answer some questions about him."

"I can try, but she sometimes works late as we get closer to the weekend." Lindsay took out her phone. "She works for a large florist and they do a lot of weddings and other events. Now that it's April, the season is getting busier."

"Let's see if she's available," Matt urged.

She punched in her sister's number with fingers that trembled. Parker was studying her carefully. Knowing he had mental telepathy, Lindsay guessed he could read her confusion. Why the heck would Norm be sending her these messages?

"Hi, Lindsay." Jessica picked up on the second ring, and Lindsay switched to speaker phone.

"Jess, do you have a few minutes to talk? I'm here with Matt, the security expert for the Lightning Center, and Parker. They have some info on the messages I've been getting."

"Sure. I'm home now. I didn't have to work tonight, but I will tomorrow, so I can talk now."

Matt introduced himself and Parker, who'd met Jessica when she visited to see where Lindsay worked, said hello.

"The individual who's been sending these messages to Lindsay is named Norman Brown," Matt began without preamble.

"Norm?" Jessica sounded astonished. "Why would he do that?"

"We were hoping you might have a clue," Matt said.

"No. I can't imagine why he'd be bothering my sister. I haven't seen him in—oh, wait. At Christmas time I saw him at Target when I ran in to get a few things. He was shopping, too."

"Did you talk?" Parker asked.

"Only to say hello, how are you doing," Jessica told them. "It was short. He told me he had a new job, but during December and January, they laid off most of the crew."

"Did he ask you out?" Matt questioned

"Yes. Yes, he did. But I wasn't interested. I'd just

broken up with Sam, and wasn't interested in seeing Norm."

"Did he say anything about his social life?"

"No. Nothing. I got the impression he wasn't seeing anyone, at least not seriously. He was a bit of a loner."

"Did he seem disappointed that you wouldn't go out with him?" Lindsay asked.

"Not especially. Why do you think he's harassing my sister, Matt?"

Matt sighed. "Perhaps he thinks she has a lot of influence on you?"

There was a moment of silence. Then Jessica said slowly. "He used to ask a lot of questions about her once he met her at my apartment. At the time I thought maybe he was attracted to Lindsay or something."

Lindsay sat back, surprised. Parker sent her a look she couldn't read.

"But when we broke up, I didn't think about it again," Jessica continued. "Lindsay, has he been bothering you in other ways?"

"Not at all." Lindsay blew out a breath. "I haven't heard from him or seen him since that time at your apartment. I always thought he didn't have much personality."

"He didn't," Jessica stated. "So this—this harassment—is a surprise."

"He may be looking for attention," Parker said, "or a way to get back with you, Jessica."

They could hear her "humph!"

"If anything, he may be looking to get together with Lindsay," Jessica observed. "But why do it this way?"

"Perhaps to make me feel vulnerable?" Lindsay guessed.

Parker gave her a nod. "That's a possibility.," he

said. "We should bring Pam in on this discussion. As a psychiatrist, I'm sure she might have insight."

Matt frowned. "I don't like it. I think we should keep an eye on him."

"Well, he hasn't bothered me at all," Jessica said. "I haven't gotten any messages like that."

"How do you think he got my phone number?" Lindsay asked her sister.

"I don't know, unless at some point he looked at the contacts on my phone. He used to sleep over a lot when we were going out," Jessica said.

Not, Lindsay thought, that that was surprising. He seemed like the type who would sponge off a girlfriend who was making more money than he was, and Lindsay knew he had a history of periods of unemployment.

Parker sent her a look and she knew he'd read her thoughts.

"Well, I'll have Lindsay share my cell phone number," Matt said. "Please contact me if you hear from him, even if it's a brief call; or if you see him around."

"I will definitely," Jessica said.

They all thanked her and Lindsay promised to call again soon.

"Well, that was a surprise," Lindsay told the two men when she disconnected. "I never would have guessed that quiet Norm would be bothering anyone."

"Sometimes it's the quiet ones you have to watch for," Matt stated.

Lindsay nodded. She hadn't been aware that Norm had ever had a crush—or whatever—on her, but now that she knew, she felt uncomfortable.

"Is there something I should do?" Lindsay asked Matt.

"Not now. However, I'm going to have a couple of people keep an eye on him after work," he said. "I don't like this."

"That's a good idea," Parker said.

"But that's expensive," Lindsay protested.

Parker waved her protests away. "It's to protect you. Besides, with that latest donation from Ben Greenfield's charitable foundation, we have extra money to protect our employees."

Matt agreed. "It's for your and your sister's safety. Please don't worry about this."

"Alright," Lindsay agreed. She was so used to having to worry about stretching her budget while she was in grad school, that knowing the money was provided for the employees' safety was a welcome relief. Now that she was working at a job that paid well, it was wonderful to feel she could pay for rent, her car plus her monthly expenses, and still have some left over for fun and clothes. And she was saving a little to go on her dream trip to Greece. Since her mother had left her and Jessica some money for their educations, at least she hadn't had to struggle for the whole amount of her student debt, and she'd gotten a big scholarship towards grad school.

With the meeting over, she went to her desk to get ready for her next client.

Friday. Brian arrived early to meet with the Costigans and Neal Wu.

He'd texted Lindsay Thursday night to ask if he could see her at 12:15 before his meeting, knowing the employees left around twelve on Fridays.

She'd replied "yes."

When he got to TLC, the receptionist was just leaving her desk.

She recognized him. "The Costigans want to see you in the conference room at 12:30."

"I know. I just want to run upstairs for something."

He hurried up the stairs, anxious to see Lindsay, to the research area. Lindsay was the only one present except for an Ashish. whom he'd met before. Lindsay appeared to be packing up her tote.

She glanced up. "Hi," she said breathlessly as he approached.

"I'm looking forward to seeing you on Sunday." He pitched his voice low, but Ashish appeared to be busy on his computer, not listening.

"Me too."

"Six o'clock? And what can I bring?"

She pursed her lips. "A dessert?"

"That would be fine." There was a great bakery in Morristown. He could run over on his way home from work. "And I'll bring wine too. What kind?"

"A white wine."

"What are you making?"

She smiled. "Chicken cordon bleu. I've made it before," she added.

He licked his lips. "Sounds delicious. Perfect. I'll see you then. Bye. I have my meeting." Smiling, he turned to go.

"Good luck," she called after him.

There was a bounce to his step as he moved towards his meeting.

Lindsay had a good feeling as she stepped into the spring sunshine.

She intended to stop at the grocery and get the items she needed for Sunday's dinner. She could cross off dessert and wine from her list.

She'd made this dish once before with Carolyn. She shopped quickly, crossing items off her list once they were in her cart. She drove home with them, put everything away and had a quick sandwich, before going to have her hair trimmed.

Once she was home she made a cup of coffee, deliberately putting aside her concerns about Jessica's old boyfriend and his antics. She tried Jessica but wasn't surprised when she got voicemail. Her sister was usually busy at the florist's on Fridays. She probably had a Saturday wedding to prepare for. Now that it was April, Jessica's job would get busier and busier.

Lindsay relaxed for the rest of the afternoon, looking forward to the girls' day she'd have for Courtney's bridal shower.

She couldn't help wondering if she'd ever be in the same position, preparing for her own shower and anticipating her wedding.

Brian's face flashed before her mind.

Lindsay pulled into the parking lot behind TLC. Laura's car pulled in right in back of her.

Alicia was already parked in the lot. The assistant director of their Research and Testing department was always punctual, often early.

Lindsay got out of her car. As she did, a shiny limo pulled into the parking lot. Within five minutes the other female employees were arriving, except for Pam, Meredith, Sabrina and Kathleen Coatigan. Since those women were in the bridal party, they had planned to get their own limo and go in early with Lorna, their head volunteer, and Kathleen.

"This is going to be so much fun!" Madison said, pulling a heavy package from her car. It was wrapped in clear cellophane, so the gifts at the shower could all be put on display. It would have been difficult for Courtney to open each and every one. Lindsay had heard there were going to be at least seventy women there.

"Let me help you with that," she said, stepping over to her colleague. Laura and Alicia joined them and each took a package.

The co-workers had chipped in for a comforter and matching linens Courtney had registered for. Madison and Tanya , who had become close friends as interns at TLC, had volunteered to wrap them.

Lindsay helped her co-workers to carry over the gifts to the limo's trunk as the chauffeur opened it. Afterwards, the women started piling into the car.

"I can't wait until the wedding!" Tanya said. "It's going to be spectacular."

"Well, Ben is a billionaire," Laura said. "I'm sure it will be wonderful and exciting. My own preference is for something a little more private and low key, though."

"Me too," Tanya confessed. "Besides, my family couldn't spring for anything so lavish."

"Are you bringing a plus one to the wedding?" Madison asked Priscilla as she slid into the seat.

Priscilla sighed. "I'm not sure. I started dating a new guy… but I don't know how it's going to go. I don't know whether to ask him or not. The invitations are supposed to go out next week, Courtney said. So I have to decide fairly soon."

Madison turned to Lindsay. "What about you, Lindsay? Are you bringing someone?"

Brian's image popped into her mind. "I don't know."

"What about that good-looking architect you've been hanging around?" asked their receptionist, Emily.

"Yeah, he seems to be a really nice guy," Dawn said. She was their newer, part-time social worker. She was a young mother who lived nearby and was thrilled to get a job with them.

"Yes, he is," Tanya added.

"He is," Lindsay agreed. "But, I don't know… it's not as if we have much of a relationship now."

Not yet.

"But didn't you have a relationship in the past?" Madison asked.

"That's true." She and Brian hadn't kept it a secret. And since he was a client the staff had shared background info.

"I guess I could ask him, but I don't know if I want to."

"I would do it!" Madison urged. "You'll have a lot of fun if you bring a date."

"Maybe she doesn't think so," Dawn observed.

Everyone looked at her. Lindsay shrugged. "I haven't given it much thought." She decided to steer the conversation in another direction. "It's formal, Courtney said. What's everyone wearing?"

That launched a lively conversation on what people were planning to wear.

"I'm getting a new dress!" Priscilla said.

"I have a gown from my cousin's wedding that I really like. I'm going to wear it," Tanya said.

With the women discussing what she considered a

safer topic, Lindsay sat back. She caught Alicia staring at her.

Had she guessed the tumultuous feelings Lindsay was experiencing?

Lindsay sighed inwardly, then joined the lively discussion.

The trip into the city passed quickly. Once the car got them to their destination—a beautiful catering hall in a large hotel-- they entered. A young woman—wearing a white sash that said "Bridesmaid"—handed Lindsay and Laura flutes of champagne. The beautiful decorations and flowers added to the festive atmosphere, and Lindsay started chatting with Meredith.

They were soon sitting down at their assigned tables. Lindsay sat between Laura and Alicia.

The maids of honor, who introduced themselves as Courtney's sisters, Melissa and Sherry, proposed a toast and everyone stood and raised their champagne flutes.

"To Courtney!" everyone shouted enthusiastically.

The bride- to-be flushed with pleasure. She wore a beautiful white dress with a slanting hem and frills on the short sleeves, which made her look like a bride.

Before luncheon was served, they played a trivia game to see who knew the groom best. Ben's sister won, and received a basket with some scented candles and lotions.

Courtney made the rounds of the tables, greeting everyone. She wore a white sash that said "Bride" in gold letters, and looked radiant.

As the waitstaff began bringing in salads and Italian bread, an older woman—who was sitting beside Courtney's mother, called out "What will your first dance be, Courtney?"

"It's a secret," Courtney answered.

"In my day, we told people what our first dance would be," the woman grumbled.

"I once went to a wedding where the bride and groom hadn't even thought about the song until that day," another woman at the same table said loudly.

"Now they all pick the song and practice a dance to it, Irene," the first woman declared.

"A choreographed dance," another woman chimed in.

Alicia looked around the table. "I think Pam and Evan's first dance was the most romantic one I've ever seen," she said.

Several of the women murmured agreement.

"And it was also sexy," Tanya said.

That started a discussion on first dance songs which continued through the salad course, until they played another game. A cousin of Courtney's won that one. Then their meal was served.

The food was excellent and tastefully presented. Lindsay enjoyed the female camaraderie at her table. There was also white wine to accompany the meal.

Someone called out another question to Courtney.

"Where are you going on your honeymoon?" the middle-aged woman asked.

"The Fiji Islands," Courtney answered.

"How exotic!" someone exclaimed, and heads nodded all around the room.

That began a conversation about destinations. Lindsay knew that Sabrina had gone to Greece and some Greek Islands; Meredith to the Hawaiian islands and Pamela had traveled to Paris and the French riviera. All of these trips sounded so romantic and exciting, and once again Lindsay felt a twinge of envy. Would she be planning a honeymoon someday?

When Brian had broken up with her, and throughout years she spent in college and getting her doctorate, she had pushed aside any thoughts of marrying. She hadn't dated much, instead concentrating on her studies. She didn't know if she'd ever find Mr. Right, or if she'd even want to marry after having her heart broken.

She tried to focus on more positive thoughts now. Maybe she'd someday go on a honeymoon to an exotic location.

They played another game in which some of the ladies made raunchy comments. The wine flowed freely during the main course—a choice of chicken or salmon or a vegetarian option. The food was tasty, and conversation was upbeat. There was a break when guests got up to view the many gifts displayed on different tables. Then their dessert and coffee were served.

"Did you see some of those nightgowns?" Priscilla fanned herself. "They would turn any man on!"

"Some of them were beautiful," Alicia said wistfully. As far as Courtney knew, she wasn't dating anyone and hadn't volunteered in the car if she was bringing a "plus one." Lindsay still thought there were sparks between Alicia and Neal.

Dessert was made up of some small pastries like Cannoli and fancy cookies placed at the center of the tables, and a delicious cake..

The bridesmaids all wandered to different tables throughout the meal, checking that everyone was enjoying themselves. Pam came over to their table to chat with her coworkers.

Dawn asked how Courtney and Ben had met. Pam

spoke about Courtney recognizing Ben from their past life together in Venice, at Pam and Evan's wedding.

"Oh, that's romantic!" Dawn exclaimed.

"Not only that," Pam said, "but he had been murdered in their past life. Courtney was determined to prevent that in *this* life, and the reincarnated killer was finally caught."

"Wow," Dawn said. "What a story to tell their future children and grandchildren!"

Everyone at the table murmured agreement.

Some lively discussions continued about how people met their husbands or current boyfriends as they ate the delicious desserts.

"Sabrina met Parker when she came in as a client," their receptionist said. Lindsay knew that story.

"And Meredith met Richard when she was trying to persuade him to come work for TLC," said Tanya.

Laura turned to Madison. "How'd you meet Keith?"

"At a party his best friend was hosting. My apartment is right next door."

Lindsay listened with half an ear. So many of her colleagues at work were married or going with someone. She felt a little envious. Would she meet the right person someday?

Had she met him already? She couldn't help the little voice that piped up in her mind.

She concentrated on what Tanya was saying about where she'd like to go on a honeymoon.

"I've wanted to visit Ireland for a long time," Tanya said.

"Meredith and her husband are going there this summer," Priscilla told them.

"And Sabrina and Parker are planning to visit Spain,

and Pam and Evan are going in July to Scandinavia—Norway, Sweden and Finland," added Alicia.

"They always have such nice trips planned." Tanya sighed. "I'm trying to save for a trip now."

"I'd love a honeymoon where I get to sit on a beach with a pina colada," Priscilla said.

Conversation turned to the expanding staff at The Lightning Center. Once the renovations were done upstairs, they'd have room for a bigger research and testing staff.

Some of the women, who said they had to catch a train back to Long Island, began departing. Everyone got a scented candle with a picture of Ben and Courtney on the jar as a favor.

"I love the scent," Alicia said.

"Me too," Lindsay agreed. "It's a nice memento."

Her group got ready to leave. Before she knew it, they had said goodbye to Courtney and her bridesmaids and family, and were back in the limo heading to New Jersey.

Talk was centered on Courtney and Ben's love story on the return trip, and the romances that had occurred at The Lighting Center. Content to mostly listen, Lindsay said little.

She thought about the dinner she was making for Brian, and couldn't help looking forward to it. She did enjoy cooking, and didn't do much with only herself to feed.

Alicia mentioned that next weekend was Easter, but she wasn't flying home to Nebraska.

"It's too difficult to fly there on Friday, then turn around and leave right after Easter dinner at my brother's on Sunday, and try to get back at a decent hour. I tried it a couple of years ago."

"So do you have somewhere to go?" Madison asked her.

"Yes, a friend invited me to join her family." She didn't elaborate.

"I know what you mean," Laura added. "Flying home to New Mexico would take too much time out of the weekend. So I'm going to spend the time with a distant cousin. She also invited Eddie, an old friend of mine who relocated to Jersey City for his job, and got in touch with us. I have been thinking of asking him to be my 'plus one' at the wedding," she finished, looking uncertain. "As a friend."

Madison urged her to do it.

As they approached The Lighting Center, it got quieter. People became wrapped in their own thoughts. Lindsay's thoughts turned to Brian again, much to her annoyance. She wondered about inviting him to the wedding.

When they arrived at TLC, she felt content. It really had been a fun girls' day.

Everyone hugged and said goodbye, and Lindsay got into her car and drove home, feeling good..

Once she was home, she kicked off her shoes and slid out of her dress, getting into jeans and a T-shirt.

Jessica called a little later, asking about the shower, and about the texts Lindsay had gotten.

"Should I call Norm and tell him to stop?" Jessica asked.

"Matt said no, not at this point,": she told Jessica. "In fact, if necessary, he and Parkee offered to do it, figuring he'd respect another man more."

"Okay. Tell me about the shower, and the flowers they used."

She did, then told Jessica she'd see her next weekend. She lit the candle she'd received at the shower, then curled up with the cozy mystery she was reading,

Again her thoughts wandered to Brian. Why was her mind revolving around him so much? She felt annoyed. Had it been a mistake to invite him over?

She let her mind drift. Would he attempt to kiss her? And would she let him?

That was an important question. Would she encourage a relationship that was physical as well as friendly?

She shook her head, confusion seeping through her. Was she ready for anything more than a casual friendship?

She could invite him as a "plus one" to the wedding. But once she did that, it would elevate their relationship to a new level. Was she ready?

She took a deep breath, remembering how her heart had broken when he'd ended things with her all those years ago.

No, she wasn't ready, she concluded. She'd keep the status quo.

That decided, she got ready for their dinner, changing to casual pants and a pretty short-sleeved red top. The days had warmed up now that it was April and the kitchen in her apartment would grow warmer while she was cooking.

She started cooking the chicken, then the rice. She would save the asparagus til Brian got here. Once the rice was made and the chicken was cooked, she left those dishes to keep warm.

Her doorbell rang. She glanced at the clock, noting Brian was right on time

When she opened the door, she was impressed. He looked neat but masculine in khakis and a navy polo, and she observed he'd had a haircut. He was holding a box from a bakery, and a bottle of white wine, along with a bouquet of colorful flowers.

"These are for you." He thrust the flowers at her first. She recognized colorful daffodils and red and white tulips. She didn't know what the purple flowers were.

"They're beautiful! She exclaimed. "I'll put them in a vase right away. Thank you!"

A warm glow settled over her as she gazed at the bouquet. It was very thoughtful of Brian.

And romantic. So maybe *he* wanted to take their relationship to the next level.

They went up her stairs, and she found a vase in the cabinet she had in the living room. The flowers fit nicely, and she filled the vase with water. Placing the vase on her table, she said, "it looks beautiful"

"I'm glad you like them." He smiled widely.

She looked at the bottle of wine. "This will go with the chicken." Next she cut the string on the bakery box. "Oh—chocolate layer cake. Yum!"

"I remembered you like chocolate," he said.

"I love chocolate." She waved at her couch. "Why don't you have a seat. You can turn on the TV if you like."

"I'd rather spend the time with you. Can I help?"

She was surprised. Her last boyfriend, back in grad school years ago, used to come over and promptly turn on a ballgame.

Brian was soon tossing the salad for her while she cooked the asparagus, leaving it on a low heat to keep it warm.

They sat down and began the meal with the salad.

He asked her if she'd enjoyed the bridal shower, and she described the food and the games they'd played. "It was a lot of fun," she concluded.

"I guess all the women from the Lightning Center were there?"

"Yes, even the people who work part time, like our new social worker." She focused on him. "Tell me a little about your architectural plans for TLC."

He described his ideas for making individual offices, including utilizing a large closet that was hardly used. "You have another large closet on the second floor near the library which isn't being used much at all. With some shelving, your staff could make better use of the space and keep all the supplies there."

"That could work. What did the Cosigans think?"

"They were very enthusiastic. We're submitting the plans to the town tomorrow. I don't see why they would object, but the process takes a while."

"Great." They ate for a couple of minutes, while he described a few towns that had given him a hard time about some plans for other office buildings. "I'm also working on a commercial building which has an upstairs office that the owners want to convert to living space. That's meeting challenges from the town. Not here." He shook his head. "It's about a half hour from here."

She went to get the main course, and Brian helped her carry the dishes to the table.

When they sat down again, he took a generous piece of the chicken, cut a piece and ate it, his eyes widening.

"It's chicken cordon bleu," she told him.

"Wow. I'm impressed." He dug into the rice pilaf next, chewed and swallowed. "Lindsay, this dinner is absolutely delicious."

She felt her cheeks flushing with pleasure. "I'm glad you like it. I made extra, so help yourself."

It *did* taste good, she admitted to herself.

She knew she was a decent cook, starting when her mother's cancer got worse and she and Jessica had to take on more responsibilities. But she didn't want to think of that now. She concentrated on the meal and Brian's company.

"Home-cooked meals are the best," he said, taking another large forkful. "And this is wonderful."

"Thanks." She smiled at him..

"How do you like the wine?"

She took another sip. It was light and crisp. "Good. It's refreshing and smooth. It's perfect with dinner."

"Glad you like it." He scooped up more rice.

As a teenager she'd noticed he had a hearty appetite. The same was still true.

She took a moment to feel glad that he really appreciated her cooking. It had been one of the most challenging dinners she'd made in a long time. Satisfaction wove through her.

"Tell me about some of the things you're doing at TLC," he began.

She described some of the research projects she was working on. She knew he was aware of their various studies into different areas of psychic research, including a project they'd had from the beginning: research on how, when two or more subjects were together, their psychic abilities were all enhanced. These studies were not secret; they discussed them at conferences, and schools.

"The Costigans told me about that one," he said. It's an ambitious project."

"Yes. And we have other, smaller projects. Like one Courtney and Sabrina are heading up about past lives."

"Any very unusual abilities you've met up with?" he questioned.

"Yes. There's someone who can predict earthquakes twenty-four to forty-eight hours before they occur. I had never seen or heard of that one before. And there's someone who has an extraordinary ability to find lost objects, like keys. And someone who can speed read though they never took a class on that, and their retention of the material is amazing."

He looked surprised. "I never heard of that. You did tell me about the earthquake-predictor."

"And of course, some of our subjects have their talent to an extraordinary degree. Like Sabrina."

"Parker told me she can astral project. That must be an unusual ability."

"We've had a couple of subjects who can do that," she said, "but not to the degree that Sabrina can. She's had enormous success, even finding lost children."

"Wow."

She switched topics. "Tell me what you're working on besides The Lightning Center."

"I have a customer with a building with a store, and the space above was rented as an office previously. But the company moved out, and now they want to convert it to residential space. And I have a dentist who is working on a new office, bringing the place up to the standards that he needs."

"Are they in the area?" she asked.

"Nearby. One is in Netcong and one in Roxbury," he answered, naming two towns in the vicinity. "Those two projects will keep me busy this week, and hopefully I'll hear from this town with approvals of my TLC designs."

"I hope you will hear soon. The design sounds great, and means we'll all have more personal space."

He switched to more personal topics. "How's Jessica?"

"She kept changing careers for a while. She left college after her first year, claiming she just couldn't focus." Lindsay sighed. "Our mother's death was very hard for her."

"As it was for you," he acknowledged. "Is she married?"

"No. She goes from one relationship to another. When something seems to get serious, she usually breaks up with the guy."

He raised his eyebrows. "Oh."

"I think she's afraid to commit," Lindsay admitted honestly. "After all, we had a terrible example with our parents. When my mother was diagnosed with cancer and started treatments, she looked awful. She and my father were very into their looks. And my father couldn't stand the fact that she used to be gorgeous, and no longer was." She didn't try to hide the bitter note in her voice. "Even though my mother used to be very vain, and had fallen for him because he was so handsome, she was shattered when he told her he wanted a divorce.

"It was awful for us all! And the fact that he would leave a sick wife and their kids was absolutely disgusting." She cut a piece of asparagus ferociously.

"I felt very sorry for you all when you told me after we started going out," he said. "And when I met your mom, I felt even more so. She was a decent person—and by the way, she still looked pretty good for someone going through aggressive cancer treatments."

"She was decent," Lindsay agreed. "And my father was a lousy person to do this. He could have waited until she got better-or-or until the end, when we knew she wouldn't make it. There was no reason to do it when he—did." Her voice broke, and she had to fight back sudden tears..

Brian laid a hand on hers and squeezed it. A tear escaped and trailed down her cheek. "I'm sorry to get so emotional," she choked out, feeling her throat tighten with grief.

"Don't apologize," he stated firmly. "I would be feeling the same as you, I'm sure, if it happened to my family. What a horrible thing to do. It's a wonder you and Jessica weathered the storm so well."

"Not really well," she said shakily. "Jessica is afraid of relationships—and I'm afraid too," she confessed, her voice wavering. She met his eyes. She felt embarrassed admitting that to him. After all, he was one of the causes of her fear, not just her father's behavior.

He squeezed her hand again. "Please don't be afraid of me, Linds. For what it's worth, I am very sorry I added to your hurt. I wasn't ready for a commitment when I was eighteen, but I should have stuck around and considered your feelings more. I feel guilty, and I'm truly sorry." His voice shook.

She met his eyes. Surprise swept through her. Her throat loosened. She felt a tremulous smile start on her face.

"Th-thank you." She wiped away her tears. "I appreciate your—saying that."

Brian got up and came around to her side of the table. He pulled her into his arms. "I am truly sorry. I should have been kinder. I won't hurt you again." He held her tightly.

She clung to him, crying as relief swept over her. He's said what she'd needed to hear long ago—late, but he'd finally said it. Brian had acknowledged how much he'd hurt her, and that's what she had wanted for so long. Her tears stopped. She felt his heart thud beneath her face as he held her tightly. He sounded so steady and dependable.

Her fears began to slowly evaporate. She felt something unusual. Trust and hope bloomed deep inside her, spreading warmth throughout her, even to her shaky limbs. She pulled back to stare at Brian's face. "Thank you. I feel better."

"I think you needed to cry," he said quietly. "You can trust me and lean on me." He angled his face to kiss her gently.

But could she really trust him? That negative voice inside her questioned. *Shut up!* She replied sternly. Time would tell. Either he would prove trustworthy, or he wouldn't.

She pulled back to stare at him for a minute. Then she grabbed at her napkin and wiped her remaining tears away, then blew her nose. "I'm really glad you apologized. Really glad."

Stepping back, she suggested "let's finish our dinner." Her voice still trembled.

"Okay, he agreed, heading back to his seat.

They resumed the main course, chatting. He asked her about her Aunt Jane and Uncle Bill.

"Uncle Bill just retired," she said. "Aunt Jane—she's younger—wants to work for another two years. They've started traveling. This summer they're going to Scotland."

"Interesting. My parents were there last summer, and this year they want to go to Ireland. One of my great-grandfathers was born there."

They talked about places they'd been. Lindsay hadn't traveled much since she'd been so wrapped up in school. But she and Carolyn had gone to Boston last year when she'd graduated. She told him of her desire to see Greece, and he described his trip to Italy with his friend, where he'd had a chance to look at architecture from long ago. "It was fascinating," he told her.

"Sounds like it," she remarked.

They ate small pieces of the cake he'd brought for dessert, then Brian helped her clear the table. She had no dishwasher in her apartment, so she started washing plates and utensils by hand and he moved beside her. "Let me help."

Together they did it all in a short amount of time, and put away a few leftovers. Lindsay asked Brian to take some home, guessing he didn't cook much for himself. Most men didn't.

He surprised her, saying he did make himself a nice meal at least once a week. "Take out gets boring, after a while."

"Let's sit down," he said as they finished.

They sat on her couch, cozily close, and he pulled her even closer.

"This feels wonderful," he murmured, kissing the top of her head lightly.

"Yes," she agreed, snuggling closer.

After a moment, he turned her face toward his, and brushed his lips against hers.

His lips were gentle. She pressed against them.

An electric jolt hit her as they kissed. Like being struck by lightning, she guessed. The spark inside her flamed. Her whole body warmed and she instinctively pressed closer, molding herself to him.

He returned her kiss, pressing his mouth against hers, tightening his hold on her with an urgency she hadn't expected. She felt like they both had been ignited—and it was overwhelming.

Her heartbeat had accelerated much too fast. She wasn't ready for this intensity.

She quickly disentangled herself and leaned back.

"Lindsay?" Brian sounded dazed and uncertain.

"Brian—I'm not-not ready for this." Her voice shook. She pulled further away.

His eyes had darkened with passion. "I understand, Lindsay." It came out reluctantly. He disentangled himself further. "I get it," he said. He sounded both understanding—and disappointed.

"I'm sorry. I'm just—not at that point. Yet."

"Maybe another time."

"Maybe another time," she echoed. She was surprised that she wanted this so much. But she was cautious. Maybe too much—but experience had made her that way.

"I better go," his words came out slowly, reluctantly.

"Y-yes," she agreed. She felt both relieved and disappointed.

She didn't really want him to go. But if he stayed here she didn't know if she could keep from falling into his arms again, and not ending up in bed with him. Her body had responded so quickly to his kiss, and she didn't yet trust him enough to make love right now.

He stood up, pulling her with him, and kissed her forehead. "Can I see you next weekend?" His voice was hoarse.

"It's Easter weekend. I'm going back to Monroe to see my family."

"I am too."

She thought rapidly. Trying to juggle seeing him

while spending time with Aunt Jane and Uncle Bill, her sister and cousins, would be too difficult. She wasn't ready to let her relatives know she was seeing him again. "How about the weekend after?" That was the last weekend in April, but she had nothing on her agenda but a half day of work that Saturday.

"The weekend after is perfect. I'll call you during the week," he promised.

"Don't forget your food." She moved to the fridge and removed a sealed bag with one of the pieces of chicken, and another with some asparagus, and a third with rice. "Want some cake too?" She tried to keep her voice even but was afraid she hadn't succeeded.

"You keep the cake. I can enjoy my dinner tomorrow with these delicious leftovers.".

She walked him downstairs to the door.

"Thanks again for a great meal,": he said.

"I enjoyed it," she replied.

He gave her a swift hug and left.

Lindsay shut the door and backed against it. She touched her lips, which were still hot.

Obviously, she still had the same old reaction to Brian—excitement and desire. If she hadn't put a stop to their kiss, they would have been headed eventually to bed. She was certain of it.

And she wasn't yet ready for such intimacy.

She trudged up the stairs. No, it was too soon. He had given her the apology she'd always longed to hear— but it had been a long time coming. She wasn't ready to totally trust him. And she needed that trust, she thought, in order to be intimate with him. Much as he made her hot and physically ready, she wasn't ready psychologically. She didn't know if she would ever be.

It wasn't just that he had hurt her badly. He hadn't believed in her either. No, she wasn't ready for anything more.

She sighed and went to finish cleaning up.

What would happen the next time they got together?

She had no answer.

CHAPTER IX

The week before Easter passed quickly.

Lindsy met some new and interesting patients, continued testing of some existing patients and did two annual patient reviews. She also was on two conference calls with some other colleagues listening to info about some recent studies that had been conducted in Canada and in Oregon.

The weekend was fun although her sister was in a decidedly negative mood. Neither Jessica nor Lindsay had heard further from Jessica's old boyfriend, fortunately; and Lindsay hoped he had dropped his interest in sending semi-threatening messages. She tried to cheer up her sister, whom she suspected was lonely. At least her cousins Erica and Tom were cheerful and fun to be with. Some second cousins from south Jersey joined them at her aunt and uncle's and she enjoyed seeing them for the first time in several years. Aunt Jane made a good meal to which Lindsay added a carrot dish she'd made and Jessica brought a salad. They all had fun, and when she returned to her apartment late Sunday afternoon she felt happy.

Her mind turned, as it often did lately, to Brian. He'd called her once during the week to see how she was, but their conversation had been brief, just asking each other how they'd been doing.

Monday brought a small surprise. Matt, the security expert, texted Lindsay asking if he could speak to her since he'd be in the building in the afternoon. She had no one to test at two o'clock, so she offered to meet him in a small conference room then.

When she entered the room, he was already sitting at the table.

"Why did you want to see me?" Lindsay asked the tall, muscular man as she sat down.

"Norm Brown, your sister's old boyfriend, was arrested on Friday," he stated.

"Arrested?" She stared at Matt. Norm didn't seem like the type to break the law. But then, he didn't seem like the type to send vaguely threatening messages either. "I'm surprised," she added.

"He got into a brawl at a local bar Friday night," Matt said, "with a couple of other guys. They arrested four people total, but the consensus was that he started it." Matt frowned. "He's definitely the kind of person you and your sister should avoid. If you see any sign of him, or Jessica does, or you receive any more messages, please let me know immediately."

"I definitely will," she told Matt. "Thanks for letting me know. I'll call Jessica right now."

She got voicemail, but left her sister a message. She thanked Matt for keeping her in the loop and then went back to her office, her stomach tightening at this news..

Should she be really concerned? Norm was sounding more and more unstable.

She went back to her computer. She had work to do, and so far all Norm had done was sent her some cryptic and annoying messages.

After retrieving her ham and cheese sandwich from the fridge, Lindsay sat down in the conference/break room for lunch on Wednesday.

"So I decided to ask my old friend to be my 'plus one' at Courtney and Ben's wedding," Laura was saying to Pam and Priscilla, who sat beside her.

"Is he the guy who grew up near you in New Mexico?" Pam asked.

"Yes, he's from a distant branch of my Navajo tribe," Laura stated. "Not really related except his great grandfather's second wife was my great grandmother's cousin."

When Lindsay sat across the table from Laura., Laura looked at her. "What did you decide to do, Lindsay?"

"I'm still not sure," she admitted, opening the can of soda she'd brought with her.

As Ashish entered the room, Laura directed her next question to him. "Ashish, what are you doing about bringing a guest to Courtney's wedding?"

He grinned. "Over the weekend I ran into an old friend, Chetna, from my town. She's lots of fun and I spent some time with her on Saturday. I ended up asking her."

"Nice," Priscilla remarked. "How about you, Felipe?"

"I'm bringing Manuel," he said. "We've been seeing a lot of each other during the last few months."

Priscilla sighed loudly. "Maybe I should invite someone. Although I am not really sure about that guy I went out with a couple of times."

"Do you have any friends who you'd enjoy being with?" Pam asked.

"Yes," Priscilla answered. "Now I'm thinking of

asking a friend from high school who still lives in the area."

Lindsay began eating her lunch and wondered about asking Brian again.

They'd had fun together when they'd gone out. But she was hesitant, thinking maybe she would appear too serious, and wondering if he was still skittish about that sort of thing.

Laura looked at her, the question still on her face.

What was there to lose? Lindsay's brain demanded. What, indeed?

Why not? He could always say no. If he did she might feel hurt, or annoyed, but… it wouldn't be the end of the world.

"I guess I have nothing to lose by asking," she said slowly to her friends.

"That's true!" Laura stated. "So why not?"

"You're right, Lindsay," Priscilla said. "I think I will ask my friend too."

"I guess I'll ask Brian. If he says no, I'll go alone." This time her voice sounded more firm.

With that decided, Lindsay actually felt relieved. Brian could always say no if he didn't want to go, she reminded herself. She knew he'd met Ben several times and of course he'd know Parker and Evan and some of the staff who'd be there.

She was still thinking of Brian when she finished her lunch and returned to her desk. She heard her phone ding with a text. It was from Jessica.

I'm surprised to hear about Norm being arrested, her sister had typed. She'd called Lindsay back on Monday night and learned about Norm's arrest. *I still haven't heard a word from him,* her text read. *Good riddance!*

Lindsay typed *Agreed!* And sent the text to her sister.

Less than five minutes later, she heard another ping from her phone. She pulled it from her purse, knowing she had another fifteen minutes until her next client showed up.

This one was from Brian, almost as If he knew she'd been thinking about him.

I have to stop by The Lightning Center late this afternoon. Any chance you're free for a quick dinner and hanging out?

She didn't usually work Wednesday evenings, and had no plans except for reading and watching TV, so she was available. Why not see him and ask him about the wedding in person?

. She sent back a text immediately: *Yes,*

Great. I should be around by 5. I'll come over after that and we can figure out where to eat.

Okay, she replied.

She was looking forward to seeing him again.

CHAPTER X

When she got home, Lindsay hurried to freshen up. She didn't change from her light green top and black pants, but she did replace her short black boots with nicer black shoes, added more make-up, and brushed her hair, adding an extra spritz of cologne. She was ready ten minutes before Brian arrived, and she switched on the Sirrius radio app on her phone which played classic and softer rock and roll. She had her mother's collection of CDs and often heard music on this station that she was already familiar with, like the Beatles. .

Listening, she always felt less isolated when she was alone.

She'd have to ask Brian if he'd seen any sign of her mom.

When the doorbell sounded, she turned off the music and went down the stairs to let him in.

"Hi," she greeted him, her voice a little breathless.

"Hi." He bent to kiss her cheek.

Warmth from the brief kiss spread over her face. She smiled at him. "Where do you want to go to eat?"

"The diner again?"

"Perfect. I'll grab my purse." She hurried up the stairs, and clambered back down them a minute later, purse in hand.

He took her hand after she locked the door and they walked to his car.

During the week the air had grown warmer, and the April evening felt good. His hand surrounding hers warmed her in an unexpectedly pleasant way.

Once at the diner they sat in a booth and studied the menu.

"I think I'll get a deluxe cheeseburger again," Brian said.

After the waitress took their orders, Brian asked her if she was working on any special projects?

"I'm working on a paper about the people who've had pre-cognitive dreams, along with Pam," she said. "We've been working on that for several months."

"Interesting. Have you found anything unusual in your research?"

"It's been proven that women have more vivid dreams than men, and dream more often. I'm working on the theory that they also have more precognitive dreams than men. So far, my theory is holding up."

She decided she might as well bring up the topic of the wedding. Nothing ventured, nothing gained, her grandmother used to say.

"You know Ben and Courtney are getting married in June, right?" she asked him. *Smooth, Lindsay, really smooth,* she chastised herself.

"Yes. I've met them both."

"Well, everyone at TLC is invited to the wedding. And all of us who are single are invited to bring a—a 'plus one'." She swallowed. "Would you like to be my date?"

He gave her a large, delighted smile. "I'd love to be your date."

Warmth and relief suffused her. Brian seemed sincerely glad to be invited.

"Great," she said. "It's Saturday June 8th. I can give you more details when we return to my apartment. I have the invitation there."

"It should be fun," he added, grasping her hand. "Everyone I've met from the Center has been very nice, and interesting. We'll have a good time."

She waited to see if she felt regret at extending the invitation, but what she felt was happy. Happy that she'd invited him, and that he'd accepted so enthusiastically.

She squeezed his hand, then let it go as the waitress brought their cheeseburgers over. "It's going to be a formal wedding," Lindsay told him.

"Black tie?"

"Yes. I hope you don't mind."

"Not at all." He shook his head. "I'll rent a tux."

"Ben is sparing no expense, and giving Courtney the wedding of her dreams," Lindsay told him. "It should be quite an event."

Brian dove into his burger with gusto.

Lindsay followed his example and began eating, but slower. "Our entire staff is planning to be there with husbands, wives, and significant others."

"Evan and Pam too, I presume."

"Yes, They're both in the wedding party," she added, "along with Parker and Sabrina and Meredith and Richard. The Costigans have known Ben for years, and everyone else has gotten close to him, and Courtney."

"Where is it being held?"

She described the well-known, large catering facility in Bergen county. "It will be a traditional Reform Jewish ceremony, according to Courtney. Do you know the story behind how she and Ben met?" she asked.

"No," Brian admitted, "although Parker said something about them knowing each other in a past life."

Lindsay described Ben's and Courtney's love affair and past lives together as Brian listened, eating his meal.

"Wow," he said. "That's really fascinating."

"Yes." She nodded, dipping a fry in ketchup.

Brian polished off his cheeseburger.

They left the diner a little later. She felt very comfortable with Brian when he took her hand. Since she often felt edgy when she was with him—kind of sexually aware and with the pull from the past—she welcomed this more comfortable sensation. Although she still felt the tingly, sexual awareness she always did around him.

Sitting in the car beside him felt cozier now. She invited him to come up to her apartment for coffee.

As they sat on her couch, sipping their coffees, they talked a little about past lives. Brian seemed curious.

"I never heard of anyone having the ability to recognize past lives in others," he said, "until I met Courtney."

"It is an unusual ability," Lindsay admitted. "At TLC, Courtney is the only one we've met who has exhibited it. She doesn't mind telling people, by the way," she added. "Especially those who, like you, have abilities of their own."

"Did she ever tell you about your past life?" Brian asked, his brows raised.

"She said I had several very happy ones in Greece," Lindsay said. "I'm guessing that's why I have a strong desire to visit there one day." She didn't tell him that Courtney had seen him sharing at least one of those lives with her. She didn't think he was ready to hear that information yet.

"That makes sense."

She turned the topic to his family, since he'd spent the Easter weekend with them. He talked a bit about his brother as they finished their coffee.

After a few minutes Brian said, "I have an early morning meeting, so I better get going." He placed his mug on her coffee table.

"Okay," she said, putting hers down as well.

He leaned forward and kissed her gently. She slid her hands up his shoulders.

In seconds, the kiss changed, became electrified. Suddenly he was pressing his lips hard against hers, and she was clinging to him like he was a life raft. Like he was necessary to her very existence.

The kiss became more demanding. It swept her away, and Lindsay hung on, wanting more, needing more of Brian as his tongue tangled with hers. She tasted coffee and a prelude to something more intense.

There was a sweet familiarity to Brian's embrace. But also an exciting flame of charged awareness— desire—piercing through it all. She almost gasped as he freed her lips and kissed her cheeks, her forehead, then her mouth again. Her heartbeat sped up.

"Lindsay," he murmured, his hand stroking her side.

It was too soon. If they kept this up she was well aware they could end up in her bed—and she wasn't quite ready for that.

Not yet.

She disentangled herself. "Brian," she gasped.

He pulled back and stared at her for a moment, his breathing heavy. "I better go."

She heard the reluctance in his voice. She shivered from the desire underlying it.

"Okay," she agreed.

When they stood up, she felt cold, bereft without his closeness.

"But," he finished, "I'll see you Saturday. Six thirty?"

"Sounds perfect."

They walked down the stairs to the door.

"I'm looking forward to it already," he whispered, his voice husky.

"So am I." She smiled. Her heartbeat was still rapid.

"See you then." He stepped into the vestibule, then opened the outer door. She waved as he left the building.

She was looking forward to Saturday immensely, she thought, touching her lips.

They could have ended up in her new, queen-sized bed. The idea was tempting, but… she wasn't ready yet.

But she suspected she would be in the near future. And the kiss permeated her dreams.

CHAPTER XI

The weekend always started for Lindsay on Fridays, when she had the afternoon off. Right after work she ran to the mall and selected a new dress to wear for Saturday's dinner date with Brian. She chose a seafoam green dress and decided to wear her beige pumps with it. She could add either a classic gold necklace or some costume jewelry she already had.

She wanted to get something new for Courtney and Ben's wedding, but would save that for a Saturday when she could spend the whole day shopping.

Once back at her apartment, she did her nails and listened to classic rock on the Sirrius FM radio app on her phone. It always reminded her of the music her mother loved. She and Jessica had grown up hearing her mother's favorite musicians—the Beatles, the Stones, Fleetwood Mac and others—and listening to their music reminded her of her mom, but in a good way. A comforting way.

Her thoughts drifted often to Brian. Was she ready to start over with him? He seemed to want that. Despite her sister's warnings, she was afraid she did want to take a chance on him again. She *liked* the man he had become.

Could she trust him again? she wondered for the hundredth time.

She called Carolyn, who was still encouraging her to spend time with Brian and "see what happens."

"If you don't try," her best friend urged, "you may regret it later."

When she went to bed at eleven, she still felt more confident in her decision to be with him.. She thought about their love-making when they were young. It had been hurried because often they didn't have much time.

Brian had never pressured her, but it seemed everyone she knew was sleeping with their boyfriends, and she was eager to find out what it was all about. They had to sneak around, of course, either in his or her basement recreation rooms or once in Brian's bedroom when his parents were away for the weekend and his older brother had gone out with his own girlfriend.

Their lovemaking had been more sweet than passionate. He had been tender with her, and she had responded with enthusiasm, finding she loved the closeness of being with a Brian, the caresses and sweet touches.

In the ensuing years she had had a couple of boyfriends whom she'd slept with—but none of the affairs had been more than casual and the sex had been unremarkable. She had missed that sense of closeness and intimacy she had shared with Brian, and believed it was because her feelings had never been seriously involved with any of the other men she'd dated.

She finally fell asleep, and slept late. When she awoke she scrambled out of bed and showered, eager to start the day, letting her hair dry into soft waves.

She managed to pass the time by reading, listening to music again, and chatting with her friend Krista.

Like Carolyn, Krista urged her to go out with Brian and see what developed. But she cautioned Lindsay to tread carefully. "You don't know if you can completely trust him," she warned.

Lindsay got ready early for her date, feeling anticipation. She was going forward with Brian, seeing what might happen.

And he was going with her to the wedding. So he expected they would keep seeing each other.

The day had continued the warm spring trend, but now the sky was overcast and predictions were for rain tonight.

Brian showed up right on time. When she opened the door, already holding her purse, she paused to look at him. He looked appealing in his navy sports jacket, a solid light blue shirt and striped tie.

He surveyed her, a smile on his face. "Lindsay, you look gorgeous."

"Thanks. You look pretty good yourself." She felt her cheeks warm. She inhaled, and that crisp, clean and masculine scent invaded her senses.

They were both dressed appropriately for the fancy restaurant he was taking her to. It was about a forty-minute drive to Mendham, and once in Brian's car, Lindsay felt a little self- conscious. Her knee-length dress slid up her thighs and before he started the car, he sent her an admiring look. "You look wonderful. I know I'm repeating myself," he said with a chuckle. "But it's true."

"Thank you," she replied, smiling.

They chatted as soft popular music played in the background. She asked him about the jobs he had worked on that were most satisfying, and he described designing a whole office building with another architect in his firm; and also remodeling a historic brick building to fit the needs of a group of lawyers.

"They wanted to keep the character of this beautiful building," Brian told her, "but make it convenient, and also accessible to some of their injured clients."

"Oh, I'd love to see it," Lindsay said. "It must have been a challenge."

"I can show you photos on my phone. We finished it just about a year ago,"

"Great. I'd love to see them."

He asked her about some of her most challenging cases. She described a woman who was in terror whenever there was a storm since she had been struck, and was now having visions of future events. "She worked with Pamela for a long time to overcome her fears. I gave her the basic tests and then some follow-ups; Courtney, who saw a troubled past life in her, followed up with other, more specific tests."

"And how's your special project going?"

She was glad he was showing an interest in her career, her achievements. She settled further back into the seat. "Well. I didn't get to spend much time on it this week, though. Next week I'll be able to do more."

When they pulled up to the restaurant's parking area, Brian gave the keys to a valet, and escorted Lindsay inside. She caught the scent of his masculine aftershave as they waited to be seated at the table he'd reserved.

She had never been to this place. The sign said it had been a stop for coaches since the American revolution. She'd heard about it from some others at TLC. It was beautiful and historic, and the interior was tasteful and posh, with gleaming woodwork and glowing lanterns along the walls.

The menu included some high prices, but everything sounded delicious. "I've never been here before," Lindsay admitted. "What do you recommend?"

"I've only been here once." He didn't elaborate, and Lindsay felt a twinge of envy-- it probably was with another woman.

"I don't remember what I ate," he said, "but I think I'll have the surf and turf special."

Lindsay had seen it on the list of tonight's specials. It was steak with a lobster tail.

She studied the menu. The chicken Milanese, with a crispy coating, sounded appealing. When the waiter returned, she ordered that with a baked potato and asparagus and a glass of Chardonnay. Brian ordered his meal with a baked potato too, and ordered a red wine.

They sat and sipped their wine and ate the homemade brown bread that the waiter placed before them. The fragrance made Lindsay hungry despite the butterflies kicking up in her middle at being with this handsome, attentive man. How would this evening end? Was she ready to take this relationship to the next level? She wasn't usually nervous about this kind of thing. But this was Brian, whom she'd once known intimately. .

Through the meal, he sent her some flirtatious looks and she responded in kind with warm smiles and lowered eyelids. She found herself blushing when he complimented her about the meal she'd cooked for him which he labeled "better than any restaurant."

They finished with coffee and shared a generous piece of apple pie.

The waiter asked if they wanted an after-dinner drink.

Lindsay took a deep breath. *Might as well go for it.*

"No thanks," she told the waiter, and then she whispered to Brian, "why don't we have a drink at my place?"

He smiled widely. "I'd like that."

It was drizzling when they left, and they waited under the awning for the valet to bring his car. Brian reached out and put his arm around her, pulling her close.

Once in the car Brian turned it west and drove them back. They spoke little. Lindsay had enjoyed the delicious meal but now was feeling nervous again.

When they got back to Mount Olive, she led the way to her apartment. Once upstairs, she automatically kicked off her heels. "I don't like wearing shoes inside," she explained.

"I remember," Brian said. "I'll be glad to take off my good shoes too." He slid them off.

Somehow, without shoes, Lindsay felt that they were both partially undressed. Which was ridiculous, she told herself.

She opened the liquor cabinet in her wall unit and asked him what he wanted. "I have Scotch—my uncle likes that if he and my aunt come over—and my favorite, Midori, a melon liqueur." Jessica had brought her that at Christmas because she knew Lindsay occasionally liked a sweet drink.

"Scotch is fine," Brian answered.

She poured him a glass over ice, then took some Midori for herself. She sat beside him on the couch.

He scooted over so their bodies were touching.

For a moment they simply sat, sipping their drinks. The sweet melon taste with a sharp tang slid through her mouth and down her throat as she looked into Brian's eyes. He gazed back.

Then Brian reached out and played with a curl of her hair.

"You have the most beautiful hair," he whispered. "And… I'm excited to know you better now than as a teenager."

She leaned closer.

"Thanks," she murmured, her heart beating rapidly

at his touch. "I like learning more about you too." And she did.

"I admire the woman you've become," he murmured.

But she wondered, did he really admire all her achievements? The ones she had worked towards, sacrificed for?

She wouldn't think of that now. She shoved those negative thoughts aside with ferocity. *Concentrate on the here and now. On Brian being close to you.*

He abruptly took her glass and put both their glasses down on coasters she'd placed on her coffee table.

"I've been wanting to do this all evening," he declared. And he gathered her in his arms and crushed her to him, his lips coming down on hers.

It wasn't a gentle kiss. It was a sweet but demanding one. A passionate kiss. He kissed her hard, holding her tightly. She met his lips eagerly as the heat of their kiss burst through her whole body. She kissed him back, the kiss quickly escalating into passion, and she gasped against his lips. The desire spiking through her was exciting.

"Lindsay, Lindsay." He kissed her cheeks, her forehead, and then swooped to her lips again, kissing her repeatedly. "God, I want you. So much."

Her voice shook. "I want you too, Brian." It was like throwing herself off a diving board into a deep pool. A pool full of sensations.

"Are you sure?" he pulled back a little. "Are you certain? I want so much to make love to you, Linds." He held her face and gazed into her eyes. "I've dreamed of making love to you. Having you beneath me, hearing your cries—" he kissed her again.

She felt no uncertainty now. "Yes," she breathed.

With that he kissed her again, harder, and slid his hand down to grasp her breast. Even through the cloth of her dress she felt the searing heat of his hand. She leaned into it, letting the warmth and passion ignite her further.

He squeezed her. She heard a soft moan and realized it was her own.

"Lindsay…" he whispered.

"Let's take this into my bedroom," she whispered.

"Yes. Yes."

She opened her eyes and stood, holding his hand. She led him down the hall and to her bedroom.

He barely glanced at the room as she turned on the nightstand light, leaving it on the low setting.

He pulled off his tie, then his shirt, as she quickly shed her dress.

Standing half-dressed next to Brian after all these years was better than she recalled. His shoulders were broader now, his chest had more dark hair sprinkled over it as he pulled her close. His chest hairs brushed against her, stimulating her. His chest was hot and his fingers trembled slightly as he unhooked her bra.

He dropped it on the floor.

He pulled back and his hungry glance swept over her. Bared to him from the waist up, she felt emboldened by the huger in his eyes.

She started to move her hands and he stopped her.

"Let me look at you," he whispered. "Lindsay, you are even more beautiful than I remembered. You've always had the most gorgeous breasts and of any woman I've ever seen—" He bent his head and suckled one, then the other.

She felt the pull of longing right down to her core. Grasping his head, she moaned.

Desire cascaded through her. She pulled him towards her bed. They tumbled down and he unbuckled his belt and she helped him shed his pants. He pushed aside his boxers and she felt his hard shaft.

It was like steel covered by satin. She held him firmly.

"Lindsay…" now he was groaning. "That feels— so—good."

He tugged at her lacy bikini panties and slid them off. His hand returned to touch her reverently.

"Brian," she whispered in a throaty voice she barely recognized.

Sex with Brian had always been warm and caring, but this—she had never been so turned on. She was going up in flames. He had ignited her whole body and soul. She kissed him deeply, their tongues tangling.

He pulled back and said "Lindsay" in a tender voice, then swooped in again to capture her lips. She held onto him tightly.

His mouth traveled down to pull at her nipple and desire speared through her whole body. "Brian," she gasped.

He pulled back slightly. "Are you certain Lindsay?" he asked.

"Yes. Oh yes."

He fumbled with the pants which he'd thrown to the end of the bed and withdrew a foil packet. A rush of gladness wove through her. He'd always been a careful and considerate lover, and she was happy to see he hadn't changed. Although she had a few in her nightstand, she hadn't used them in forever. "I do have some in my apartment if we need more."

"You were planning..?"

"Just in case." She gave him a provocative smile.

He slid next to her again, taking her into his arms, and cupped her where she wanted him most.

She moaned again. It felt so good—so wonderful—to have Brian beside her, caressing her after all these years.

He inserted a finger into her. She bucked up as the first sensations hit her so strongly, so unexpectedly—

He rolled on top of her. "Lindsay, sweetheart—" He thrust into her, deeply, tightly.

"God, you feel so good—" he panted—"so wet and hot—"

He pulled slightly out, then thrust again, harder and further.

The orgasm rocked her whole body. "Brian!" The scream erupted from her.

And he followed, yelling her name.

She felt him vibrating inside her.

Electrical aftershocks shook her whole body.

She had never felt so good.

Brian held her tightly as vibrations of pleasure spiraled through him. She seemed to be just as intensely affected.

Making love to Lindsay had been better than all his dreams. Better than he remembered or even imagined. He felt more passion, more tenderness, more everything--like the lightning bolt had struck him all over again—but this time, leaving pleasure, not pain, in its wake.

He kissed her again, holding her tightly.

"Brian?" she asked in a sleepy voice.

"Yes, sweetheart?"

"Would you like to stay here tonight?"

He hugged her tighter. "There's nothing I'd like more."

"I'm glad." She burrowed into him.

She wanted him to stay here. She wanted their closeness to last through the night.

He felt immensely happy at that realization. He wanted that same closeness too.

Within a few minutes her breathing evened out, and he knew she was drifting into sleep. He kissed her cheek again and drifted off himself.

Lindsay gradually became aware of the warm man next to her.

Brian. His breathing was soft and steady, and it felt extraordinarily good to be snuggled against him, under the covers. His heart thudding near her, their legs tangling.

She opened her eyes. A dim light still shone on her nightstand. She moved to turn it off, careful not to disturb him. *Brian, her lover.* She slid back beside him and closed her eyes.

Pleasure flowed through her, and a sense of rightness. Their lovemaking had been the most passionate, the most stunning lovemaking she'd ever experienced in her whole life. She'd do it again in a heartbeat.

She had the opportunity now.

Brian moved against her. "Lindsay? Are you alright?" His voice was sleepy but with a note of concern.

"Better than alright," she murmured, and kissed him.

His reaction was instant. He kissed her hard, tightening his arms around her, and she could feel his warm penis growing against her body.

He groaned. "Linds, I want you again—"

This feeling of importance was like no other. He wanted her as much as she wanted him!

She moved against him too, increasing the heat and friction between their bodies. When he rolled on another condom, whispering that he'd have to get more of these, she felt more powerful than she ever had before.

He boldly thrust into her, and she zoomed right to the stars, gasping.

"Lindsay!" He followed, pumping into her.

It was morning when he woke again.

The bed was messy from their passionate love making—three times—last night. He and Lindsay were tangled up in the soft comforter. As he moved slightly, she opened her eyes and smiled.

"Good morning." Her voice was a sexy, throaty whisper.

"Good morning." He bent down and kissed her.

"I need a shower," he said. "Want to take one together?" They had never done that before.

"Sure," she responded.

Her apartment's bathroom was cramped, but they showered, laughing, and ended up making love in bed one more time. While they were laying together afterwards, his stomach growled.

She propped herself up and looked at him, her mouth tilted in a smile. "You must be hungry."

"Starved. We worked up an appetite." He touched her face tenderly. "This was a spectacular night."

"I agree," she said in a husky tone.

"How about," he suggested, "we get dressed, I run

back to my apartment—with you—and get clean clothes, and then I take you out to breakfast?"

"Sounds like a good idea."

"And then " he added, "we can spend the day together. And I can go to a drug store and get more condoms."

She smiled, a wide smile that touched him deep inside. He gathered her and held her close.

They did exactly that. He drove them to his condo—which she liked, exclaiming over the large closets he had and the luxurious bathroom—then went to a nearby, large diner for brunch. After a quick visit to a nearby pharmacy, it started raining, and they decided on seeing a new suspense movie. They enjoyed it, then went back to her apartment and made love again.

This was so much more than their quick, furtive lovemaking when they were young. They could bring each other to the peaks of pleasure. They could take their time and appreciate each other's bodies, and bringing each other pleasure while enjoying each other thoroughly.

He loved seeing her climax, and hearing her cries of ecstasy.

"Lindsay," he said after as they lay on her bed, "you make me feel so wonderful." He stroked her hair.

"You make me feel wonderful too," she told him, and kissed him deeply.

When they came up for air, he asked, "Can we get together next weekend—Friday and Saturday and Sunday?"

"I'd love to," she replied, "But Saturday I'm working in the morning."

"That's right. Okay, how about Friday night we go out and then again on Saturday and Sunday?"

He wanted to spend the whole weekend with her!

She nodded, happy to hear his words. "Okay." Pleasure washed over her. "You can plan to stay here too, so pack a duffle bag."

"Great. I'll stay Friday night but leave when you go to work. I promise not to distract you from getting in on time.," he teased.

"I was going to go shopping for a dress for the wedding."

"I can go with you."

She hesitated. Did she really want to model different formal dresses for him? No, she decided. She'd rather find something attractive and surprise him with it.

"We'll see," she said lightly. "I may go during the week with a friend from work. But we can always shop for something else."

That evening they went back to the local diner again, and then returned to her apartment and made love one more time. Before he left on Sunday night Brian kissed her thoroughly. "This was a wonderful weekend," he murmured, nuzzling her ear. " I had a great time with you." He pulled back to stare into her eyes.

"I did too." She kissed him. "I can't wait til next weekend already."

That night as she lay in bed, she thought about all their love-making. It had been absolutely spectacular. Everything she had ever wished for, and more. He'd brought her to the heights of passion, yet he had been a considerate lover, always making sure she was satisfied, She couldn't have asked for a better lover.

Brian. Her lover. She shivered as she recalled his kisses and caresses, and hearing his throaty cries as he came., feeling him pump into her—

She'd never get to sleep if she kept thinking like this.

Instead, she concentrated on the warmth of his arms, how safe and cared for she'd felt as she sheltered in them…

The week both dragged for her and rushed by.

When she looked at her face in the mirror while applying make-up, she noted she had color in her cheeks. Had Brian put that there? And her eyes shone. She knew that was from a weekend of good love-making.

But she missed Brian. Although she got to work on time and Meredith said "you look good!" to her, the morning crawled.

Brian texted her at ten AM saying he missed her. She replied "Miss you too!" She was tempted to add a heart emoji to the text, but decided against it. She didn't want to come on too strong.

His text did add a spring to her step for the rest of the day and she was smiling when she entered the lunch/conference room.

"You look cheerful," Laura said, looking her over. "Have a good weekend?"

"Yes, I did," she answered her friend. And in a low voice, she added, "I took your advice and asked Brian to the wedding. He's coming!" She could hear the lilt in her voice when she said that.

"Oh, great!" Laura said.

"What's great?" Priscilla asked, joining them and unwrapping a sandwich which smelled like tuna fish.

Lindsay explained as Meredith entered the room.

"Good for you!" Meredith declared. "I think you'll have a great time together. The wedding should be a lot of fun."

"That's funny! I decided to ask my friend to come to the wedding this weekend too!" Priscilla said. "Now, what are you all wearing?"

They launched into a discussion of dresses, long and cocktail-length. Since it was a Saturday night wedding and formal, most of the women discussing the topic wanted to wear formal long gowns. The bridesmaids were.wearing that length, Pamela said.

Lindsay always enjoyed feeling an essential part of the female-centric group at the table. Lindsay had missed that camaraderie when she first left grad school, but now she was an accepted—and valued—member of the team here at TLC. Happiness spread through her at the realization.

That feeling continued through the afternoon, and between that and the glow from the weekend with Brian, the afternoon moved more quickly than the morning had.

She did see some interesting patients, but in between she thought constantly about Brian When she had a few moments alone she found herself missing his touch, his kiss… oh, hell, him. She had it bad. She longed for Brian.

It was almost a relief to return home although her apartment seemed empty without him. She paused after kicking off her shoes at the top of the stairs, and grabbed her cellphone. She texted him "My apartment feels lonely without you here." Then she went to change out of her work clothes to her favorite pink yoga pants and a matching long sleeved T shirt.

Ten minutes later, as she removed a salad from her fridge for dinner, she heard a return text. Picking up her phone, she read: "I can't wait to see you this weekend!' from Bian. Her heart jumped up and she responded, "Me too!"

Brian missed being around Lindsay. It was worse at night when he climbed into his big bed and she wasn't beside him to hug. To ignite him.

Thinking of her soft curves and silky skin made him hard. If he kept thinking like this, he would never get to sleep.

Tuesday was no better. Thoughts of her kept interrupting his workday, and once when he was in a meeting with several others in his firm he had to turn to Larry, an older man whose ideas he admired. "What did you say?"

When he got home he was actually relieved, though he loved his job. At least at home he wouldn't have to pay close attention and he could relax and let his mind wander.

After he ate the dinner he'd picked up on his way home—chicken tenders and fries and a coke—he went up to his home office and sat at his desk, intending to look over some ideas for an office remodel he was doing in conjunction with Larry. Sitting there, he unrolled the preliminary sketches they'd worked on.

He saw something out of the corner of his eye. Swiveling his chair to the right, he turned to look at it head on.

The figure standing there wavered, then appeared to solidify. A woman, looking to be in her forties, with dark wavy hair, wearing a red dress, looked back at him. With a start he recognized Mrs. Hughes, Lindsay's mother! He stared at her image.

He was seeing her spirit, he realized. Just as he had seen other people.

"Mrs. Hughes," he breathed.

She gave him a soft smile. Her lips moved. But Brian couldn't hear the spirits he saw--unlike some people.

"Don't hurt her." The words seemed to float through his brain, and he realized it was Mrs. Hughe's thoughts he was "hearing" with a sixth sense.

"I won't hurt your daughter," he affirmed. "I will not hurt her." He repeated it emphatically. He had vowed never to do that again. .

Lindsay's mom gave a brief nod, and then with a small smile her image began to fade.

"Should I tell her I saw you?" But he was addressing vacant space. She was gone.

He sat frozen for five minutes. He hadn't seen a spirit for at least a year, and now to see Lindsay's mother… it was mind-blowing.

Mrs. Hughes must have wanted reassurance that he wouldn't hurt Lindsay, he concluded.

Not that he would. But should he tell Lindsay he'd seen her?

He sat thinking, for a good twenty minutes. Should he? She might be happy, then again, it might bring up sad memories of her mother's death. Should he not? If he didn't, and it came out later she might feel hurt or mad that he hadn't said anything. Besides, maybe it would contribute to the research The Center was doing.

Maybe he should ask Evan. He checked his calendar. Yes, he had an appointment on Thursday afternoon right after a work commitment.

That decided, he went to relax and watch TV.

"You're looking good," Evan said as he escorted Brian into his office on Thursday.

It's amazing what a great woman and great sex can do for a man, Brian thought. But he didn't say that to his friend. Instead he said, " I had a great weekend." He sat in the chair in front of Evan's desk,

Evan raised his eyebrows, then sat behind his desk. "Oh?"

"I spent most of it with Lindsay, and we got along great. I think she's trusting me again. At least it appears that way. She invited me to come with her to Ben and Courtney's wedding." Brian relaxed his body.

"Nice. You want her to trust you?"

"Yes, it's important to me. But something happened afterwards. I'm uncertain about sharing it with the team since that group includes Lindsay." He furrowed his brow.

"You tell me whether to share it."

"I do value your advice." Since high school, he'd admired Evan's logic and wisdom. Having counseling and discussion sessions with him here had brought them closer, and he truly valued his opinions.

He described the sighting of Lindsay's mother's spirit, and his confusion afterward about whether to tell Lindsay or not.

Evan listened, steepling his hands.

"What does your gut tell you?" he asked.

"My feeling is, I should tell her," Brian answered.

"Then I'd go with that," Evan advised succinctly. "But perhaps… choose your moment carefully."

"What do you mean?"

"Women are very sensitive." Evan waved his hand in a "what are you going to do?" gesture. "It's important to have a discussion when she's not upset, when you think she's feeling good and can speak about her mother without much emotion. Lindsay was a teenager when she lost her mom--a difficult time in anyone's life."

"That's true." Brian considered Evan's words. "I'll have to be sensitive to her needs."

"Yes," Evan affirmed.

They were silent for a moment, then Evan asked, "have you had any other experiences lately?"

"No. I'm not sure why they sometimes happen more often, then I can go months without one."

"I don't think we at the Center have figured that out yet," his friend said candidly. "But if you get any glimmerings of an answer, let me know."

"I will. And I'll tell you when I have another—visitation—whether it's Mrs. Hughes or someone else."

Brian had sent Lindsay a text that morning, saying he'd be at the center in the afternoon. He knew Thursdays were their busiest day but asked anyway if she'd have a chance to meet him, have a cup of coffee, or just say hello.

She'd replied that she was all booked up, but could plan to stop into the break room to grab a soda after his appointment with Evan. Apparently, she knew the Center's schedule for the entire day.

It was better than nothing. So he had texted yes, he could meet her.

He casually stopped into the conference room when his session with Evan ended. He felt like he was back in high school, scheduling breaks to catch a few moments with his girlfriend—Lindsay then, and Lindsay now.

She hurried in a few minutes later. "Hi."

"Hi." Since they were alone at the moment, he bent and kissed her, then took hold of her arms and held her close to him. Being close to her made him feel better than good. He stepped back reluctantly. He didn't think Lindsay wanted to broadcast their relationship yet. "I can't wait to spend the weekend with you."

"I can't wait either." Her voice was throaty and husky, reminding him of good whiskey.

She shot him a wide smile. "I want to grab some cold water." She opened the refrigerator and took out a bottle.

"I'll come over after one o'clock tomorrow when I can wrap up my day."

"Great. See you then." She pivoted, sending another smile over her shoulder, and hurried out of the room.

He had hoped for a longer amount of time with her. He sighed.

<hr>

When the knock came at her door at one thirty, she practically skipped down the stairs of her apartment.

Opening the door, she found Brian standing in the vestibule, an eager, wide smile on his face. His masculine scent preceded him.

"Lindsay. I missed you more than I can say."

"Come in."

He stepped inside and pulled her up into his arms, crushing her against him.

She kissed him fervently, and he kissed her back just as hard. They stumbled up the stairs together, still locked with their arms around each other. They made it to the top and began shedding each other's clothes. His kisses heated her all over, and without words they moved toward the bedroom. She couldn't wait to get him into bed and make love, and his fervent kisses told her he felt the same way.

"Brian." She was actually breathless. "Brian. I missed you too."

Then there were no words. They tumbled together onto the bed, as they finished pulling off each other's clothes. He lavished kisses on her, sucking on her nipples as the heat in her tightened to one place, one spot. He sheathed himself quickly, paused a second above her, then thrust into her, burying himself deep inside of her.

The intense thrust brought her to the peak. She cried out, seeing stars.

"Brian!"

He followed a second later. "Lindsay!"

They lay tangled together for several minutes. She couldn't say a word. She had never experienced such sudden passion. It was Earh-shattering.

That was her only coherent thought for several minutes.

He couldn't think; could barely breathe.

Their love-making had been so intense, so sudden and spectacular, that Brian could only feel intense pleasure enveloping him. He lay there, stunned, on top of Lindsay's blanket as her body entwined with his intimately. Finally realizing his weight must be pressing hard on her, he shifted so they lay side-by side. He kissed her softly.

"Lindsay. That was—that was—amazing."

"Yes." Her voice was muffled as she pressed her face against his shoulder and kissed him. "And exciting!"

He couldn't remember getting so instantly and

thoroughly aroused before, even as a teen. And coming so hard and so fast.

"You are—" he fumbled for words—"beautiful and sexy and—oh hell, the most sexy woman. Ever."

He could feel her smile. "Thanks," she whispered. "And you got me so turned on."

He hugged her.

After a few minutes she disentangled herself. "My one arm is getting numb."

"Oh. Sorry." He sat up. "I didn't realize, I was so… overcome." He leaned down and kissed her.

Slowly, they searched for their clothes and re-dressed.

Lindsay watched him, suddenly feeling cold without his arms around her, and with the realization of what that meant. In a short time, Brian had become *important* to her.

Maybe too important.

CHAPTER XII

They had originally planned to eat out at a nearby restaurant Lindsay recommended.

But Brian was happy that Lindsay agreed with him to stay in and order food instead. He relaxed with her on the couch as they studied the menu from the Chinese restaurant in town, his arm holding her close.

Brian could see Lindsay had carefully made the living room cozy with pillows, spring-like decorations of dried flowers, and framed photos.

During their love-making the gray and cloudy skies outside had turned stormy. Rain began to pelt the windows.

The guy who delivered their food wore a raincoat with the hood up. As Brian gave him a generous tip, the rain began to come down hard.

Lindsay was putting out dishes and utensils as Brian brought the food up the stairs. They dug in. He was starving, probably from their frenzied lovemaking.

"This is good," Brian said. His pepper steak and pork friend rice, which they were sharing, was delicious.

"Try this." Lindsay gave him a sample of her sweet and sour chicken.

"That's delicious too," he told her.

Afterwards, they cleaned up, then went back to bed and made love, taking it slower this time. Linsday's exclamations as she came were the most stimulating and satisfying he'd ever experienced. It was amazing that he could feel this wonderful each and every time they made love. He'd never experienced that same satisfaction with any other woman.

They showered and watched an old episode of the original Star Trek, which they used to watch reruns of in high school—and snuggled together, making love again, before Lindsay turned off the bedside lamp and they both fell into a contented sleep, with the soothing sound of rain hitting the building's roof above them. Before he drifted off, Brian felt an enormous contentedness wash over him.

Lindsay woke at seven o'clock before her alarm shrilled, to a cloudy morning, but she felt as if it was a sunny day, happy and optimistic.

She quietly slid out of bed and left Brian sleeping.

After a quick shower, she started her coffee maker.

Brian stumbled into the kitchen. "Good morning." He reached out and engulfed her in a hug.

"Mind if I take a shower?" he asked.

"Of course not. Grab another towel from the linen closet." She watched as he left the room. He'd decided last night that when she left for work, he would go back to his office, check on a few of his project plans, and do a little work. Then, when she went to the mall to shop, he'd finish up and meet a friend to watch a baseball game at a sports bar. He would meet up with Lindsay in the late afternoon and go to the Italian restaurant they'd originally planned to go to yesterday.

Lindsay kissed him when they parted, promising to see him later.

The Saturday TLC meeting was brief. Lindsay sensed that she wasn't the only one in good spirits. She asked if Laura wanted to join her at the mall, and her friend said "Yes!"

"As soon as I stop at home and walk my dogs," Laura said. "I can't wait until we have that doggy daycare they're planning here!"

Lindsay smiled. She would love to get a dog, once she had a house or condo. Her apartment didn't allow them, and besides, she wasn't home very much. It would be unfair to the dog. That's why, Laura had told her, she had two—to keep each other company. Of course, once they had an on-site doggy daycare, it would be wonderful for any dog she had.

"I can meet you at the mall at, let's say, one," Laura added. "We can eat lunch there."

"Good idea," Lindsay agreed.

The morning sped by with one annual retest, and administering the basic test to two new patients. One man had come all the way from Maryland. But he had cousins in the area, he told her, so he was visiting and staying with them while he was tested.

By twelve they were all finished. Lindsay left for the mall, knowing she'd soon see Laura.

They ate at a salad place, and discussed the guys they were bringing to the wedding. Then they went to look at formal dresses and gowns at Macy's.

Lindsay loved looking at the different styles, colors and fabrics. Her mother used to say "It's bad to wear black at a wedding. It's like wishing the couple bad luck."

"It's not that way anymore," Lindsay had protested. But it must have stuck with her, because she usually wore different colors to weddings. Besides, she liked colorful dresses.

She chose five dresses to try on—all varied colors and styles; and Laura selected four.

They had fun comparing necklines and fit. Laura's native skin tone and midnight-black hair made her look great in bright colors. She chose a beautiful turquoise dress from among them as her favorite.

"I have jewelry from my reservation that will match perfectly." she said. Lindsay knew she came from New Mexico.

Lindsay selected a very dark blue, clingy dress that she thought would make her look sexy. She pictured dancing with Brian when she wore it at the wedding.

They put their dresses in their cars so they wouldn't have to carry them around the mall, then returned to look for nice shoes to go with their dresses.

They each found high heels they loved, plus sandals for summer casual wear..

When they parted to head home, they hugged before leaving the mall. Lindsay felt warm and satisfied with the friends she was making at TLC. And triumphant over finding the perfect dress and shoes.

It was almost four o'clock by then, and with Brian due to meet her at five, she drove back to her apartment to spend a little time relaxing before he arrived.

As she drove home, she listened to the radio—a soft rock and roll station on Sirrius. Though the day was cloudy and gloomy, she felt as if the sun was shining. She was a woman going to meet her lover. *Her lover, Brian.* Delight swept through her.

She hummed along as the lead singer sang about really wanting to see an old girlfriend. How apropos. She and Brian had really wanted to see each other. She didn't know what the future would bring, like the people in the song, but they both really wanted to see each other, to spend time in each other's company. She relaxed and tried not to think about the future.

Did their taking their relationship further mean that he was now her boyfriend? she wondered. Whether he was or not, she was basking in the relationship now.

She enjoyed driving with the music. When it ended, she hummed along with two others tunes. Traffic was light as she got off the interstate.

It might be a gloomy day, but she was spending the rest of the weekend with a fabulous guy whom she was coming to like more and more.

And that's when the niggling doubt crept its way into her mind: was she coming to care too much about a man who had disappointed her before, and could do it again?

When she pulled into her parking lot, Lindsay turned off the engine and texted Brian: *I'm home!*

She hoped he'd arrive soon. In the meantime, she wanted to get her dress, wrapped in the store's dress bag, into her apartment before he could see it. She didn't want to reveal it until she wore it to the wedding.

Which reminded her, she had to suggest they book a room in the block at the hotel near the banquet hall. There was a block being held for the wedding guests, and there would be available buses to transport people to the banquet hall. She was pretty sure Brian would want to stay there and be free to drink without worrying about driving. Her colleagues were doing the same.

The minutes that had flown by with her friend at the mall seemed to crawl now. She glanced at her phone several times.

160

Then, a ping alerted her to a text.

I'm nearby, she read. *I did a couple of errands on the way over. I should be there in ten minutes.*

He would be here soon! She felt like a teenager waiting for her date to arrive.

Lindsay got up and quickly changed to a nicer pair of black pants and a bright yellow top. She added a costume jewelry necklace and matching earrings, ran a brush through her hair and touched up her make-up. She was ready when Brian knocked on the door.

She flung it open. "I'm glad you're here early."

He pulled her into his arms. "So am I." He kissed her thoroughly, not waiting until they were even inside her apartment. When she came up for air and they stepped inside, she realized he held a large bouquet in his hand.

"For you," he said, handing them to her.

"They're beautiful!" she declared. The bouquet included yellow daffodils; pink, red, and white tulips.; and purple flowers she didn't recognize. "Let me put these in water. Thank you!" She kissed his cheek.

Upstairs, she opened one of the doors to her wall unit, taking out a large glass vase which had been her Mom's. She'd always liked the cut crystal design. The flowers fit in perfectly once she'd trimmed the stems. She added water and smiled at Brian as she put them on her kitchen table where they were easily visible from the living room. The scent perfumed the area and she took a deep breath.

"You look like spring with that yellow top," Brian said.

"I feel spring -like with you," she quipped, feeling her cheeks warm.

He slid a soft finger down her cheek, then kissed her. "You're very special, Lindsay."

She wasn't sure what to say to that, so she kissed him. He drew her into his embrace and hugged her. "Are you hungry?"

"Yes, but not for food," she whispered, and pressed her body against his.

"I feel exactly the same."

Within minutes they were undressed, under her comforter, and he sifted his fingers through her hair as he pressed her into the mattress. "Your hair is like satin, Lindsay," he murmured, kissing her again and again. Then he moved his clever fingers to her breasts.

When he plunged into her, she cried out as her world shook. He yelled at the same moment.

They lay together as dusk settled outside, sneaking a little light through her blinds. She felt something she'd rarely felt. She felt complete.

"You always satisfy my appetite, Linds." It sounded like he'd read her thoughts. He smiled. "But how about we get dressed and go out to eat now?"

She kissed him. "Okay. As long as we can come back here and do this again."

"It's a deal." He studied her for a moment. "Next weekend, how about you come over to my place?"

"Sure."

They dressed leisurely, then she brushed her mussed-up hair and they went out for a nice Italian dinner. During their meal, she brought up the idea of staying at the hotel for Ben and Courtney's wedding. Brian agreed immediately.

She was unsure how to ask about the financial aspect. Would he want to share the cost? Before she could figure out how to frame the question, he spoke. "I'll pay," he volunteered.

"Are you sure? I'm certain this hotel is going to be pricey. It's supposed to be wonderful, and everything is high-end."

"Yes." He sipped his wine.

"Thank you. I think we'll have a lot of fun at the wedding."

His eyes gleamed. "Especially the part we spend in our room," he teased.

Sparks sizzled in her when she thought of spending any night with him. She raised her glass and clinked it against his.

He grinned at her.

After a few silent moments, he asked "What should we do for a gift?"

"She got a lot of things she wanted at her bridal shower. Money would be best." Although Ben had plenty.

"Not that they need it," Brian added. "Everyone knows Ben's a billionaire."

"True." She frowned, thinking. "I think I'll ask Pam if she suggests anything else. She knows Courtney well."

They lingered over their delicious meal. She had ordered chicken parmigiana, and Brian had ordered the seafood fra diavlo.

He met her eyes as he polished off his food. "I guess I worked up an appetite." He grinned.

"Me, too."

They both enjoyed their wine and ordered coffee with cannoli for dessert. When they were finished, he drove them back to her apartment.

They went on line, and reserved a hotel room for Friday and Saturday of the weekend. Afterwards they watched a little TV, and made love again.

Lindsay curled up close to Brian. She'd never experienced the kind of earth-shattering sex she had with Brian with any other man. It was wonderful.

Her mind drifted as they lay in each other's arms. She could smell his masculine, light aftershave, and feel the strength in his arms and chest as he held her..

She really should go on the pill, she thought hazily…

They must have dozed for a little while. She awoke when thunder boomed. Brian hugged her.

"I love holding you," he whispered, his voice husky.

"I love it too," she said.

He fell back to sleep. But she was left pondering if she loved it too much, if she was getting too dependent on him…

That niggling doubt wove through her brain. With determination, she finally pushed away the negative thoughts and matched his breathing. It took a little while, but she fell asleep, thinking instead about how safe and content she felt in Brian's arms…

She could hear Mom and Dad arguing. She huddled on her bed with Jessica, trying to avoid hearing the raised voices—but not succeeding.

Their mother's voice from the master bedroom sounded so sharp. "You're a liar and a cheat! How could you do this to me?"

"Lindsay! Lindsay! Wake up, sweetheart!" Someone was calling and shaking her shoulder. "Wake up!"

She opened her eyes and recognized Brian.. "Wh-what?" she stuttered, shivering.

"Lindsay, honey, you were having a bad dream," he said. "It's okay. You're here with me."

She blinked, and focused on him.

"Brian!" she exclaimed, clutching him.

"Shh, it's alright, Lindsay." He hugged her and stroked her hair. "It was only a dream. You were yelling."

"It seemed so real," she stammered. "I—I remember when it actually happened."

"Want to tell me about it?" Sympathy wove through his voice.

"Tomorrow." She held him harder until she felt warm instead of cold, and they could fall back to sleep.

But before she slept, she wondered, could the same thing happen to her?

CHAPTER XIII

Brian kept his breathing even and soft, hoping it would lull Lindsay back to sleep if she thought he was sleeping too. He desperately wanted to ease her distress, get rid of the nightmare that had enveloped her.

She had called out "No! Mom! Dad!"

He remembered only sketchy parts of the story of her parents' break-up. In the morning he would ask her about it. He needed to understand this caring woman better. He recognized that he was rapidly becoming attached her.

He continued to breathe deeply and slowly, until she sagged in his arms and he was certain she was asleep. Then, he followed her into slumber, where his dreams were fleeting and light.

When they awoke in the morning, they made languorous love, then showered. The day was partially sunny and partially cloudy, but no rain threatened, and the air was warm. A perfect May morning.

"Why don't we go out for breakfast?" he suggested.

"Okay."

They decided on the local diner for breakfast.

Fortunately they didn't have to wait more than five minutes for a small booth. The place was crowded with couples, singles in a few large groups and many families with small children dropping food that the employees were quick to sweep up.

Lindsay ordered waffles and bacon. He chose the complete breakfast of pancakes, sausage, and scrambled eggs.

Over their coffee, which was served immediately, Brian asked Lindsay, "want to tell me about your dream?"

She took a sip of her coffee. "Ahhh. I needed that." She paused, frowning. "It was about something that actually happened."

"Oh?"

"One night, after we went to bed, my mother and father started arguing. At first it was low, but then it got louder and louder. Jessica came into my room and both of us were so scared. We huddled on my bed together, arms around each other, listening to my mother accuse my father of cheating. She used the word infidelity several times. At the time, we weren't sure what it meant."

"How old were you?"

"I was about fourteen, and Jessica twelve."

"That must have been awful for you." He paused while their meals were served.

"Yes." She stirred her coffee, inhaling. "It was the first time I can remember their having such a terrible fight."

"You two must have been really upset. Understandably so." He tried to infuse his voice with sympathy.

He picked up a forkful of sausage.

"It was." She sighed, and poured syrup on her waffles. "I looked up the word infidelity the next day. That was the first huge, really huge, fight. Oh, there'd been others arguments over the years—but nothing as ferocious as this. I remembered—" she stirred her coffee again, "Jessica saying that she was afraid Mom and Dad would get divorced. And she started crying."

His heart went out to the two frightened young girls who had huddled together at an impressionable age. He reached across the table, grasping Lindsay's soft hand. It was cold in his.

She withdrew her hand, picking up her coffee cup and taking another swallow.

"After that," she continued, "they didn't even try to hide their fights from us anymore. They would fight right in front of us. Once when we were in the kitchen, Jessica and I both started crying. My mother flung out her arms and screamed, 'See what you've done?' to our father. 'See how you're causing your family such pain?'"

"What did your father say?"

"He screamed back. He said my mother had only married him for his looks—she loved being with a handsome man, a big man on campus, a football star from a well-known, rich family. Now he'd found someone who loved him for himself, for his character." She put down her coffee cup, her hand trembling.

"Then my mother started crying and screaming at him. 'You only married me cause I was the most beautiful girl on campus'! she yelled at him."

"'I guess we were both vain!' he screamed back. And he stormed out of the room. My mother threw a dish after him, and it broke." Lindsay's voice choked up.

He covered her hand again with his, and this time

she grasped it. But her other hand fumbled for her purse and she withdrew a tissue, dabbing at her eyes. He could see the tears in them.

Lindsay pulled her hand away when the waitress came to refresh their coffees, bending her head.

"And that's when they got divorced?" he asked gently.

"Not right away." She cut her waffle and lifted a piece. "They continued to fight, but not as loudly. I think they both realized how much it was upsetting Jessica and me." She chewed and swallowed. "Then you asked me out a couple of years later. For a while I could block out my family problems—my parents were still arguing, but not as terribly. I was so— so engrossed in our relationship." She met his eyes.

"I remember some of our first dates." He better tread carefully here, not wanting to stir up resentful feelings on top of her other hurtful emotions. "You were so sweet, so caring, always treating everyone—especially me—so nicely." *I never had such a sweet girlfriend.*

Her voice fell to a whisper. "I remember our first time."

"So do I." He matched her tone. She had been a virgin with a beautiful body that turned him on, despite her inexperience. He'd had sex prior to her—with a girlfriend who was two years older, and experienced— but he'd known it was Lindsay's first time. He'd tried to be tender and gentle. She'd been naïve, but subsequent times she'd surprised him with growing enthusiasm, and soon the two of them were constantly hot for each other, looking for ways to be alone and sneak into his basement. "They were wonderful times," he said, reaching for her hand and bringing it to his lips.

"Yes." Her hushed voice shook.

"But these last few weeks," he added, "have been even better." He squeezed her hand.

She blushed, looking even prettier than usual. "I feel the same." She met his eyes, and her own were no longer sad, but shining.

"No one—no one—I've ever been with has made me feel as good as you do." He said it emphatically. He hoped she believed it.

She squeezed his hand back, then dropped it and fiddled with her fork, appearing nervous. She lifted her knife and cut more of her waffle. "It was the one part of my life that was bright." She stopped. "But then…"

Her expression darkened.

"But then…?"

"My mother got diagnosed with cancer. Stage four breast cancer." She looked down at her coffee, and drained it.

"I do recall how upset you were. Naturally."

"We were—devastated, since the prognosis was very grim." She set down her cup with a clink against the saucer. She met his eyes again. "I cried every night, but I tried to do it quietly so Jessica and my mom couldn't hear."

His heart seemed to twist at the pain she had gone through. Pain, he realized, that as a teenager he hadn't recognized was so deep. His own life had been pretty happy.

"But the arguments started up again, nastier than ever. My mother accused my father of continuing his affair again. I could hear him swear he wasn't, but then she discovered—I don't know how—he was having an affair with *another* woman this time. She started screaming at him almost every night. She went on social media and somehow discovered the woman was beautiful. By that time they'd scheduled my mother for a double mastectomy and she cried that she'd be 'ugly and look like a freak'. Her words, not mine."

"I remember you telling me she had cancer," he said. "But you never shared how bad it was… until we broke up." Seeing she had stopped eating, and he was nearly done, he suggested, "would you like to leave?" He could see how emotional she was getting.

"I… yes." She nodded. "I'm really sorry, but I lost my appetite. Even though the food was good."

"It's okay. I understand." He waved the waitress over.

"Was everything okay?" she asked, glancing at Lindsay's half-eaten plate.

"Yes," Lindsay reassured her with a wan smile. "I'm just not very hungry."

Brian gave the waitress a generous tip so as not to insult her. Then he steered Lindsay out and they quickly returned to her apartment.

Once inside, he led her up the stairs and to her couch. He sat down and pulled her onto his lap. She rested her head on his shoulder.

"Want to tell me the rest?" he asked, his voice soft and sympathetic.

"My mom… my mom went through the operation and then was more depressed than ever. She refused the reconstructive surgery because she said she was going to die anyway. I tried so hard to convince her to do it, that she wasn't going to die. Jessica did too. But my father—he's so selfish—didn't. He kept telling us—in his most condescending voice—''you girls have to accept the fact that your mother is dying'."

"'She has a chance--she won't die' Jessica argued back. And I told him 'you can't assume that she'll die. No wonder she's depressed'." Lindsay started crying softly into his shoulder.

"And she got worse?" Brian asked, hugging her to him.

"Y-yes. She went downhill quickly." Lindsay clutched his shoulders. "And you broke up with me."

He'd felt at the time she was way too clingy. He'd felt hedged in. Plus she war always asking him about his experiences. So he'd also felt like a human experiment on top of feeling stifled.

All normal teenage feelings, he'd been told, and not just by Evan, but by another counselor he saw in college. But he hadn't known the extent of—had been oblivious to-- the depths of her pain.

"My mother basically gave up. She didn't try to fight the cancer. She kept saying, 'I'm ugly and I'm going to die anyway, so why fight it?' She was miserable to be around. My father left. He sat us down and told us he couldn't take it anymore. He went to live with his girlfriend."

"He couldn't wait until she passed?" Brian couldn't believe it.

"No. He was a total, in-insensitive jerk."

Brian tightened his grip. Poor Lindsay. Poor Jessica. The man hadn't considered what his daughters were going through, only his own feelings.

And neither had he, Brian. The little voice in his head arrowed through his brain.

"I'm so sorry, Lindsay,' he told her, hugging her. "I didn't realize—didn't understand—how much pain you were in, how you were hurting," he said. He stroked her hair. "I should have been a lot kinder."

"I know teenagers tend to-to be self—involved—" she hiccupped—"But you were usually so thoughtful, I couldn't understand why we broke up." She leaned into him more. "And—and—I tried to support your dreams of being an architect—but…"

"But…?" he prompted.

"But you didn't support my goals to be a psychic researcher." She sniffed.

"For what it's worth," he said, "I won't hurt you again, Lindsay. And I will support your achievements." He kissed her gently.

I will keep that promise.

CHAPTER XIV

Could she trust Brian to keep his word?

She wanted to believe him. Oh, how she wanted to believe him! She clung to him desperately. She needed to hear this. That he was sorry. That he wouldn't hurt her again. She'd prayed years ago that she would hear those exact words.

He sounded so sincere.

She took a deep breath, as if about to dive into a pool. She *would* take a chance and trust him.

She wasn't sure how she and Jessica had dragged themselves through the following weeks when her mother was dying. Or once they did, how she'd gotten through the remaining year of school. She'd had to move in with Aunt Jane and Uncle Bill. They drove her to school for the remainder of the year so she could still be with her group of friends. Jessica had barely squeaked through the last months of her years. Somehow, with some counseling, Lindsay had picked up the broken pieces of her soul and flung herself into her studies. She'd determined that she was going to study parapsychology and excelled in her psychology class. She'd leaned on her friends Carolyn, Krista and Jade. Jade's parents were divorced and Krista's mom was widowed young, so they understood a little about her pain and grief. But it was

Carolyn who'd been her greatest champion, encouraging her to date others; to use her time to study effectively, to do some fun things with their group of friends; to continue with the activities which she liked like glee club, instead of dropping all activities; and to go for counseling to find the support she needed so much.

She stopped sniffling and blew her nose, sitting up. "Thank you for letting me spill like that."

"I want to be there for you, Lindsay."

She snuggled into his embrace. His lips grazed her cheek. God, she needed this. Needed *him*.

"I won't hurt you again," he repeated. His tone was so emphatic, and his words sounded so sincere, that she couldn't help believing him.

She turned her lips to meet his, and his gentle kiss reassured her. Brought her a peace she hadn't realized was lacking.

She kissed him back harder, and he returned her kiss with intensity.

Suddenly she needed him. Like a parched flower needed rain. She kissed him hard, pulling at his shirt, and he kissed her back with equal fervor. They made sweet love, each caress slow and tender. In a matter of minutes, they had stripped each other's clothes off and were naked on her couch. She couldn't stop kissing him and touching his shoulders, his chest. He lingered over her breasts, then stroked her intimately

"Condom—" he whispered, tearing his lips away as she started to touch his member.

He fumbled for the foil packet in his pocket. And when he sheathed himself, she wriggled so he was right on top, grazing her where she wanted him so much. He entered her slowly. She gasped with pleasure.

"Brian!"

"Lindsay!" he exclaimed as he pounded into her.

They lay together. That had been beautiful. She felt cared for, cherished, as never before. She didn't think they'd ever made love so sweetly.

They slowly drifted back to reality, the couch's smooth fabric beneath her, the distant sound of music somewhere outside.

'Oh, God," was all she could say.

He nodded, seemingly unable to speak. A few minutes later their breathing slowed, and he said, his voice husky, "Lindsay, that was—that was—" he paused, at a loss for words.

"Beautiful."

"Yes," he agreed, kissing her neck.

She was certain their passion had given way to something else—what, she was unable to define.

Tangled together, they held each other as weak sunlight filtered through the blinds and afternoon moved towards sundown. Her legs began to feel cool. After a while, she whispered, "Let's shower. Together."

"Yes."

They did that, their shower full of sweet touches and cuddles. Lindsay suspected they were both spent. Both physically, and for her, emotionally too. Her story and his tender treatment had literally worn her out. But now she felt safe and warm.

After they'd toweled off and sat on the couch, she told him that Matt had traced the ominous texts to Jessica's former boyfriend, Norm.

Brian was concerned and questioned her. "Why?" He furrowed his brow.

She didn't want to discuss Jessica's past. "They're

trying to figure it out." She switched to talking, instead, about how Jessica was showing signs of becoming a happier person.

They spent the rest of the afternoon watching a little TV, and sending out for a pizza for dinner.

When it was time for him to leave, he hugged her tightly. "I'll talk to you soon. We'll figure out the time we can meet at my apartment."

"Yes," she agreed, kissing him tenderly.

Later, he texted her. *I miss you already.*

Sweet words. But… would they last?

Monday Lindsay and Brian exchanged a few texts, but, busy at work, they didn't speak.

Tuesday's meeting began with a discussion of new clients. One, a man who had been struck by lightning down in the shore area of New Jersey five years ago, but only just learned about the center. He was eager to be tested and share his experiences with ESP. Tanya was doing the basic test with him this morning.

Another was a foreign language teacher from Bergen County who had been struck by lightning only last year. She'd always had a flair for languages and spoke and taught Spanish and French, and also spoke a little Italian and German.

"But since she was struck," Parker told them, "She has developed the ability to pick up languages much more rapidly. She is now proficient in Italian and Germans as well as Spanish and French; and can now speak fluent Swedish *and* is quickly learning Mandarin, a difficult language."

There were surprised and excited murmurs and exclamations all around the table.

"I'd like to test her; the first time in English, the second time in Mandarin," Neal stated. They all knew that Neal had been born here in the United States; but his parents spoke fluent Mandarin at home.

"That's a good idea," Parker agreed. "I know we have never seen this ability before," he continued. "It's fascinating! Sabrina is now researching if any ESP center, anywhere, has encountered this particular talent."

"Yes," Sabrina added. "So far I've come up empty. But I'm going to devote a good part of the day to researching this."

"I'll help you," Alicia said excitedly.

"Great," Sabrina said.

Parkerd continued, "perhaps Priscilla can later test her in Spanish, since she is a native speaker. She also is conversant in Italian. Priscilla, do you agree?"

"Yes!" Priscilla declared. "I'll be happy to do both."

There were more excited whispers. Lindsay exchanged a look with Courtney. This was indeed exciting! Being at a place where she was researching brand new subjects and ground-breaking work was not only thrilling, but also an honor.

They went on to discuss their other clients for the day. When Parker dismissed them all at ten o'clock, the buzz of conversation was louder than usual. It was like being at an excellent seminar where a speaker had shared brand new information; everyone was discussing it.

"You look happy today, and I noticed that Monday," Courtney said from beside Lindsay.

"Yes, she's been sending off good vibes the last few days." Laura added. Laura had the ability to have precognitive dreams, like Pam; but hers were in symbols. A bird in her dream might symbolize a particular cousin or friend. "Have a good weekend with *him*?" Her voice dropped to a whisper.

Lindsay could feel her cheeks warming. Courtney sent her an appraising look.

"I—yes." She dropped her voice as they exited the room. She wasn't ready to broadcast to the entire staff that she was having a relationship with the architect working for the Center. "We've been—spending the whole weekend together."

"I knew it!" Laura said, her voice pitched low.

Courtney smiled widely. "I guessed something was going on. My ESP is not much better than normal, but there's been a lot of hot vibes between you and him, and now you have that glow on your face."

Lindsay smiled at her friends. "I guess it shows."

Both women said "yes!"

It must be obvious, Lindsay thought, her cheeks growing hotter. But she knew it wasn't just good sex.

She guessed it was much more.

Shortly after their meeting, the receptionist sent Lindsay an email that her four o'clock appointment was cancelled because the woman, an elementary school teacher, had come down with strep throat. So with a free hour, Lindsay went to get a cup of coffee and then sat in an available testing room and practiced her ESP with the standard cards. Meredith was proof that practicing could increase even average skills.

She was pleased when the two tests revealed she was scoring higher than before. Not by an extraordinary amount, but enough to take notice.

When she finished, she checked her phone.

There was a text from Brian, asking how she was and adding *I've been thinking of you all the time.*

The same, she texted back.

There was also a text from Pam asking her to stop by her office before dinner.

When she did, she found the psychiatrist with a smile on her beautiful face.

"I've been asked to give a workshop on precognitive dreams at the state university," she told Lindsay. "I'd like for you to give it with me, since you've been heavily involved in the research the last few months."

"I'd love too!" Lindsay declared, warming with pleasure. It was flattering to be asked to speak along with one of her bosses at an important workshop. It meant she would be noticed in the research world. Her work was being touted by a well-known institution. It was an achievement!

"But Laura does have precognitive dreams too," Lindsay pointed out, in fairness to her colleague.

"True. But I wanted someone who doesn't to also speak," Pam said.

"Thank you! It's an honor." And it was. *It reaffirmed what she was doing.*

"Of course, we can't announce this on the web or anything, until the contract comes in," Pam said.

They discussed the workshop briefly, agreeing to meet and outline it once the contract got emailed and signed. The workshop wouldn't occur until fall; but they could start to prepare for it.

Happy, Lindsay left and went back to her desk.

She also sent Parker an email, describing her progress on the ESP test and asking that one of their psychic researchers test her officially again.

After dinner, she got a text from Brian.

I'll be in the area tomorrow. Can I see you for dinner? You usually don't work late on Wednesdays, right?

She replied, *Yes! And you can stay over at my place.*

He replied with a smiley face.

Meredith walked into the break room, smiling at Lindsay. Lindsay took the opportunity to tell her about her improved ESP testing results.

Meredith smiled even more widely. "That's great, Lindsay. And I see that's not all that's new for you. Pam told me you'll be presenting a workshop with her."

Lindsay smiled. "Yes. I'm honored to be asked."

"You deserve it. You've been working hard since you joined the staff.".

Lindsay and several others worked late on Tuesdays. By nine o'clock she was tired but satisfied with her day.

She felt lucky as she drove home. She had a job she found fascinating, that paid her enough so she could live—not a life of luxury, but certainly comfortably. She lived in a decent place and had friends.

And now, a boyfriend who made her feel special.

She was home only for twenty minutes, when she got another ominous text.

I know your secret and Jessica's.

Huh? And Jessica's?

Suddenly the texts took on new meaning.

With a snap, she realized the texts, allegedly from Norm Brown, all made sense.

She could vividly recall the day that Jessica got arrested, and dragged home from the police station by their angry dad. Her sister had begged them not to call their mother, who was pretty sick by that point.

Their father had closeted himself in a room with Jessica, his voice raised. Lindsay had heard the gist of it. Their mother had already been in bed, weakened from a treatment the day before.

She'd heard the phrases "ashamed of you" and "how could you stoop so low?" for a while, and Jessica's tearful replies. Apparently, she'd been caught selling pot, not just smoking it, which Lindsay knew she'd done before. No, this time she was in trouble, real trouble.

After their father departed, Jessica had come crying to Lindsay. "She'll be so ashamed of me! I'm glad she's sleeping already. I don't want her to know." She'd wiped tears away, sobbing softly.

"Why did you do it?" Lindsay had asked, her heart hurting. Her sister a drug dealer?

"I—I had some idea that I'd make money quickly, and—and I could get Mom some drugs to ease her pain." Jessica had cried softly into a wad of tissues.

They'd sat in Lindsay's room that evening discussing the situation. Jessica had been mortified. When she was brought to the police station, she told Lindsay, she had insisted that they not call her mom. She'd had them call her dad. Of course he was livid that his daughter could be mixed up in selling marijuana, which at the time was illegal, but she was a minor, so she hoped she wouldn't have a permanent record.

Lindsay, who was already taking a psychology class at high school and reading up about personalities and motives, had secretly thought that night that Jessica, was seeking attention, not just trying to get money. Perhaps Jessica was also trying to seek revenge on their father for abandoning his family.

So Lindsay simply held her younger sister and murmured soothing words to her. "It's gonna be alright Jessica. Just don't ever do it again."

Their father had hired a good lawyer. Because Jessica had no previous record and was underage, and their mother was dying, the judge had gone easy on her. He'd commanded her to do community service. And her record was sealed once she became an adult.

Lindsay had helped her choose her project: volunteering at a women's shelter.

Lindsy had sworn to Jessica that she wouldn't tell a soul, other than Aunt Jane. Their mother had died without knowing of the trouble Jessica had been involved in.

Lindsay kept that promise. She knew how mortified Jessica had been, and she wanted to support her so she'd never do something like this again.

Now Jessica had a secure job which she liked, a decent apartment, a car she had recently finished paying off, and now stayed away from drugs. She had been so scared by the experience that she'd managed to turn things around.

Their father rarely referred to that incident. Even his current wife didn't know about it.

As she stared at the text message, she concluded *now* was the time to tell Parker and Matt what the rather threatening texts probably referred to. But she needed to let her sister know first.

She stared at the phone message for another two minutes, then called Jessica.

"Hi Lindsay," Jessica said. "How are you doing?"

"Okay." She told her sister first about the weekend.

Jessica's reaction was pretty much what she'd expected. "Lindsay, you better not trust Brian."

"I don't." Not completely anyway. Although the more time she spent with Brian, the more she did trust him. "Right now we're having a good time together. And the sex is fabulous."

"That's always a nice perk."

"Yes. And Sunday we talked a little about the past." Lindsay kicked off her shoes and put her feet up on the coffee table. "He apologized for hurting me back then. He seemed very, very sorry."

"I don't know," Jessica said. "I still wouldn't trust him."

"I'm being cautious," Lindsay reassured her. *I better be,* she told herself. The last thing she wanted was another fissure in her heart.

"Jessica," she continued, pushing the thought aside, "I just got another text from Norm Brown. I checked, and it's the same number. And he said, and I quote, *'I know your secret, and Jessica's.* I'm feeling nervous about these texts. I think it's time to tell Matt about your—being arrested."

"You know I never wanted to share what happened," Jessica protested. "I never should have gotten involved with drugs."

"I know. But others in your group of so-called friends pressured you, and you paid the price. You did your community service. It was a long time ago. But obviously Norm knows."

Jessica sighed. "I guess we can tell Matt."

"Yes, because maybe he can find out *why* Norm is doing this. And he can advise us whether to go to the police or not. The idea is for us to be safe."

"I know." Lindsay pictured Jessica's grimace.

"How do you think he found out?" Lindsay asked her sister.

"Remember I told you that he and I went to his friend's wedding? And I had a little too much to drink?"

"Yes."

"Well, I told him. I guess it was a moment of weakness. He had confessed shoplifting when he was twelve, and he got caught. I told him about my—mistake. But after we broke up," she added, "he kept annoying me, asking for another chance. I blocked his number."

"Oh. I'm surprised you said something to Norm about your arrest. I never did," Lindsay said.

"I know." Jessica paused. "I always knew you were trustworthy. Our father never told anyone either, because he was ashamed of me."

"He's not—"

"You know he is," Jessica interrupted her. "He thinks I'm a failure. I never graduated college or got a professional job. I heard often enough how I should have aimed higher." Her voice faltered. "Like Sharona. She's a school administrator, for God' sake. I can't imagine her being an example for little kids." Lindsay recognized the bitterness in Jessica's voice. She had taken their parents' divorce especially hard.

"But you have been successful at your career. You work for a prominent florist and you're making a name for yourself in the world of wedding flowers."

"I guess so. But in his eyes, I'm not as successful as you. You have a PhD, and you're working at the foremost research center in your field."

She could tell Jessica was frowning. "You have worked your way up to be an important part of your company," Lindsay declared. "And you live in a nice area, with a good apartment and you're on your own, independent of our father and his family."

"I guess so. But I'm not married. I don't even have a boyfriend. Not that I really want one," Jessica stated.

Was she trying to convince herself? Lindsay wondered. Even though Jessica had a habit of breaking things off when her boyfriends seemed to be getting more serious—or she felt she was getting too involved and panicked—Lindsay wondered sometimes if deep down, Jessica did want to find love but was paralyzed by fear.

Lindsay took a sharp breath. "But dad doesn't know."

When they ended their call, she wondered if she should call Matt and Parker now, but decided it could wait for tomorrow. It was almost ten o'clock. She was safe at home. No sense disturbing them now.

She showered and got into her pjs. After she'd toweled off her hair, she got into bed and looked at her phone, ready to charge her phone on the nightstand.

She'd missed a call from Brian. His voice message said he just wanted to talk to her and say good night.

Eagerly she returned his call. They chatted for a while about their plans for the weekend. She didn't say anything about the texts from Norm Brown. She would deal with it all in the morning, when she could tell him about whatever Matt recommended.

When she hung up, she realized she'd forgotten to mention the workshop she would be presenting with Pam.

That could wait til tomorrow, too.

Brian's caring tone made her feel good, important. She scooted under the covers, smiling.

She took out the romance novel she'd been reading this week—one recommended by Meredith, a romantic suspense book—and read for a while. By eleven, she placed it on the night table and turned off the light.

But she couldn't turn off her brain quite as easily. She thought about Norm, Jessica's old boyfriend. What could his motive for bothering *her* possibly be?

She switched to thoughts of Brian, laying in his arms after fabulous sex, being cuddled and hearing his heartbeat by her ear, and fell asleep with a smile.

When she awoke, Lindsay texted Parker and Matt: *I have info to share about my sister and Norm Brown.*

Parker replied a minute later. *"Let's meet privately this morning. Can you get in early?*

Matt followed up with *I'm flexible.*

She answered *yes.*

She rushed to get ready for work. Once at the building, she went to the small conference room on the second floor. Matt was already there.

"What did you want to tell us?" Parker asked, entering two minutes later.

She wondered if he had read any of her thoughts about Brian.

He shot her a look. *Maybe he had caught that last one.*

She cleared her throat. "Uh, my sister finally gave me permission to tell you about a secret we've been keeping about her past. I really don't want this to get back to her acquaintances, especially her coworkers."

"What is it?" Matt asked, while Parker raised his eyebrows.

Briefly, she told them about Jessica's arrest when she was young. "Because she had no previous record, and our mother was dying, the judge showed leniency and gave her community service to teach her a lesson. And it didn't go on her record cause of her age."

Matt frowned. "I guess those records were sealed. I didn't find any court records about this when I first did research on your sister, too, since I wanted to know any possible motives for someone sending you threatening texts."

"Because she was under seventeen," Lindsay explained. "So I'm thinking this is why Norm Brown is sending those vaguely threatening texts," she concluded.

"That's very possible. Probable, in fact." Matt frowned. "I'm not sure why he's sending them to you."

"Jessica said she's blocked his number."

"So he figures he'll get to her through you," Parker added.

"Maybe." Lindsay nodded.

Matt looked at Parker. "Will it be ok if we go back to our former surveillance of Lindsay and Jessica, to make sure they're safe?"

"Of course. We have plenty of money in the budget, thanks to Ben and his charitable foundation."

Lindsay felt relieved and, at the same time, a little guilty. It was probably Jessica who was being threatened, not her. Norm knew that they were close. She voiced her opinion to the two men.

"We have to keep you safe," Parker insisted. "You're our employee."

"He's sending you the messages, Lindsay, so we must look out for you too," Matt said.

"Okay," she agreed.

"Any other thoughts?" Parker asked.

Lindsay shook her head.

"We'll go back to our surveillance," Matt told them. "And Jessica's of course. We'll also keep a close eye on this building." He met Parker's eyes. "Just in case."

"In case what?" Lindsay asked, furrowing her brow. "In case he escalates his threats."

The rest of the day passed quietly. Lindsay texted Jessica to let her know about the plan. Later her sister texted back *Thanks, but I don't think it's necessary.*

They're doing it anyway, Lindsay answered.

Lindsay didn't see the text til later, and she replied, *it's a precautionary measure.*" She intended to call Jessica and discuss it with her when she got home this evening.

When she did reach her after returning home, Jessica kept repeating "I'm sure it's not necessary. I've never felt threatened by Norm."

"Then why did you block him?" Lindsay asked. She twirled a lock of her hair.

"Because he kept texting and calling me after I broke things off. He thought we could get back together. I was getting annoyed."

"You never felt threatened?"

"No," her sister answered immediately. "Just annoyed."

"But he is obviously an angry man. He got into that bar fight."

Jessica sighed. "But that's not my problem."

Lindsay was silent, unsure what to say. After a few seconds she said, "promise me you'll be careful."

"Of course. You're sounding like you're a bossy big sister."."

Lindsay could picture Jessica scowling at this point. "I'm just worried about you."

Jessica sighed loudly.

She went to bed that night thinking about how she'd see Brian on Friday.

Lindsay sipped coffee on Wednesday morning with her colleagues at their meeting. They went over the usual patient reports, brief reports of any progress on research or studies, and testing results.

Parker did mention the vague threats to Lindsay regarding her sister, but not why. "I have to ask you all once again to be extra vigilant about your own and the Center's safety. Matt and his staff are on it, of course, but please be extra cautious."

Heads nodded around the table.

Lindsay hadn't noticed anyone tailing her on the way to work, but she assumed that meant it wasn't obvious. She knew someone would be there. Matt had texted her last night that all was in place for her security, and Jessica's.

The day was full of both annual testing and a couple of new clients who'd been struck by lightning. One was a teenage girl who was having trouble adjusting to her ability to have precognitive dreams that predicted danger. She hadn't told one of her friends what she had "seen" and that friend had gotten into a serious car accident. The patient, Taylor, was relating well to Pam, and working through her feelings and acceptance of her new-found ability. Especially since Pam had the same gift, although she also had dreams foretelling happy events, like her own relationship and marriage to Evan.

Brian texted and asked if he could come over in the evening. He didn't want to wait until Friday to see her.

Lindsay was happy to agree.

When he arrived, he folded her into his arms.

"I have some good news I wanted to share with you," he said once they were sitting on her couch.

"Oh?"

He grinned. "I found out today that an office I designed in a Victorian residential building converted to offices won an award from its local Chamber of Commerce." He smiled proudly.

"Brian! That's great!" She threw her arms around him and hugged him hard.

"I'm going to get the award at a dinner sometime in September," he announced. "I hope you can come with me."

"I'd love to." Lindsay thought of telling him about the paper she'd been asked to present with Pam, but decided to wait. She didn't want to steal his limelight.

She could wait for her kudos.

On a future date she'd get her chance to bask in the spotlight.

And he'll get the chance to acknowledge my achievement.

The rest of the week sped by, with interesting clients to test and reports from her colleagues and suggestions for further studies.

Thursday evening Lindsay packed for the weekend at Brian's place. She was eager even though she'd seen him recently.

Friday was busy since she was scheduled until twelve. Once she had picked up her suitcase, she stopped at a nearby mall and did a little shopping. Now that the weather had turned warmer, she wanted to treat herself to a new pair of sandals. Then she wandered into a couple of stores, looking for nothing in particular. A sexy red nightgown caught her eye, and she bought it to wear tonight.

She still had a little time before she knew Brian got off work, so she continued to browse, buying a stylish top for her cousin Erica's birthday.

When she got the text from Brian that he was on his way home, she left the store and drove to his condo.

The weather had grown warmer all week and this weekend was predicted to be close to or at ninety degrees, so she'd brought summer clothing, She wore a bright pink top and newer jeans with her comfortable, older white sandals on her feet.

She found his condo easily. When Brian opened the door he was wearing a dark green polo shirt and khaki pants.

"Lindsay." He pulled her into his arms and kissed her, his lips leaving a hot trail where they touched the sensitive skin on her neck. She loved being in his arms like this!

He pulled back, and she sensed he was disturbed about something.

"How are things?" she asked as they went up the stairs to his main level.

"Do you want a tour?" He sounded distracted.

"I saw it a few weeks ago, so I'm fine. Let's sit down and catch up."

"Okay. He ran a hand through his hair. "Want some water or a soda?"

"Water's fine."

While he went into the kitchen area, she glanced around.

Some mail had been left haphazardly on the dining room table. And a pillow lay on the floor near the couch where she sat.

She wondered if he had thrown it. Bending, she

picked it up and smoothed it out while he removed two water bottles from his fridge.

"Brian. I'm glad to be here," she said simply. She was. Spending the weekend at his place—well, that proved he cared and wanted her to see his environment, didn't it?

He sat beside her.

She laid a gentle hand on his knee. "What's going on?"

"I had a rough afternoon at work." He sighed, then turned to look at her fully. "I had plans all drawn up for an office re-design. Then the client called and said he had had an idea; he decided he wanted other major changes in the floor plan and he wanted me to implement those into the re-design. It meant a complete overhaul of my plans and I'm not sure I can make it work. I spent the entire afternoon on them." He frowned.

"Oh, that must have been frustrating," she agreed. "Maybe if you get away from it for a few hours, you'll get a different perspective."

"I guess so." He didn't sound positive.

She had rarely seen him discouraged. Now she tried to help him feel more positive. "I'm sure, with all your good ideas, you can work this out." She hugged him.

He held on to her for a while. Then easing back, he looked into her eyes. "Thanks,, Lindsay. I always feel better around you."

It was on the tip of her tongue to tell him about her workshop invitation, but she held off. This was about him. There'd be time to tell him later.

"Maybe after dinner and a drink, you'll feel more optimistic?" she asked. "And I have another idea for afterwards."

"What?"

"You know that big spa/tub in your master bath? Maybe we could relax in it." She raised her eyebrows.

"That would be perfect," he agreed.

They went to a small, local restaurant for dinner and a glass of wine. Afterwards, they soaked in his luxurious tub, which ended up with their touching and kissing, and making love. After they dried off, they moved to his bed for more love-making and serious cuddling. Brian fell asleep with a smile on his face. Satisfied that she'd made him feel much better, Lindsay followed him into slumber.

As she fell asleep, she remembered that she hadn't yet told him about her being asked to present the workshop. She'd brag about it tomorrow.

Somewhere in the early hours of the morning, she saw herself through a mist, in a generously sized kitchen, her little daughter playing with a toy at the kitchen table, her newborn son napping in a portable crib nearby. Brian entered the room, bending to kiss her, then scooping up their little girl.

She smiled with pure joy. She was so happy as she stood in the spacious kitchen, in the house Brian had customized to make it their own.

The images started to dissipate, like fog in a burst of wind.

She struggled to hold onto the happy picture. She gasped out.

"Brian!" she said as the images started to fade.

She must have cried it only in her head, because when she sat up and opened her eyes, the room was dark. Brian lay peacefully beside her, breathing slowly. She stared at his face. His eyes were shut, his breaths even.

The dream reminded her of the daydreams she'd had when she was a teenager: dreams of forever with Brian beside her, getting married, moving into a home, having a family.

But it had been just a dream.

With a disappointed sigh, she rested her head on the pillow again. It was only a dream.

But it had been so real!

Was that what her mind was wishing for?

Brian moved slightly beside her, then settled back into slumber.

She tried to do the same, but it took her a while to doze off.

When she awoke, Brian had already left the bed.

She found him in his home office, staring at the blueprints spread out before him.

"Still worrying about the office changes?" she asked, trying to make her tone light.

"Yes." He frowned. I'm not sure how to get this done."

"Maybe you should ask a colleague for their input."

"Maybe."

She wrapped her arms around his shoulders and hugged him. "I have something interesting to tell you."

"Yeah?" he sounded distracted.

She described Pam asking her to join in on presenting the workshop on their recent research on pre-cognitive dreams, and how flattered she was.

"That's great, Lindsay." He hugged her.

But his tone suggested his mind was still focused elsewhere, and she felt a pang of disappointment in her stomach.

It brought back the fact that he hadn't supported her desire to go into psychic studies all those years ago. She swallowed the sudden lump in her throat.

"I'm excited about it." But her voice sounded flat to her own ears.

He smiled. "Good for you."

"Let's have coffee," she suggested.

"Good idea."

She tried not to dwell on his lack of enthusiasm. Men weren't as boisterous as women about this kind of thing, she told herself.

But disappointment still echoed inside her.

Over breakfast, Brian suggested going to the carnival in a nearby town later. Lindsay agreed.

"I remember the county fair we went to when we were in high school. That was so much fun!" They'd gone with a bunch of his friends, and had had a blast. She determinedly shoved her hurt feelings into a corner of her mind.

"Yeah. I still keep in touch with Harry and Colin," he said.

"Did Harry ever end up with Kayleigh?" They'd dated for a long time.

"No. They broke up their second year of college. She married somebody else pretty quickly after their break-up. Harry ended up marrying someone he met after graduating from U. of Delaware," Brian said. "She's nice."

Lindsay nodded. What was there to say? She and Brian had been tight in those days. But they hadn't ended up together.

But now they were dating again. *Don't think about that now.* She needed to simply enjoy the present moments.

The minute they arrived at the carnival grounds—an open field near a school—the smell of hot buttered popcorn made Lindsay's mouth water. She'd been pushing aside thoughts of Brian's rather neutral response to her career news all day. Now she could concentrate on just having fun.

Brian must have remembered she loved it. "Want some popcorn?" he asked after buying their tickets.

"Maybe after we walk around for a bit," she replied. The warm May air was soft, as dusk began to fall.

They walked, holding hands. Lindsay felt warmth flow through her at the familiar coziness of this simple act.

The first ride they passed was a kiddie ride. They wound through the crowd to get beyond it, and now she spotted the vendor selling popcorn and another with pink and blue spun sugar cotton candy.

"There's the Ferris wheel," Brian said, pointing at the large wheel. It moved slowly. "Want to take a ride?"

She wasn't crazy about heights, but she'd ridden on a Ferris wheel in the past with Brian, so she answered "yes," and they got in line.

Once they were seated, and the Ferris wheel moved up, she could see more of the carnival. On this warm evening it appeared busy, with even more people entering through the gates. Children squealed from a neighboring ride and someone hawking hot dogs in a booth near the wheel yelled. "Hot dogs. Git yer hot dogs."

She gripped Brian's hand as the wheel moved higher.

Once they were at the top, she could barely look down. They seemed to be awfully high.

"Don't be scared," he said, hugging her.

She held onto him tightly. "I'll try." Once they started down again she felt marginally better.

But then the wheel started its endless rotations. Brian wrapped his arms around her shoulders. She caught the scent of his familiar aftershave, fresh and a little spicy as he held her close.

The people beneath grew smaller as they rose in the air, then larger as they descended again. She leaned into his strong body, shutting her eyes briefly. She could stay like this, going round and round with Brian—

Whoa. She couldn't go there. She couldn't think beyond the here and now. There were no guarantees their relationship would last.

But her mind speeded along with the thoughts of doing just that.

She could go on with him forever.

She firmly told herself not to think of the future. Just to enjoy these moments together.

Don't think beyond now. Just think of today. Not beyond that.

She tried to ease back to look at his face. He was staring down at the people below, a smile playing on his face. He glanced at her.

"Feeling better?"

"Mmm… maybe," she murmured, snuggling into his shoulder again.

His smile grew wider. "I'm glad," He said it softly, but she could hear it above the screams and laughter below.

The remainder of the ride didn't seem so scary. Ensconced in his arms, she felt safe. Warmth surrounded her.

When they alighted at the end of the ride, he suggested walking around. "I know you like the Tilt-a-Whirl ride."

"Yes. Let's find that one," she said.

They walked around passing a scary-looking roller coaster, which she didn't want to try; and a carousel, which she didn't mind. They went on that one but sitting on a bench and going in circles was pretty tame.

"I think I see the Tilt-a-Whirl." He pointed further along the avenue after they alighted.

"Brian? Brian. Is that you?" A female, loud voice pierced the others nearby.

CHAPTER XV

Brian almost groaned as he caught sight of Amber Sanford.

Amber.

He had no desire to see an old girlfriend. The one who'd left him in the dust when she'd met a wealthy, high-powered lawyer shortly after declaring she loved *him*, Brian.

The slim blonde was with a few other young women. Amber wore sandals that were too high for the precarious ground, and the predominant red lipstick emphasizing her mouth reminded him of a clown. Her hair was carefully braided in a single chain and swung beneath her shoulders. It looked way-too blond and artificial under the carnival's harsh lights.

"Brian!" She repeated and flung her arms around his neck, depositing a smacking kiss on his lips before he could move.

Not again, Brian thought, observing Lindsay's frown. How many old girlfriends did he have to run into in the present?

Stepping back, Amber studied him while flashing very-white teeth in a wide smile.

"I'm so glad to see you!" she gushed.

He gave her a small, tight smile. "Amber." He

turned to Lindsay, who was standing stone-still beside him. "Lindsay, this is Amber Sanford. Amber, this is Lindsay Hughes, *my girlfriend.*"

Lindsay smiled. "Hi, Amber." Her posture relaxed a little.

But Amber stiffened. "Hello," she said cooly. Turning to Brian, she continued. "How are you, dear? I think about you so often and was going to give you a call this week."

"I'm fine," he replied shortly. "Nice to see you." And he started to turn away, intending to walk in a different direction, pulling Lindsay with him.

"Brian, why don't we talk this week?" Amber called after him. Not giving up. She sounded a trifle desperate to him. He concluded she was single, and free of any involvements.

"No, sorry." He purposefully made his voice cool.

Lindsay smiled at him as he led her towards the left.

Another female voice hissed, "Amber, forget about him."

He knew he wasn't supposed to hear that.

He led Lindsay further away from the group and let the crowd swallow them.

Once they were close to the Tilt-a-Whirl, Lindsay stopped him.

"Was she an old girlfriend?"

"Yes. I'll tell you about her later. Let's enjoy the carnival right now."

"Okay," Lindsay agreed.

They kept moving and she didn't say another word. Once they were safely on the Tilt- a-Whirl ride and the attendant had pulled in the bar to secure them, he looked over at Lindsay. She wore a soft smile.

He kissed her on the lips, erasing the feel of Amber's lips pressed against his. Lips he didn't want to feel.

The ride began, tilting them one way, then the other, as the seat swayed in a circle at ever-increasing speed. Soon they were also tilting up and down.

Lindsay shut her eyes and leaned into him, giving the occasional screech. He put his arm around her and held her tightly against his body, squeezing her as they went faster and faster. She squealed at one particularly fast turn.

He basked in the warm feel of her as the ride jolted them tightly together.

"Just hold on!" he shouted to her.

She gripped his other hand on the bar as the ride jammed her into his side, hard.

She held him until the ride slowed. Only when it completely stopped did she open her eyes and ease her hold.

"That was—fun!" she declared, her breaths uneven.

"Yes. Especially with you," he added.

As they got off, she wavered.

He caught her. The ride was causing a lot of people to walk unsteadily.

"Want to go on that?" He pointed toward the high swings.

She shook her head. "Ugh-uh."

"Okay. How about something to eat?" he asked. "I could use a soda."

They wandered over to the refreshment area, where he bought two colas and hot buttered popcorn to share.

They found seats at an empty table.

"That was fun!" Lindsay declared. "I love the Tilt-a-Whirl,even though it's a little scary. Especially when you can hold me and make me feel less frightened."

"I enjoyed it too." He gave her a quick kiss.

She paused and looked at him.

"Want to tell me about Amber?" She inclined her head towards where they'd seen his old girlfriend.

He sighed. "How about if I tell you after the carnival? I don't want to ruin our good time by talking about her."

She sent him a sympathetic look. "Okay."

After they ate, they wandered around the carnival, playing some games. Brian won her a stuffed, soft turtle.

She gave him a kiss. "Thank you!" She felt warm all over, and she knew it wasn't just from the summery air.

"I still have the stuffed owl you won for me at the county fair," she said. It was tucked away in a closet in her hall. She hadn't been able to part with it when they sold her mother's house. And she'd kept it all these years.

His eyebrows rose. "You do?"

Yes," she confessed. "I couldn't get rid of it. I guess I'm too sentimental." She had tossed out other paper mementoes, tickets to a Blink 182 concert and that sort of thing. But she couldn't part with the snowy owl.

He smiled, and she felt her body warm. He slid his hand over hers, and squeezed it.

She couldn't think of anything to add. Jessica had said she was crazy to keep something an old boyfriend won for her after they'd broken up, but she'd kept it anyway, through all her moves—to Aunt Jane's, her apartment in grad school and now her new place. She rarely looked at it, because remembering all the good times with Brian sometimes pierced her with longing. But she had never been able to throw the owl out.

As darkness descended and stars peeked out, they wandered around the carnival for a while longer. They didn't run into Amber or anyone else either of them knew.

When they returned to the car, Brian drove them home. They arrived at his condo quickly and he offered her a drink as he led the way up the stairs.

"Yes," she agreed.

"I bought Midori melon liquer for this weekend, knowing how much you like it."

"I'll take a glass of that."

He poured some into a small tumbler. "Ice?"

"No thanks."

He indicated the couch and they sat down.

"I'll tell you about Amber," he said. "I met her during college." He'd gone to the state university, and lived on campus although it wasn't too far from home. He knew Lindsay had gone there for grad school.

"I met Amber in the student center. She was fun and we started seeing each other almost every weekend."

Kind of like us, Lindsay thought.

As if he'd read her mind, he echoed her words. "Like us, but I never felt as comfortable with her as I do with you, Lindsay." He hugged her.

He took a sip of the whiskey he'd poured himself. "She kept trying to persuade me to become a lawyer like my parents. In fact, she started pushing hard for it. I began to resent it. You know I'd fought with my parents over my choice of career; but in the end they respected my aspirations to become an architect, and they did become very supportive when they realized that was my goal, and it wasn't just a fleeting interest. And it was a worthy career."

"I'm glad they ended up supporting you," Lindsay said. She sipped her own drink The melon flavor slid over her tongue. She savored the sweet taste with its sharp tang, then swallowed.

"They did." He gazed off into the distance. "But back to Amber… she kept nagging me, and I resented it. She had this notion that in the end I'd be a lawyer like the rest of my family. And she wanted a successful lawyer for a husband more than she wanted *me* as a person." He grimaced. "So, I broke it off."

She felt a sudden burst of relief inside. Brian hadn't broken up with Amber because he was unwilling to get serious about someone—he'd broken up with her because she wouldn't accept or support his goals and dreams. So there was hope for *her* relationship with him.

It wasn't until that moment that she realized how much she really had hopes and dreams for a relationship with Brian. A relationship that would go far into the future—

She fought with the little voice in her mind. *It isn't as if I'm in love with Brian.*

Yes, you are that voice declared, quite loudly. The words reverberated in her brain.

CHAPTER XVI

She was hit with a dizzying delight, followed by a rush of anxiety about their relationship.

"It must have been difficult having a girlfriend pressuring you like that," she said. She hoped he saw the comparison between Amber and her.

"It was." He looked at her, taking another sip of his whiskey. "I ran into her last year and she was with some guy. We said hello but that was all. I actually felt relieved that it wasn't me with her." He shrugged. "I guess they're not together now."

"Sounds like she would like to be again," Lindsay said, hearing the cattiness in her voice.

He grinned. "Let's talk about something else." He played with her hair. "I've been concerned about those texts. And wondering if Matt figured out why you've been getting them."

"I think I realized what they were about." She hesitantly described the circumstances of Jessica's arrest and community work, and how she'd kept the secret all these years, but Jessica had spilled the story to Norm. "Please don't share this with anyone else," she said.

"Of course I won't."

"I had to tell Matt and Parker that's why I believe I'm being targeted," she said, sipping more of her drink.

"Frowning, Brian said, "I don't like it. I'm concerned about you. Why are you getting these texts?"

"I'm not sure."

"I'm surprised Matt didn't discover this stuff about your sister. He seems pretty thorough," Brian said, sipping his own drink.

"Because she was underage, her record was sealed," She explained to him. "My father was pretty good at convincing all of us to forget about it. That's why Jessica does tolerate him—but not much," she finished.

"I see."

"Anyway, let's not talk anymore about our pasts," Lindsay suggested, draining the rest of her sweet drink.

"Fine with me." He finished his, and reached for her. They kissed, which soon led to more, and they made love in his big bed. He made Lindsay forget all her worries and conflicted thoughts about her feelings—all she could do was simply enjoy the ride. Literally.

The following morning Brian awoke before her again.

But when she located him in his study, he was bent over his drafting board, busily sketching.

He must have heard her pad into the room in her bare feet.

"I woke up with an idea," he said, looking at her and grinning, "And I think I can make this work!" He bent over his drawing again.

"That office remodel?"

"Yes. I think I figured out how to do what the customer wants without sacrificing the other parts. If I move this partition..." he began pointing out different aspects of his redesign.

"That's great?" She hugged him enthusiastically.

He hugged her back. "Thanks for believing in me."

They ate breakfast and had coffee, but Brian didn't linger. Lindsay gave him space as he finished up drawing a rough plan and got all his ideas down on paper.

"Now we can plan our day," he announced when she emerged from a shower.

Once he'd showered, they made plans to do a quick stop at a discount store, then go to the movies.

When she left Sunday evening, she had to promise him she'd text when she arrived home and was safely inside her apartment, which she knew was being watched. She didn't know if anyone had watched her at Brian's place. She certainly hadn't been aware of anyone, so they must have been careful.

The next two weeks were filled with time spent on her demanding but satisfying job, the testing and research, the camaraderie with her colleagues—and with Brian. The quiet moments with him, the discussions about beautiful architecture and psychic phenomenon; the sweet and thrilling lovemaking that always left her satisfied made her feel like her life was wonderful. Then it was Memorial Day weekend, and she was looking forward to Kathleen and Edward's annual party for the staff of TLC that weekend.

Their big house was situated on a lake in a historic neighborhood. Many of the homes were designed by a famous architect Edward Hapgood, according to Brian. Kathleen had even promised them a tour. Brian was especially eager to see the Costigan's house.

Lindsay could see her pride as Kathleen Costigan showed them the house. The rooms were classical yet large; a huge formal dining room, large kitchen which had been updated over the years, formal living room; family room and rec rooms; a beautiful library; and multiple bedrooms. There were guestrooms and a smaller study on the third floor; and all the bathrooms had been updated

Everything was decorated with classic furniture with some modern touches, tastefully combined with antiques. It was very, very impressive.

Lindsay added her positive thoughts to Brian's admiration of all the authentically preserved architectural details. She was conscious of the many antiques, some of which had been in the Costigan family for decades, others which the couple had acquired over the years.

She also noticed the smaller antiques—carnival glass vases and bowls. She recognized them because Aunt Jane had a few pieces which had been her mother's; and some silver candlesticks which were highly polished but appeared old.

She could have spent hours in the library, where she noted hardbound Agatha Christie mystery novels plus others, which looked old *and* well- read. Lindsay guessed that Sabrina must have spent hours here when she visited.

. The furniture looked like it was used, not just there for show; and well cared-for. But the styles were classic and probably expensive.

Lindsay had heard Pam, Meredith and Parker speaking about their parents and childhood and knew that the Costigans were a successful doctor and nurse; but also they had come from wealthy families. Living in this expensive neighborhood, right on the lake, meant they had not only the means to buy the house but also to maintain the large structure.

Kathleen pointed out from the window that Ben Greenfield, Courtney's fiancé and a billionaire in his own right from his scientific discovery had been raised diagonally across the street from them. His house was equally large and historic.

"Your house is just lovely," Lindsay said to Kathleen.

She smiled modestly. "Thank you so much."

"And the architecture fascinating," Brian said. "I remember learning about Hapgood and his houses in architectural school. Thanks for the opportunity to study it close up."

Lindsay had noticed him poking around, studying details of woodwork surrounding doorways, windows and more. He had even asked if he could take some photos and Kathleen had permitted him to do so.

"I thought you would enjoy the tour. And I'm glad you were able to come to our party," Kathleen said with a sincere smile.

"I'm glad Lindsay invited me." He sent her a warm smile.

Even that made Lindsay feel tingly.

They joined the others on the large deck at the back of the house, overlooking Mountain Lakes. The day was breezy but very warm, typical of May in northwestern New Jersey. Edward was grilling some hot dogs, hamburgers and chicken on the outdoor grill, with Parker and Evan and Richard assisting.

"Salads and desserts are set up in the kitchen," Kathleen announced. "So after you get your main course, please help yourself."

People started lining up for the grilled items. Lindsay noticed that some people had brought dates or partners, while others like Priscilla and Alicia had come alone. Although they were bringing "plus ones" to Courtney's wedding.

Courtney and Ben arrived late, with his family in tow. He began introducing his parents, his brother and his fiancé, and his sister to the other employees of The Lightning Center. Lindsay gathered that while this had always been an employees' barbeque, the Costigans had decided to include the Greenfield family since they lived across the street and Ben was marrying Courtney as well as his being a not-so--secret investor in The Lightning Center.

Lindsay found herself relaxing as she and Brian sat with Pam and Evan and Neal at one of the tables which had been set up. The guys started discussing the chances the New York Yankees had this season to win the pennant.

Pam turned to her and asked if Lindsay had a dress for the wedding.

"I do."

"What color?"

"Midnight blue," Lindsay answered, thinking how she was anticipating Brian's reaction to the sensual dress.

"Any room for me?" Alicia stood in between Pam and Neal.

"Of course." Pam slid over a little, close to her husband. Alicia wedged herself in between her and Neal, and placed her paper plate in between theirs.

"What are you wearing to the wedding?" Lindsay asked, continuing the conversation.

"I bought a beautiful sea green dress with a handkerchief hem," Alicia said, picking up her hamburger.

"I love that color," Lindsay said. "My gown is a very dark blue. I loved the style and it didn't come in any pastel colors."

"Blue is very popular this season," Alicia remarked.

They chatted about dress styles while the guys continued to talk about baseball teams. Apparently, Neal had played baseball in high school but admitted he was not more than an average player.

Lindsay enjoyed the warmth and friendship of her coworkers, and the graciousness of their hosts. When she and Brian left to go back to his apartment, she could tell he'd enjoyed the evening too.

"You work with a really nice group of people," he observed.

"I do," she agreed. "I love my job; and the people I work with make it even better. I am so lucky I was selected to be on the staff."

"You always wanted something like this." He approached a red light and stopped.

"Yes. Before you were struck by lightning, I used to think I wanted to study to be a teacher or a social worker; but after you were struck, and started having those experiences, I became so fascinated by paranormal abilities. So I majored in psychology with a concentration on parapsychology and a minor in sociology.""

He nodded. "I remember."

It didn't take long to reach his condo.

Once inside, he pulled her close. "I've wanted to make love with you all day," he said, nuzzling her neck.

She wrapped her hands around him and kissed him. The love she felt welled up in her, but she didn't speak the words. Not yet. Not until she thought he was feeling the same way. She hoped that would be soon!

He covered one breast with his hand, stroking it, and her nipple peaked. She kissed him harder, feeling the desire shoot through her whole body like a warm wave of water at a sandy beach.

He moved them swiftly to his bedroom, where they made passionate love.

The next weeks passed rapidly.

Lindsay was conflicted about her feelings. She had fallen in love with her former boyfriend. But could she trust him completely with her heart? He seemed to care about her a great deal, but was it love or was he just having fun?

She flipped from highs of emotion, riding a magic carpet of delight, to depressing lows, recalling her feelings when he'd broken up with her years ago. There were times when anxiety crawled through her at the thought that Brian didn't care as much as she did.

The week before Courtney's wedding everyone noticed that Courtney kept dropping items like pens and books. The others in the Psychic Testing and Research department teased her.

"Having second thoughts?" "You must be nervous!" "You need a massage!" were some of the remarks directed at the bride.

Courtney smiled and admitted at lunch that yes, she was a little nervous.

"Not that I feel anything different for Ben," she declared. "Just this big wedding is making me on edge. There're so many details to think about."

"On that day, your bridesmaids will all be there to support you," Meredith reminded her. "Your sister Melissa has *everything* under control. I spoke to her last night."

"She *is* organized," Courtney agreed. "And she reassures me all you ladies will take good care of me!"

"We will!" Pam added.

Tuesday was Courtney's last day of work before the wedding. Everyone wished her luck and assured her she'd be a beautiful bride and things would go smoothly.

The rest of the week went smoothly. Lindsay went on the pill as her doctor had prescribed. She didn't see Brian until Friday afternoon. She planned to surprise him with that news.

She finished packing for the wedding weekend, and he picked her up and drove them to the very nice hotel where they'd reserved one of the rooms. The wedding was on Saturday after sundown, but festivities would start this evening.

Since some of her coworkers were in the bridal party, they would be attending the rehearsal dinner this evening. Lindsay and Brian had been invited to join other staff members staying at the hotel tonight at a restaurant nearby.

Lindsay and Brian went up the elevator to their room on the sixth floor, which featured a king-sized bed and a sitting area with a dresser and desk. The bathroom was luxurious.

"This is a very nice room," Lindsay said, glancing around as they brought their suitcases inside. She immediately hung up her fancy dress and Brian did the same with his tuxedo.

Then he looked at the bed and turned to her, his eyebrows raised. "We got here early to avoid Friday rush-hour traffic… so we have a couple of hours before going out to dinner. Have any ideas what to do?"

She walked slowly to him, swaying her hips, then sliding her hands around his neck. "We haven't seen each other all week since we've both been busy…" and she'd been getting her hair cut and nails done for the big event… "So… I can think of something I've been missing. How about you?"

He gave her a teasing smile. "I think I know what you want… and the funny thing is, I want the same thing." His lips crushed hers.

The kiss became heated and Lindsay and Brian were soon pulling at each other's clothes. At some point he remembered to close the curtains and the room became dark as he pressed her onto the large mattress. Soon the only sounds were her murmurs as his hands and mouth caressed her body, and his whispers as she stroked him.

"Lindsay… yes, right there…"

She stroked his nipple as she slid down and covered his cock with her mouth.

"Ahhh… sweetheart… I can't hold off much longer…" He pulled her head back and she grazed his chest with her lips, moving upwards.

He paused to reach for a foil packet.

"I have a surprise," she whispered huskily. "I'm on the pill. We don't need that anymore."

His eyes widened. "Really?" His breath caught. "Oh, sweetheart—" He hastily moved over her, and she opened her legs, inviting him.

He plunged into her, and she arched her back, crying out. He felt so *good*. He started to move, moaning with pleasure, and she cried out as he took her over the edge. He immediately followed, and she felt his spurting more keenly than ever without the condom, as she spasmed around him.

"Oh, God Lindsay!"

They panted and clutched each other as they rode the wave.

She felt complete.

They slowly came back to earth.

"That was spectacular," Brian said, his voice husky.

"Yes," she agreed breathlessly. She'd never, ever felt such powerful love-making.

It's because you're in love with him, whispered that little voice in her brain. *It's good sex, yes, but it's more than that.*

I know, she whispered back. She recognized the truth of it.

But on top of that a seed of doubt slipped in and took root.

Did Brian feel the same?

As he got dressed for the dinner, Brian kept sneaking peeks at Lindsay.

Not only was his girlfriend a wonderful, passionate lover—she made him feel so good—but she was also loving and giving. He saw how she interacted with her colleagues. She was always respectful and kind. She brought the same consideration to their relationship. She'd reassured him when he was frustrated by problems. He recalled how encouraging she'd been when he couldn't figure out a solution immediately to his client's sudden change in wishes for his office.

He'd lucked out when she'd agreed to go out with him again. Now, somehow, she'd become his significant other.

It had happened so gradually he hadn't been aware at first how important she'd become to him. But as he observed her getting dressed, her smooth and sensual moves and curves in all the right places—he knew he was one lucky bastard. But most of all she was a kind, giving person, caring about others and about him.

And he'd tread on her heart long ago, discarding it.

Would she ever forgive him? Did she have it in her?

He stopped, looking at her as he took out his sports jacket. She had donned a casual dress, in bright green with white and pink flowers, looking very summery. She slid her feet into white sandals that had a small heel.

She met his eyes, smiling.

"What are you thinking about??"

"You." He took her arm, pulling her close. Grazing her lips, he said "You're beautiful and sexy, Lins. And the most caring person I've ever met."

"Thanks." She sounded breathless. "You're handsome and sexy and wonderful, too. And you make me want you like no one else ever has."

He felt a totally male satisfaction. He wanted to puff out his chest, but refrained..

At the elevator they met Meredith and Richard, whose room was also on this floor, and Priscilla and her date, Rafael. They exchanged pleasantries and when they got to the main floor, Meredith and Richard departed for the rehearsal dinner while he and Lindsay went to his jeep.

He invited Priscilla and Rafael to join them and he drove to the nearby restaurant where the other coworkers who were not in the wedding party were meeting up for dinner.

It only took a few minutes to get there. Alicia, who he'd observed seemed very detail-oriented, had made the reservation for their large group. She was there already as were Neal, Felipe and his boyfriend, and Tanya and her fiancé. The other coworkers of Lindsay's soon joined them and they were shown to their long table.

Brian had heard this was a classy place, known for good food.

At least Ben and Courtney were getting married in an area of New Jersey that was close to New York City, not in the city itself. Then the prices would probably be double for the hotel and meals.

He'd heard that the large catering hall where the reception would be taking place was a very elegant one, so he was looking forward to a good meal tomorrow, plus drinks and dancing.

He and Lindsay sat down next to Laura and her boyfriend, and Rafael and Priscilla took the seats to his right.

Dinner was fun. The conversations between Lindsay's coworkers flowed; they discussed everything from theatre to books to New Jersey sights. The food was excellent too. His steak was cooked just the way he liked it—medium—and Lindsay said her chicken with a lemon sauce was great. He was pleased that everyone accepted him as Lindsay's boyfriend, not merely the Center's architect or a client.

Rafael asked how Courtney and Ben met. When Priscilla explained, that launched a discussion of past lives.

The evening went by rapidly, and before he knew it, Brian was having coffee with his chosen dessert of chocolate cake.

When the dinner party ended, he drove Lindsay, Priscilla and Rafael back to the hotel.

A few of their group was meeting at the hotel's bar for after-dinner drinks.

"Want to join them?" he asked Lindsay.

She shook her head. "I had two glasses of wine at

dinner and I'm full, so not tonight. But feel free to join the others who are going."

"I'd rather spend the time with you." It was true.He linked hands with her. He always enjoyed himself with Lindsay—not to mention they could go to bed and enjoy themselves there.

Which was exactly what they did. He'd gotten up early for work and then taken half the day off, so after making love he was content to sleep with Lindsay snuggled close. He thought if he could sleep with this woman in his arms every night, he'd be wonderfully content…

When she awoke on Saturday morning, Lindsay felt great. It was not just that she'd had a good night's sleep, but that Brian had been beside her, his arms surrounding her, and she felt more than comfortable. She felt… valued.

Knowing she loved him was exciting—but scary too. How did he feel?

Maybe she would dare to tell him her feelings… one of these days.

He must have felt her stirring, because he opened his eyes and smiled. Pulling her in even closer, he nuzzled her, and she could feel his hard member.

"I want you, Lindsay. Again."

Their love-making last night had been deeply satisfying, but now she could sense excitement and his urgency. She felt a growing desire so she rolled over him. Quickie sex with Brian was just as exciting and satisfying. She'd never, ever been with a man she desired as much-- and it was always wonderful.

Once they'd showered and dressed, they went downstairs to the hotel's restaurant. Lindsay glanced around, looking for any other co-workers who had come down for a late breakfast. She spotted Laura and her boyfriend Ed, who were sitting with Ashish and his friend Chetna, whom he'd introduced to them yesterday. They all waved them over.

"Come join us," Laura said. "We just got here."

They did and ate an enjoyable breakfast, chatting about the wedding to come and weddings they had been to recently.

The guys decided to watch a Mets game together on the big screen in the hotel's parlor area, and sent a mass text to everyone from TLC staying at the hotel. Lindsay suggested that any of the women who were there join her, Laura and Chetna on a shopping excursion to the nearby mall.

"Great idea! I left my lipsticks at home," Priscilla texted back.

They all met up in the lobby a half hour later, and went shopping, agreeing to meet up with the guys at three o'clock.

The wedding party was busy, Lindsay knew, getting their hair and make-up done, and taking some preliminary photos.

She enjoyed the excursion with her friends. She wasn't looking for anything in particular, but found a pretty multi-colored top for the summer in Macy's.

Priscilla splurged on make-up and Laura and Chetna found summer purses they liked. Madison was more interested in going to an upscale housewares store. She selected a ceramic bowl for her new apartment.

They ate a small lunch at the food court, knowing that the food at the wedding would be plentiful. When they returned to the hotel the game had gone into extra innings, and more guests from the hotel had joined Brian and the others. The guys were yelling and cursing at the umpire. Brian said he'd join her to get ready for the wedding once the game was over.

She went to their room and dropped off her purchases, then relaxed with the book she'd started reading during the week. After a half hour, she began doing her hair and Brian returned to the room.

"That was a good game," he told Lindsay. "The Mets beat San Francisco in overtime. It was exciting."

"Glad you had fun," she told him, looping her arms around his neck and kissing him. "It's almost time to get ready for the wedding."

"Okay."

She took her time, applying her fancy make-up first, then slipping into her formal dress, then adding her jewelry. She had a gold necklace with tiny diamonds her mother had left her which once belonged to her grandmother. Jessica had received another piece.

Lindsay finally slid into her heels—ones that were not too tall, so she'd be comfortable dancing. Courtney had told them they had a great band playing at the reception and to be prepared to dance. Lindsay touched up her hair and sprayed cologne on.

When she turned to look at Brian, for a moment she could only stare at him, stunned. In his tuxedo he looked incredibly handsome! And as he carefully added the bowtie, he turned to meet her gaze.

For a moment, he simply stared, his mouth open. His expression morphed into that of a hungry wolf.

"My God, Lindsay… you look *gorgeous*." His voice was breathless.

Warmth enveloped her as he continued to devour her with his eyes, his look sweeping from her head to her feet, then back up, lingering on her breasts. Heat pooled in her stomach—and even lower.

He smiled. "If I didn't know we were going to a wedding, I'd want to keep you here with me all night. Locked in this room, so I could make slow, lingering love to you."

She laughed. "Flatterer." But she *was* flattered. "You look handsome, yourself," she added. "And as tempting as it may be—we have to catch the bus that's taking the guests to the banquet hall." Like many brides and grooms, Courtney and Ben had arranged buses to transport guests to and from the catering hall so no one would have to worry about driving after they'd been drinking.

Lindsay scooped up her fancy purse and they left the room, locking it behind them. Brian took her hand as they walked to the elevator, where they were joined by Priscilla and Rafael. Prisilla's color was high and Lindsay guessed they had spent some time making love during the afternoon. From what Priscilla had told her beforehand, this was the first time she and Rafael had spent a weekend together. She had even asked Lindsay if she thought it was "too soon."

"Not if that's what you want," Lindsay had replied to her friend.

As they waited for the elevator, she noticed Priscilla took Rafael's hand, and he turned to smile at her.

The elevator doors lid open, and Brian led Lindsay inside. There were already two other, older couples inside, also formally dressed.

"Are you going to the wedding?" One of the women, dressed in a sequined purple dress, asked.

"Courtney and Ben's? Yes," Lindsay replied.

"We are too. We're cousins of her mother's," the slimmer woman said. She definitely sounded like she was from the New York area.

They all chit chatted for a couple of minutes while the elevator went down. Once they'd reached the ground floor, the group joined the others milling in the lobby, waiting for the bus.

Lindsay and Brian approached Laura and her boyfriend. He was an engineer and he and Brian had enjoyed talking yesterday, Lindsay had observed. She knew the bridal party had gone in their own bus some time ago so they could pose for pictures.

"The bus is here!" a middle-aged woman called out, and everyone lined up to board it.

The weather outside was beautiful--the sun was just starting to lower in the sky, and the air was warm—in the 80s--without being humid. Perfect weather for a June wedding, Lindsay thought. She boarded the bus after Alicia, who'd joined them. Brian was right behind her. She found two seats in back of Alicia, who'd slid in next to Neal, and Brian and Lindsay sat beside each other. Laura and Eddie sat across the aisle. They chatted amicably, everyone in good spirits as they anticipated a fun night.

Once they'd arrived at the huge catering hall, Lindsay was impressed. Courtney had said since they were inviting a lot of friends and both she and Ben had big families, with multiple cousins, they were expecting 400 guests. The luxury of the lobby and refined demeanor of the employees who greeted them alerted Lindsay to the fact that this must be a very posh banquet hall.

They were directed outside, where a sign declared

"Choose a seat, not a side; we're all family once the knot is tied!" She'd heard of those before. She took a seat next to the aisle and Brian sat next to her, Laura and Eddie adjacent to him. Neal, then Alicia, slid in next.

Lindsay had attended Jewish weddings before. A good friend from college, Rachel, was Jewish and Lindsay had been one of her bridesmaids two years ago.

"Have you been to a Jewish wedding before?" she asked Brian in a low voice.

"Yes. My friend Dave's from college. The wedding ceremony was interesting."

So he knew what to expect. Lindsay noted the beautiful hoopah—the canopy over the bride and groom with loads of flowers climbing up the pillars supporting it.

She knew the groom would be stepping on a glass at the end of the ceremony.

A groomsman was passing out programs. She read it. Meredith, Pamela and Sabrina were listed as friends of the bride; along with other women she'd met at the bridal shower, and Courtney's two sisters were maids of honor. Ben's sister and two cousins were also listed. The bridal party was large and included many groomsmen and Ben's brother and a cousin were the Best Men.

People were filling the outdoor space where the wedding was about to take place. Some were exclaiming at seeing others, hugging and crying with happiness. Lindsay heard variations of "You look wonderful!" "Isn't this a beautiful place for a wedding?" and "It's been *so* long!"

Brian turned to her and smiled.

When the music began, the large group settled down, and turned their attention to the center aisle.

The female rabbi started off the procession, followed by ushers escorting some grandparents. Then couples began to walk down the aisle in step with the music. Many were paired with their spouses, like Meredith and Richard; Pamela and Evan; and Parker and Sabrina. Others seemed to be paired with cousins or friends.

The women wore dresses in a dusky rose color, and the men wore charcoal gray tuxedos.

Lindsay was so happy for Ben and Courtney, who had been through so much to get to this point—even someone attempting to murder them! It was so wonderful that they'd found their true soulmates, she mused now.

Ben was escorted down the aisle by both his parents, as was traditional in a Jewish ceremony.

After the flower girl had scattered rose petals down the carpet, the music changed, and everyone stood.

The bride looked absolutely stunning. Her dress, a strapless fit and flare gown, had some lace on it and her heels made her taller than usual. She was smiling as her parents escorted her to Ben, her face positively glowing.

His face, looking at his bride, was so full of love and admiration that Lindsay drew a sharp breath. Would someone look at her like that some day?

Would Brian?

She glanced at him. He seemed focused on the ceremony, but as she looked at him, he turned his head, meeting her eyes, and smiled.

She smiled back then turned to take a quick picture with her phone, as the couple went together to stand before the Rabbi and Courtney handed her bouquet to her sister Melissa. Lindsay sat back to watch, focusing on the scene transpiring.

The Rabbi chanted some blessings and spoke briefly

about the bride and groom and their love for each other. Then Courtney, followed by Ben, read the vows that they'd composed.

At the end of the ceremony, the Rabbi explained that the meaning of stepping on a glass was to remember the history of the destruction of the Jewish people's first temple. Ben stepped on a glass which was covered with a white cloth napkin.

He stepped on it, hard, and Lindsay could hear the popping noise. Then he grabbed Courtney and pulled her into his arms for a long and resounding kiss.

The audience burst into applause and cheers and cries of "Mazel Tov!" rang through the crowd. Lindsay clapped along with everyone. Some people hooted.

The happy couple started back down the aisle, as cameras flashed, and the band played the traditional wedding march.

Lindsay, tears in her eyes, snapped a photo with her phone when they drew near. Then she dabbed at her eyes. "That was beautiful."

"It was," Brian agreed.

After the wedding party followed the newlyweds, she and Brian exited their row. The bride and groom had so many guests they'd decided to forgo the traditional receiving line so guests could get straight to the cocktail hour and the food.

An older man was directing people to the rooms where cocktails and hors d'ouvres were being served.

Many people made a beeline for the bar, but Lindsay and Brian decided to get in line for some of the scrumptious-smelling food.

There was everything from seafood to thinly-sliced meat. Waiters and waitresses were also going around with little hot dogs and mustard dip that were so popular, stuffed mushrooms and wantons with vegetable stuffing.

Brian pointed out a mashed potato bar where you could add your own toppings. "That's a fun idea!"

They found a small table and were soon eating and chatting with some coworkers.

Felipe and his boyfriend sat down across from them. "A mashed potato bar," Felipe said. "I love this idea!"

His partner, Manuel "call me Manny," dove in. "This is great!" he declared. He'd sprinkled bacon and what looked like scallions on top.

Alicia, Priscilla and Rafael joined them.

"That was beautiful," Priscilla said. "I've never been to a Jewish wedding before, but I loved the ceremony."

"I have. I liked that this Rabbi explained everything," Manuel added.

They chatted and ate, and Brian went with Felipe and Rafael to get drinks for them and their dates. Lindsay had asked for a Screwdriver, which was a favorite of hers, and she could tell it was made with the finest vodka.

Brian had gotten a whiskey sour. Priscilla proposed a toast to the happy couple, and they all raised their drinks.

Lindsay got glimpses of the bridal party posing for photos outside. Even during the cocktail hour, they could hear soft music played by a small group of musicians.

"Didn't she look gorgeous?" Lindsay asked.

Everyone agreed, and Brian leaned over. He whispered in her ear, "so do you, Linds."

A shiver arrowed through her.

Once the cocktail hour came to an end, guests were directed into the main ballroom. It was huge, with fancy flower arrangements on each table. Fortunately, they didn't block the flow of conversation or obscure the other people at the table. Lindsay hated when they were so big you couldn't see your fellow tablemates, and had pointed out that problem to Jessica when she started working at the florist's; so Jessica was always conscious of that. Lindsay snapped a few photos to send to Jessica after the weekend was over. Then she took photos of her colleagues and their plus ones; and Laura took a photo of Lindsay and Brian.

Music blared, and everyone hushed when the band director took the microphone. He introduced the family. They were followed by the bridal party. Pam and Evan looked especially happy, Lindsay thought. She knew Pam had been very helpful to Courtney in understanding her past life and how it was influencing the present. Lindsay took more photos, then slid her phone back into her fancy purse. Lindsay and her colleagues cheered especially loudly for Sabrina and Parker; Meredith and Richard; and Pam and Evan.

Then, "Mr. and Mrs. Benjamin and Courtney Greenfield!" the announcer exclaimed.

The guests all stood and applauded wildly.

Their first dance started. After sitting, Lindsay watched as the romantic notes swept into the room, and the bride and groom danced to their carefully rehearsed steps.

She watched as the couple dipped, swayed and stepped together. Would she ever be in the same position, dancing with the love of her life? she couldn't help wondering.

The table with Meredith and Richard was positioned near her table. Meredith turned and stared at Lindsay. Had she, somehow, read Lindsay's thoughts?

The idea made Lindsay pause. Meredith had practiced until she had improved her slightly-above average ESP. Lindsay had tried to do the same. Had she sent out the idea from her mind and Meredith heard her thoughts?

The best man, Ben's brother Nathan, then proposed the traditional toast. And he was followed by the maids of honor, Courtney's sisters, Melissa and Sherry, proposing their own brief but sweet toasts. Everyone raised their glasses of champagne.

Afterwards, the leader called up another man. "We invite Great Uncle Joe up to say the prayers over the wine and bread."

An older man approached the leader, and made a few remarks, ending with chanting in Hebrew. People raised their glasses of wine.

Then the master of ceremonies announced the traditional Hora, and almost everyone stood up and formed a huge circle surrounding Ben and Courtney. A smaller circle of family got into the middle around the bride and groom.

Courtney had showed the TLC employees the basic steps of the traditional Jewish celebratory dance that was always played on happy occasions.

"But basically you go around in a big circle, kicking your feet and stepping to the side," Courtney had finished. Then she had demonstrated with Felipe.

The reality of the dance was much faster than Lindsay had thought, but it was loads of fun. Several strong groomsmen and friends hoisted the parents, then the bride and groom, into the air on chairs as the guests danced around. They drew closer and closer, tightening the circles around them, then moving outwards again.

First they circled right, then left. Finally, some members of the families grabbed others and swung them like a square dance, holding their other hands in the air.

Lindsay was breathless by the time the dance ended. Guests were clapping and hollering. "That was amazing!" she declared to Brian and Laura, who had ended up near her as they finished the dance amidst whooping and cheering.

"Your first course is served," the band leader announced, and people began returning to their seats.

Lindsay reached for her water, in a sparkling glass.

The band played soft music in the background as they were served a colorful salad course and bread.

After a few minutes when they were all eating and chatting, the soft music playing in the background paused, and he called up Courtney for the father-daughter dance. Ben and his mother followed with their own dance.

Then another slow dance began, and the wedding party and immediate families were invited onto the floor.

After that the band began playing another romantic tune, "Can't Take My Eyes Off of You."

"All happy couples are invited onto the dance floor," the master of ceremonies intoned.

Brian looked at her. "Shall we?" He held out his hand to Lindsay, standing up and smiling.

She stood up with him, and once they were on the dance floor, he pulled her into his arms.

Brian had always been a good dancer, and since she was too, Lindsay enjoyed dancing to the romantic tune, as they swayed and moved smoothly around the dance floor. She loved dancing with him, his arms wrapping around her protectively. She inhaled the subtle scent of his masculine aftershave and felt the warmth of his chest as he pressed close to her. She leaned into him, feeling his body slide to the music with hers. She could stay like this forever. She felt warm and secure in his arms.

She pulled her head back slightly so she could gaze into his eyes as the singer crooned about thanking God he was alive. Brian was staring directly at her, smiling softly.

The way he was looking at her… she caught her breath as his fingers tightened on hers.

"Lindsay," he whispered, his breath warming her face. "I love you, Lindsay."

Pure happiness burst inside her, like a shooting star.

Brian hadn't meant to blurt that out on the dance floor.

The truth had struck him ferociously last night after they'd made such wonderful love, and he'd held her in his arms as she drifted off. He knew at that moment that he wanted this woman in his arms forever. He'd never felt like that before. He had decided to tell her when they got back to their hotel room after the wedding, when they were completely alone.

But he couldn't hold the words in any longer as the romantic song played. So, he said them then and there.

He saw her instant reaction. Her eyes widened, and then the most ecstatic smile lit up her beautiful face.

"Oh, Brian," she breathed in his ear, "I love you too." And she kissed him.

His body warmed with the knowledge that Lindsay returned his feelings.

That was all he needed to hear. His feet were as light as if he had wings, and he swirled her around, then pulled her close again. "We're so lucky we found each other again," he said in a low voice.

"Yes," she said, letting her lips graze his cheek, making him want her in every way possible.

Another couple, dancing close, bumped into them. "Sorry," the woman said.

But Lindsay had snuggled even closer to him, so he wasn't sorry one bit. Holding her tight, her words reverberated in his brain.

She loved him too. She loved him! Despite all the heartache he'd caused when they were young. They'd miraculously found each other again. Lindsay had given him another chance at a relationship, and he'd somehow won her heart. Even though it wasn't what he'd set out to do, he'd won her love

He'd found her, fallen hopelessly in love with the woman she was today. And she'd fallen in love with him, too. How the hell had he gotten so lucky? He pulled back so he could meet her gaze. He was *one* lucky bastard.

He knew the smile he gave her was gigantic. "You're the best, Lindsay. I'm so glad—and grateful— we had the chance to know each other again. I love you." He tightened his hand around hers. "And I know I'm the luckiest guy in the whole world because you love me too." He kissed her, hard, right there amongst the crowd.

"I love *you*," she answered, breathless, when their lips parted.

They stared at each other for another moment. Lindsay's mouth tilted in a soft smile. He answered her with his own smile.

The music ended, and as the last notes drifted away, the band swung into a faster tune.

"C'mon!" he said. He hadn't let go of her hand, but

he pulled her around and they were soon dancing to Earth, Wind and Fire's "September" as they speeded around the dance floor with some other couples.

They passed Pam and Evan, doing the same, and almost collided with another couple that Brian thought were Ben's brother and his fiancé.

The happy song spurred him on to dance quickly and easily with Lindsay.

Lindsay tilted her head and laughed up at him as she matched his steps around the floor.

She'd never been so happy!

Brian loved her. He *loved* her!

Knowing Brian loved her, and that she was in love with him, made Lindsay almost giddy with sheer joy. As they danced to the fast tune she felt as if she was a snowflake spinning in the wind—so carefree and beautiful. And she was surrounded by this man's love.

When the song finished, he pulled her close for a resounding kiss.

And they gazed at each other and smiled.

As one they turned and headed back to their table. She needed a few minutes to catch her breath, and knew he did too. When they sat, Lindsay and Brian both reached for their water glasses.

"ESP," she said, and laughed with the joy welling up inside her. "That was fun!"

After they both drank some water, he grinned and raised his champagne glass. "To us," he said in a low tone.

She took her own champagne flute. "To us," she repeated. His eyes were looking at her with so much emotion. She couldn't stop herself from giving him an adoring smile. She sat back, still breathing hard from the exhilaration of the dance—and Brian's declaration.

"You two look happy." Laura said in a low-pitched voice aimed solely at Lindsay. Her friend smiled as she handed around the breadbasket.

Lindsay nodded and smiled widely.

It seemed like her senses were heightened the entire evening. Being in love seemed to make the drinks, and the laughter, sparkle with extra gaiety, the music more poignant, and cause the food to taste even more scrumptious.

When she was served her Chilean Sea Bass she was too excited to eat much. She tried to, since it was delicious and so were the side dishes. But it was difficult to savor the food when she knew something so monumental: *Brian loves me!*

All around her, people at the table were chatting amicably, remarking on the music, the food, and the sumptuousness of the wedding.

"This is the experience of a lifetime," Priscilla observed. "What a party!"

Brian attacked his steak as if being in love had sharpened his appetite. "This is delicious. How's yours?"

"Great." She sampled the rice pilaf beside it. "Everything is terrific." *Including my life.*

He snatched up her hand and kissed it.

Lindsay leaned forward and kissed his cheek. When she sat back, she felt several pairs of eyes watching her, and she smiled. How many people at the table, she wondered, who had psychic powers of some kind had caught her emotions, or Brian's? She glanced around, her cheeks warming at the smiles she saw on Laura's and Priscilla's and Tanya's faces.

A little while after the main course was served, the

bandleader invited everyone up for a conga-line group dance, and Lindsay and Brian got up with most of their table. When the band swung into a Beatles oldie, a lot of the older adults got up and danced and sang with the musicians about seeing a girl standing across a room. Then they played a Rolling Stones favorite, and Lindsay and Brian got up again, dancing with the others who crowded the dance floor.

Then they played a quieter, romantic song, the old Elvis tune "I Can't Help Falling in Love with You" and Brian pulled Lindsay close. She loved nestling her head into his neck, feeling his body warmth encompassing her, his hand holding hers tightly. At one point he pulled back to gaze at her and mouthed "I love you" and she answered him the same way.

She felt like she was dancing on air. Every dream she'd ever imagined was coming true!

When Courtney did the bouquet toss, Lindsay positioned herself at the front. It was the first time she'd *ever* done this; deliberately trying to catch the flowers. She'd never had a strong desire to get married. Not since she and Brian had broken up long ago.

But now, being in love with Brian and knowing he cared, she felt open to that possibility.

The women surrounding her exclaimed and reached up when Courtney haphazardly tossed the small, throw-away bouquet. Sherry, Courtney's sister, caught it from among the grabbing arms and there were cries from some of the women.

When it came to the garter toss, there were less men in line, but one of Ben's friends caught it.

They did the traditional cutting of the cake and Lindsay got up with many others to snap photos.

After the photos, the master of ceremonies invited the guests to the room next door for the desserts.

"I've seen Viennese tables, but never a Viennese room full of desserts," Brian joked.

And there were so many to chose from! Lindsay spotted all kinds of cakes, cheesecakes and petit fours; fruit that was artfully arranged around an ice sculpture of two hearts; a waffle station with myriad sweet toppings; and a chocolate fountain with fruit, marshmallows and pretzels to dip in. There were also containers of popular candies and an ice cream bar with every kind of topping imaginable.

Brian went for a waffle covered in chocolate and sprinkles; and vanilla ice cream with a fudge and pretzel topping. Lindsay chose a waffle with whipped cream and strawberries, and chocolate ice cream plus a few petit fours.

They returned to their table and Brian went back to get them both drinks from among the lavish assortment at the bar. He returned with a whiskey for himself and Lindsay's favorite melon liqueur.

"They have top of the line liquor," he said. leaning forward to clink glasses with Lindsay again.

"To us," she echoed his words from before.

"To us." He beamed.

For a moment they just gazed at each other.

"I've never seen such a lavish desert display," Priscilla said, returning to their table with Rafael.

"Me either." Madison's eyes were wide. "My parents could never afford to give me a wedding this grand. Not," she added hastily, seeing her boyfriend's sideways look, "that I would want something this large."

"Well, Ben is a billionaire," Laura said, scooping up

some ice cream covered with a fudge sauce. "I prefer something more intimate myself." Her boyfriend nodded and took her hand in a possessive gesture.

When the people at their table were almost finished with their deserts, the band played a popular dance routine.

Their whole table rose.

As they followed directions for the dance—with the bride and groom at the very front—they turned to the right and Lindsay was looking at other dancers. Neal was actually dancing beside Alicia, and she wondered again what was going on with them.

Then they were sliding to the right, and doing cha-cha steps. Then they turned again and she was behind an older couple.

Once they'd moved to the right again she was facing a line including Brian and Felipe and a group of people whom she didn't know at all.

The dance continued for several minutes and she found herself laughing with the others. A few people stumbled during the steps—which were easy—and she guessed they'd had a little too much to drink. Most of the women who'd worn towering high heels had changed to the flip-flops which the deejay distributed.

At the end they were facing front again. Brian took her hand as she smiled up at him.

"That was fun," she said, squeezing his hand.

The band swung into the Beatles "Twist and Shout" and a huge crowd swarmed the dance floor. She and Brian looked at each other, and stayed there, as if reading each other's desire to join in. They sang and danced with the group, twisting and enthusiastically singing next to Meredith and Richard, Neal and Alicia. When it came to the part where everyone was singing and screaming

"Ah… ah… ah… ah…!" Lindsay yelled cheerfully at the top of her lungs with the all the others.

After that, she felt the need for a break. Brian looked at her and she was aware of his silent agreement. They linked hands as the crowd slowly made their way back to their various tables.

They sat, and polished off their desserts and some chocolates that had been placed on the tables, drinking their drinks and chatting with their tablemates while softer music played in the background..

"I remember 'Twist and Shout' from the Ferris Bueller movie," Rafael said. "It was one of my favorite movies growing up."

"It's a classic," Brian agreed.

"I loved it too," Tanya said. Her fiancé nodded.

Before they knew it, the reception was wrapping up and people began leaving. They had to be among those catching a bus back to the hotel, so Lindsay and Brian lined up to say goodbye and thank the bride and groom and their parents.

"Don't forget the breakfast tomorrow at the hotel," Courtney said as Lindsay hugged her.

"It was a fabulous day," Lindsay told her friend sincerely. "And of course we'll see you tomorrow morning.

She observed Brian handing Ben the envelope with their gift—which the wealthy couple didn't need, but they wanted to show their generosity.

She was happy but her feet were tired from all the dancing. Once on the bus, she slid off her heels and allowed herself to fully anticipate spending the night in Brian's arms.

It had been the most fun wedding ever. And the most eventful!

Brian smiled at her. "That was fun!" He slid his arm around her shoulders and he kissed the top of her hair..

We're in love. The thought made her ecstatic.

"I can't wait til we're alone," Brian whispered huskily in her ear.

The desire that had been simmering in her all evening flamed to life.

She shivered with pleasure. "Me too," she said for his ears alone.

There was singing and talking on the bus; and an older man with a jovial face who looked like a hippie offered to roll joints in his room in a loud voice, for anyone who wanted.

"Shhh, Marvin." His wife swatted him on the arm. "I told you to keep it quiet; we're not supposed to smoke in the rooms."

"Of course we'll smoke outside," the man said staunchly.

Someone in the front cheered.

Someone else was passing a flask of vodka around, while a few people sang in drunken voices.

"I've had enough to drink," Lindsay whispered in Brian's ear.

Once they arrived back at the hotel, Lindsay slid her shoes back on with effort.

Felipe and Manny headed to the bar along with a small group. "Anyone want to join us?" Manny called.

"I can't drink any more or I'll pass out!" Madison declared. "G'night everyone!" and she grabbed her date's arm and headed for the elevators.

Lindsay looked at Brian. As one, they shook their heads and turned to follow Madison and a few others.

Once they were on their floor and had said

goodnight to Priscilla and Rafael, they walked to their room. Lindsay felt a little buzz from the wedding drinks, not that she was drunk, just pleasantly floating, Delight encompassed her. Brian loved her!

Just outside their room, Brian paused and looked at her. She caught her breath at the smoldering, possessive look he gave her. He wanted her—and she was *his love*.

"Lindsay," he said, his voice so low she had to strain to hear it, "I've been dreaming about stripping that beautiful dress from your beautiful body. And making love to you."

Her breath hitched and she felt a hot wave of desire flow through her at his words. "Brian," she said shakily, "that's what I want too."

He opened the door and they stumbled inside. He groped for the light switch while she kicked off her heels. The desire and wanting for the man she loved kicked up as Brian pulled her into his arms. His kiss was hard and seared her to her toes.

He backed her towards the bed, where they stood for a moment while he kissed his way down her neck, her shoulder then pulled at her gown.

"Let me help you," she whispered. She turned so he could see the zipper.

He slowly slid it down, kissing her shoulder and back while he did so. The gown slid in a puddle at her feet.

"You are so gorgeous." His voice was low, his eyes hungry for her. For her alone.

A feeling of power surged through her. She tugged off his tie, then gripped his shoulders. "Make love to me, Brian."

He kissed her chest, while she pulled at his clothes too. Soon he was naked except for his boxers and he tumbled them onto the large bed. He kissed his way to one breast and suckled it through her lacy bra.

She moaned. She could have sworn she was a candle which had been ignited, fire lighting her up all over, melting her inside.

He switched to the other breast, tugging at her nipple. "Brian," she gasped as heat spiked through her. "I love that." Her insides tightened,

"I love you. Lindsay." His fingers shook as they unclasped her bra. Without the barrier, the pressure increased. She quivered at his strokes as his hand moved up her thigh.

"Brian—I love you—" the love inside her, mixed with passion, was so intense she'd never felt anything like it. Her insides tightened.

He was breathing hard. "You are so silky, so soft. And you make me so hot--I love making love to you, Lindsay."

"I love it too," she said. "I love *you*, Brian."

"And I love you." His hand covered her mound.

She could hardly catch her breath. "Please. Make love to me. Now."

"I want to feel you, I want to make you come, over and over—" he slid a finger inside her.

She bucked up, the orgasm hitting her immediately. "Brian!" she screamed, as wave after wave of bliss crashed over her.

"I love you." He kissed her.

She was drowning in pleasure, and she didn't care. There was only this moment, this man whom she loved, who loved her too.

"You're mine," he declared. "All mine."

"Yes."

Then he parted her legs, and with one strong thrust, he plunged into her.

Her body tightened around him, and without warning, she came again. "Oh God—Brian!" she exclaimed as the earth trembled around her.

"Lindsay!" His shout tore from him.

She lay back, completely satiated. "Oh my God…" she murmured.

He held her tightly and rolled them to the side. For a moment he didn't speak. Then he whispered, "My God, Lindsay, you are the most passionate, the most wonderful woman in the universe. I love everything about you. And I've never felt so wonderful." His eyes were closed but he wore a satisfied smile on his face.

They lay together, wrapped around each other, in the dim light from the entryway of their room. After a few minutes he kissed her, then went to get a damp washcloth to wipe them both.

"Lindsay, I'm the luckiest guy on Earth. You are perfect. And not just your body." He looked into her eyes and gripped her hand.

She smiled, love welling up in her. "And I'm the luckiest woman. I love you." She kissed him.

They snuggled together, and After a few minutes Lindsay murmured,, "This has been the best night of my life."

"I agree," he said, "completely. I'm so lucky we got together again." He held her close, kissing her cheek as he caressed her shoulder.

She touched his shoulders too, stroking his hard chest, kissing his nipple. She felt his member start to harden against her thigh as she touched him, whispering words of love.

"Lindsay," he groaned, and a shot of power went through, conscious of how much she was turning him on.

He slid his hand to her breast, playing with her nipple. She moaned in response.

"I want you again," he whispered.

She suddenly thrust him on his back and straddled him. "You can have me!"

His eyes had darkened in the dim light. She positioned herself so she came down on him just where she needed him so intensely.

She cried out again as the orgasm shook her. He gripped her hips and gave a final thrust, exclaiming "Lindsay!"

After a few minutes of her resting on his chest, he rolled them to the side, kissing her gently. "My God, I love you. I love everything about you."

"I feel the same." It was astonishing how much love welled up in her at his words.

They lay contentedly for while, too spent to get out of bed.

Lindsay felt herself drifting off. She'd never been so happy, so fulfilled…

* * *

Brian woke. He felt wonderful, absolutely wonderful. Lindsay appeared to be sleeping, and he didn't want to wake her. He stared at her beautiful face and body for a moment. She always turned him on so much. She was so caring and giving, so silky, so passionate. He started to grow hard again just looking at his gorgeous girlfriend.

And she was so kind, and thoughtful. How the hell had he gotten so lucky, to have her accept him into her life.

He carefully got out of bed so as not to wake her, padding over to turn off the light in the entryway,

He slowly made his way back to bed, being careful not to stumble into any furniture.

"Brian?" Her sleepy, sensual voice made his dick twitch.

"Right here, babe. I'm right here." He slid into bed and reached for her. His dick touched her satiny skin as he settled in beside her.

"Brian." She pressed against him, seeking his mouth, kissing him hard.

His dick hardened within seconds.

Their lovemaking was slower this time, but just as satisfying. When he slid into her it was like coming home, especially when she clenched around him and spasmed, crying his name. He came with a powerful shudder.

They lay quietly together and he found himself dozing off as she turned so her back was to his front. He held her, tender thoughts of spending all his time with her drifting through his mind.

Lindsay awoke slowly, sunshine peeping through a gap in the curtains. She felt wonderful, tangled up in Brian's arms. Complete.

And she wanted him again. That was almost unbelievable. How had she become such a passionate woman? It must be his touch. And the fact that they loved each other.

She turned to him. He opened his eyes and smiled as she twined her arms around him.

This time their lovemaking was fast and exciting, but no less fulfilling. They cried each other's names as they came at the same time.

Mindful of the breakfast brunch that awaited them downstairs, they took quick but separate showers, then joined the many friends and family members who had stayed at the large hotel.

Once their plates were overflowing with everything from custom omelets to bacon and croissants, fruit and pancakes, Lindsay found them seats with Alicia, Neal, Meredith and Richard. Sabrina and Parker joined them a minute later.

"You look especially happy," Meredith murmured in a low voice to Lindsay.

"I am." *I'm in love,* Lindsay exclaimed in her head.

Meredith's eyes widened as if she'd heard Lindsay's thoughts. She smiled.

"That was quite a wedding," Richard said.

"Yes, it was," Neal agreed, buttering a croissant.

"It was so much fun," Alicia put it.

They chatted and ate. *Food tastes better when you were in love. Everything seems amplified.*

"I'm going to gain weight from this weekend!" Sabrina declared, picking up a crispy strip of bacon.

The smell of maple syrup tweaked Lindsay's nose. She bit into her delicious pancakes, savoring them and nodding in agreement. "At least we danced off some of what we ate."

"That hora was fun!" Neal declared.

Before they knew it, they were stuffed, and finished eating. They said goodbye to the others. It was getting close to check-out time. They went to say goodbye to Courtney and Ben.

Linsday hugged Courtney and told her what a great time she'd had.

"I could see you and Brian were enjoying

yourselves," Courtney said, pitching her voice low. "I think you're going to recapture the happiness you shared in ancient Greece!"

"I hope so." Lindsay gave her friend an extra hug, then moved on to embrace Ben. "Everything was spectacular. We wish you the best of luck."

"Thanks, Lindsay. I'm sure we'll see you soon."

Brian hugged Courtney and she whispered something to him, then he shook hands with Ben and wished the couple "Mazel Tov."

As they went up to their room to pack and do a video check out, Lindsay asked "What did Courtney tell you?"

"She said," he told her, grinning, "that we were meant to be together."

"Oh." Lindsay smiled at him.

Half an hour later they were departing from the hotel. Ashish and Chetna were leaving at the same moment.

"See you tomorrow at TLC," he called.

"Nice to meet you!" They chorused to Chetna. Lindsay had liked her, and hoped Ashish continued to see her.

As Brian drove towards her apartment, they discussed some of the people they'd spent time with. "I really liked Chetna," Lindsay said. "She has a great sense of humor."

"Yes. And Priscilla's boyfriend Rafael is a smart guy," Brian added. "We were talking about structures. He's an electrical engineer, and when he found out I was an architect we realized we had a lot in common."

"Maybe we can get together for dinner sometime," Lindsay suggested.

"Yes, and I got to know Richard, Meredith's husband, better. I'd like to see them again too," he said.

Soft music by the Beatles played on the radio in the background. Brian glanced at her.

"I'd really like to take you to visit my parents," he said. "I want to let them know that we're involved. That I love you."

Was she ready to face his parents after all these years? Uncertainty wove through her. She hadn't run into them in ten years-- had been relieved by that fact. She had seen his brother once at a store, but they'd only said hello to each other, not stopped to converse. She wasn't sure how the Clarksons felt about her.

And then would she have to bring Brian to see Aunt Jane and Uncle Bill? Would they feel disapproval? Did it matter? She wanted them to know about Brian. To see how much he cared for her now that they were adults and had gotten involved again. How wonderful a man he was.

"I am sure," he replied. He grasped her left hand with his right one, then put his back on the steering well. "I love you, and I want my family to know that."

"I—" she stammered, and looked out her side window. The day was sunny and warm, not yet hot, but the air conditioner in Brian's jeep was going. She felt hot anyway, and she knew her face was flushing.

"I don't know if I'm ready to tell my family about—us," she admitted. Her voice quavered when she thought of her sister. Jessica would not approve. But was that important? *No.* She shook her head. She loved Brian. That was what mattered!

"Of course we should," she said declared. "I just was worried about my sister's reaction. Which I shouldn't worry about."

"Why your sister?"

"Jessica thinks—she thinks you'll break my heart again." Her voice dropped.

He slowed, glancing at her. "I won't, Lindsay. I love you. I'm sure of it."

Now she reached over and squeezed his hand. "I'm glad." The words were simple, but certain.

For the next half hour they spoke about the wedding.

Her thoughts, though, came barreling at her. This time Brian was certain he was in love. But fear cropped up. She wanted to trust him completely… but a part of her was afraid.

She knew she loved Brian. She probably had *always* loved Brian.

But trust was another issue. A tiny sliver of fear sneaked up inside her.

Once they arrived at her apartment, Brian carried her suitcase inside and up the stairs. Then he pulled her into his arms.

"I love you Lindsay," he said. "I mean it. I won't hurt you. I'm older, and wiser, this time. We belong together. Please believe me."

"I want to." She hugged him back. "But I was so— so hurt when we broke up ten years ago. It's difficult for me."

He tilted her face up. "I do love you, Linsday." He looked completely sincere. She wanted to believe his words.

He led her to the couch, where he pulled her onto his lap. "You mean the world to me," he said, hugging her.

They spent some time just cuddling on her couch. She loved being in his arms. "I could spend days like this," she admitted.

"I always want to hold you," he told her, hugging her close. "I hope you know that."

"I do," she said. At least, she hoped she did.

They spent the remaining hours of the day relaxing together, listening to music, looking into tickets for a concert they wanted to see, and ended up listening to a local band and eating pizza at a beer brewery in town

They made love again before Brian left, kissing her thoroughly and telling her how much he loved her. "I hope you believe me," he added.

"I love you too!" she declared, hugging him tightly. She did.

She sighed after he left. It had been the best weekend—the time she spent with Brian had been exciting and blissful; the wedding was lots of fun and romantic; and hearing Brian's words was music to her ears.

She ensconced herself more deeply into the cushions of her couch and grabbing a pillow, she hugged it.

She wanted to trust that Brian really, truly loved her.

She reached for her phone and clicked on Carolyn's name. At eight o'clock on a Sunday she was probably at home.

Lindsay was correct. Carolyn was home and had time to talk. Lindsay poured out the events of the weekend to her best friend.

"It sounds like he really does love you," Carolyn said. "As for trusting him again… I get how you feel, Lindsay. I would give him a chance. You love him too."

Lindsay sighed. "I guess you're right. I'll visit his family, but maybe hold off on his seeing mine."

When she went to sleep, she felt tired from the weekend's events but happy as she hugged her pillow. Brian loved her!

She kept that thought foremost in her mind.

CHAPTER XVII

Monday morning started with their usual meeting. Of course Courtney was absent—off on her honeymoon—but the rest of them were there, looking a little tired but happy. The positive vibes around the table were easy to sense, and most people wore smiles.

It was a quiet day. Parker had tried not to overload their schedules. But with schools getting out for the summer soon, they'd be dealing with more of their teenage patients scheduling tests and re-exams, Parker warned the group.

Lindsay went upstairs with Priscilla. "Have a good weekend?" she asked her friend.

"The best," Priscilla said. "I think—I think I may be falling for Rafael."

"Really? I thought he was a friend."

Priscilla's cheeks grew rosy. "I told myself that. But he treated me so well—and we had such a good time! And we started sleeping together on Friday."

"Was it good?"

"It was the best." Priscilla's face got even pinker. "He was—he was so considerate, and sexy…" She beamed. "He made me feel wonderful."

Lindsay smiled. "I'm really glad to hear that. Brian and I liked him."

Priscilla looked directly at her. "What's going on with you two?"

"I—" Lindsay paused. "We're in love," she admitted, her voice low. "But please keep that to yourself."

Priscilla's smile was broad. "I will. Oh, I'm so happy for you!"

"I want to proceed cautiously," Lindsay said. "Because of our history. So please keep it quiet," she repeated.

"I promise. And—" they had reached the upper floor and strode to their office area. "What the heck is going on with Alicia and Neal?" she whispered the question. "I noticed some hot looks between them."

"I did too," Lindsay whispered. "And neither of them brought a 'plus one' to the wedding." They walked into their office.

"Agreed," Priscilla said, and went to her cubicle.

Lindsay sat at hers and organized herself for her day. Her first client was coming in in ten minutes.

But her thoughts kept wandering to Brian, and their declarations of love, most of the day.

What was going to happen next? Would their love deepen? She recognized that she hoped it would.

* * *

The next two days passed quietly. Brian was going to come and stay over on Wednesday. Lindsay looked forward to that, but also couldn't help some concerns which sneaked in.. What would the future bring regarding their relationship?

She found herself becoming withdrawn, spending time on introspection. What was she going to do? Jessica was perturbed when Lindsay spoke to her on Monday night and told her what was going on.

"How can you trust him?" her sister fumed.

"I don't know," Lindsay had replied honestly. "I'm going with my gut feelings. I do love him."

She hesitated about telling her aunt and uncle about Brian. Maybe in a few weeks, when she saw how Brian's family reacted to her. Even her cousin Erica was someone she hesitated to speak to. She tried to get hold of Jade but got voicemail. Krista answered, but didn't have time to talk so she promised to call back. And her best friend from college wasn't around this week, away on a vacation.

She'd have to weigh the pros and cons of deepening her relationship with someone more objective. Although she knew she was already in deep waters.

It had been a perfect weekend, Brian thought as he drove to work.

Although he hadn't meant to reveal his feelings for Lindsay in the middle of the dance floor, Brian wasn't sorry. He'd gradually come to realize he felt more and more for her, and it had felt like he couldn't hold the words back any longer. He wanted to share his realization with her, hoping like crazy that she felt the same.

And she did!

He'd been walking on air since then.

She was perfect—kind and caring for others, thoughtful towards him, and smart. Not to mention she was gorgeous and the most passionate woman he'd ever made love to. And it was making love with her—not simply having sex. It was outstanding.

He felt that she touched his soul, made him feel like a superhero whenever they made love.

It was time he let his family and friends know.

His friend Jon was not surprised. "I always liked her, man," he said when Brian called him. "She was special. I'm glad she gave you another chance."

So was he. Immensely glad.

Then he reached out to his parents.

They were surprised. He hadn't even mentioned that he and Lindsay were seeing each other.

"Are you certain you're not just feeling sorry for her?" his mother, who could be cautious, asked.

"No. I never felt sorry for her, except when I heard her mother died," he said. "I liked her but I was too young to make any commitments and I felt stifled, boxed in."

"Of course you were," his mother declared.

"She was the nicest girl you ever dated," his father said. "I always hoped that maybe you'd meet up again when you were older and more mature."

"Do you want to bring her for dinner next weekend?" his mother asked.

"I'd like that. I'll ask Ryan if he can come with Jillian too. Then you'll all get a chance to see her."

After he got off the phone with them, he called his brother.

Ryan wasn't totally surprised, since Brian had told him a few weeks ago he was seeing Lindsay. What surprised him was that they were in love.

"About time Cupid's arrow hit you, bro," he said. "Well, good luck. It sounds serious."

"It absolutely is," Brian said firmly. "Can you and Jillian make it for dinner on Sunday at Mom and Dad's?"

"I'll check and see."

Once the plans were firmed up, he called Lindsay. She sounded a little hesitant on the phone.

"You're sure your family is okay with this?" she asked in a concerned tone.

"Absolutely."

He headed for Lindsay's on Wednesday, intent on reassuring her.

Lindsay was looking forward to seeing Brian—but she was on edge about his family seeing her again. As much as she knew she loved Brian, was she ready for the next steps? Did he even desire anything more at this point? She was trusting him with her heart. She prayed all would work out for them.

When he arrived just before dinner time, he swept her into his arms and hugged her tightly.

"Where do you want to go for dinner?" he asked eagerly.

"I thought we might eat in," she suggested.

"Perfect with me."

They ordered salads from an American restaurant, agreeing that they'd had so much food over the weekend that they wanted something simple and healthy. As they waited for their meals to arrive, they spent time sharing their workweek news and catching up. Once the food arrived and they ate and put away the leftovers for tomorrow's lunches, they sat on her couch, and he told her about a new project. She in turn described some of the research she and the team were doing.

They went to bed after watching a comedy show, and their love-making was so fulfilling, she felt peaceful.

As they lay entwined together afterward, he spoke. "I told my parents and brother that I was in love with you," he whispered, "and that you felt the same."

She sat up. "You did?"

"Yes," he murmured, stroking her shoulder. "I want them to know."

A cold knot formed in her stomach. "But—but—it's so soon to tell them." Her voice sounded weak to her own ears.

He shook his head. "No, it's not. I want the whole world to know." He pulled her closer. "I'm in love with the best woman around."

"I—" she didn't know what else to say, how to react to his positive words. The knot inside tightened. "It seems—too soon to tell either of our families how we feel. Our friends, yes. But our families—":

"It's not too soon for me." He hugged her. "They're eager to see you again. My dad even said he had hoped that someday we'd reunite."

She doubted if her family felt the same. She knew for a fact that her sister didn't.

"But—can we—trust each other?" Her voice quavered.

His mouth dropped open. "Of course. I trust you, Lindsay. Don't you trust me?"

"I'm afraid," she said honestly, sitting up. He still smelled of aftershave and sex. "Because…"

"Because of what?" His mouth tightened.

"Because of our past." Her voice dropped. "I studied enough psychology that I know I have a real fear based on what happened in the past. Rational or irrational, it's there."

"But that was in the past," he protested. "We were young. I was immature, I thought I needed space. And I resented being treated like a scientific experiment."

"You did. I realize that now. You were too young to be tied down to one woman."

"And I realize I wasn't there for you." He sat up too. "But I swear to you, Lindsay, that now things are different. Everyone has issues, and I have my own after Amber's rotten behavior. But they're not as big as your losses. I told you, and I mean it, that I would never, ever hurt you."

She looked down at his hand intertwined with hers.

"And I mean it." He tilted her head up so their eyes met.

She sighed. "And you didn't believe in my dream. And the other day—" she swallowed—"I told you about the workshop I was asked to present with Pam, and you hardly acknowledged it."

His eyes widened. "I guess because I was having a bad day that day. Frustrated with my work. But you're right, Lindsay. I should have been more considerate."

She nodded. But her throat clogged. "Yes," she whispered. "I wish you had acknowledged it more. It's— it's an honor to be asked by any of the bosses to help present a workshop at a major conference."

"You're right." He kissed her gently. "And I'm sorry."

After they cuddled more, then went to sleep, she stayed awake for a while, thinking about their conversation. Would Brian be more cognizant of her feelings in the future?

Brian lay quietly beside Lindsay. He was aware that she didn't go to sleep for a while, and simply held her.

He thought he had showed her completely how much he cared. How much she meant to him. He'd tried to tell her with his words, and by inviting her to see his family again, who were so open to the idea of them being together again.

But she appeared perturbed, as she had frowned and plucked at the comforter

Actions could speak louder than words, he thought, and pulled her closer.

After a little while Brian drifted off to sleep, holding Lindsay close to his heart.

Around midnight Lindsay awoke, something edging at the back of her mind.

Then she remembered. Brian wanted to re-introduce her to his family.

He was putting too much pressure on her, she decided. She pulled on her slinky robe and padded to the kitchen, pouring herself some milk. That was supposed to help people sleep, she knew. After drinking a half a glass, she crept back into the bedroom, intending to go back to sleep.

She was unsure of the future—their future. She knew from their past experience that feelings could change and they could be pulled apart. Look at her father!

And if that happened again her heart would be broken. Perhaps irreparably.

She gazed at Brian's beloved face in the dim light of the streetlamps that came through the mini-blinds.

Could she trust him? Trust him completely?

That thought kept her awake for a while.

CHAPTER XVIII

As Brian showered and dressed the next morning, he was aware that Lindsay appeared withdrawn. As if she was thinking deep thoughts. Maybe not positive ones.

After she had showered and dressed, he hugged her. "Please don't worry. You can count on me. *Always.*"

She smiled, but to him it looked doubtful. "I believe you, but… it's just…" she paused. "Between our past and my father—"

Bingo. Lindsay's past was making her distrustful. Especially her father's walking out on her sick mother.

"I love you," he emphasized. You can trust me."

They ate a quick breakfast of cold cereals and brewed coffee. She had bought his favorite cereal, cheerios.

When they parted to go to work, he hugged her tightly. "I'll call you tonight."

She unlocked her door and slid into her car.

She smiled. "Love you," she said. But he wondered if she truly did. She didn't trust him… hadn't he told her she could count on him?

"Love you too," he said firmly. But as she drove away, he worried that his words were not enough to convince her.

Could she believe him? Dare she trust him?

She didn't know the answers.

After she arrived at work, their meeting started a few minutes later.

As Parker went over the day's schedule and people gave brief reports on anything they hadn't shared the week before, her mind wandered a bit. She thought of Brian and their night together.

She raised her eyes after a few seconds to see Meredith staring at her. Her coworker frowned.

Had she caught some of Lindsay's confused thoughts?

His workday dragged. Brian had trouble paying attention to his usually absorbing work.

He knew it was because of Lindsay. The woman he loved was having trouble believing his declarations of love. He adored her, and yet she didn't believe in and or trust him.

It left him feeling troubled.

He had the impulse to visit her after work, but he knew Thursdays were late evenings for everyone at the Center. And with Courtney on her honeymoon, he imagined Lindsay and the others in her department would be swamped with work.

He picked up a meal on his way home but he wasn't that hungry. Afterwards, he sat in his home office and fooled around with some ideas for a new project his firm was working on. He was about to go downstairs and watch TV, when he saw something from the corner of his eye. Something shimmered.

He turned in his swivel chair and smelled a faint

perfume he didn't recognize. As he stared, a figure took shape and the scent became stronger.

Mrs. Hughes, Lindsay's mother, stood in front of him.

Her ghost gave him a soft smile.

Her mouth opened. He couldn't hear her actual words, but they sounded in his head.

"Don't hurt my daughter." She appeared sad despite her smile.

"I won't," he protested. "I love Lindsay. I would never hurt her."

She smiled again, broader this time. "Love has struck you both anew."

"Yes," he agreed.

"Please… take care of her…" She wavered, and he could sense her thoughts again. "My daughters mean everything to me… Lindsay cares so much for you, and she needs your love and care…"

"She has it," he confirmed. "I love her."

She smiled again, then disappeared with a strange popping noise.

He stared at the corner where she'd stood. It was his most vivid visitation by a spirit ever. He wondered if the strength of her emotions had made her visitation especially vivid.

He should tell Lindsay, he thought. Tomorrow, he would go see her.

And reassure her of the strength of his love.

He texted her: *Call me after work.*

He would tell her about her mother's ghost tomorrow. In the meantime, he could reassure her. He added *I love you.* to his text.

It wasn't even eight o'clock, so he knew she could

be with a client or another staff member, and unable to respond.

It wasn't until nearly nine thirty that he got her response. *I'm still at work, wrapping up. I'm exhausted. Let's speak tomorrow.*

A moment later she added *I love you too.*

He had to be satisfied with that. He'd see her tomorrow. At least on Fridays she got out early, and he did too.

The following morning, he was able to wrap up his work early. He had no meetings, so he headed out by eleven fifteen, calling goodbye to the few colleagues in the office today.

He got into his car, intending to go to Lindsay's apartment, his overnight bag already in the trunk. But an unexpected shimmer caught his eye, and beside him, on the seat, Mrs. Hughes materialized.

He almost jumped. He had never had a visitation in his car before!

She turned to regard him, her expression anxious.

"Go to Lindsay's office." He could hear her clearly in his head.

Then she disappeared.

That was all of the visitation. But he felt her urgency.

He started his car and headed out as fast as he could.

Just when Lindsay was packing up to leave, her phone buzzed. Jessica.

"Lindsay?" her sister began without preamble. Her voice sounded strained. "I'm in the back parking lot. Can you come out here and see me?"

Surprise infused Lindsay. Jessica had never simply

shown up unannounced before, especially at the building where Lindsay worked. "What's the matter, Jessica?"

"Come out here please so we can—talk. Alone." Her voice quivered.

Hairs stood up on the back of her neck and a cold wave shot up her spine. Come *alone*? Lindsay didn't like the sound of that.

"Okay," she replied. She disconnected, and her hands started trembling.

She tried to text Matt. *Something is wrong.* But her fingers were shaking too badly. She clicked to call him instead.

"Matt? Listen," she said the moment she picked up. "My sister's in the back parking lot. She sounds weird. She asked me to come out—alone."

"I'll be right behind you," he said at once. "I'm in the building. I had a bad feeling this morning—"

"Okay. I'm going out." She didn't have time to say more.

"Lindsay—"

Hopefully he'd realize something was very wrong.

She closed her eyes for a moment. Her first thoughts were of Brian. She needed him--his steadiness, his support. *There's trouble at TLC!*

Parker had mental telepathy. And he knew karate. She sent an urgent plea out to him too.

Something's wrong with my sister. She's outside.

Not wanting to delay further, Lindsay grabbed her purse and tote.

She rushed past Felipe down the hall and down the stairs. She heard someone coming from the downstairs corridor towards the back door.

Meredith grabbed Lindsay's tote, making her pause and glance back.

"Lindsay," she said, her voice low, "I'm with you."

"How did—" but there was no time to question her friend.

"I caught your thoughts," she said, and followed Lindsay to the door.

"I have to go out alone!" Lindsay cried, her voice also low, but strident.

Hot, dry air smacked Lindsay as she pulled the door open and stepped into sunshine. She spotted Jessica immediately, toward the back of the parking lot, beside her small black Toyota.

Norm Brown stood close beside her, his stance tense.

And not far from them, she spotted Brian's blue jeep. Brian? Had he come to the to see her? Had he been in the area, and caught her thoughts?

No time to think about that now. She faced Jessica and Norm.

Jessica looked like she was about to cry as Lindsay approached her.

Behind her she heard someone burst through the door. "Lindsay! I forgot to ask you something," Meredith called out, her voice innocent.

Lindsay glanced back. *Meredith's trying to distract Norm and Jessica.*

Lindsay kept moving forward, her footsteps slowing while she tried to assess the situation. *Matt should be here any second.* It looked like Norm was pressing his hand into Jessica's back.

Lindsay moved faster until she stood in front of them. From the corner of her eye she saw Brian emerge from his car. She tried not to look at him hopefully. *Maybe he can distract Norm.*

"What's going on?" She attempted to sound cool as she directed her question to Jessica and Norm. But she knew she wasn't quite managing a cool demeanor. Her hands still shook.

"I want you to come with Jessica and me," Norm demanded. "We're going to the bank."

"The bank? Why?" Lindsay asked. She heard Meredith's steps slow. Then she heard the back door open again. She hoped it was Matt.

Norm revealed what was in his hand—a small gun. "I have this. I already told you, I know your secret. Both your secrets. About Jessica."

Now Lindsay was really shaking. So was Jessica.

Jessica opened her mouth, and her words stumbled out. "Everyone—everyone—"

Lindsay heard the back door open again, and several sets of footsteps coming towards them.

This time she recognized Pam and Evan's low-pitched voices. They sounded like they were disagreeing about something.

"What?" Norm asked dismissively, focused on Jessica.

"Everyone knows about that little episode." Lindsay tried to make her voice derisive, stalling for time. Surely Matt would get here momentarily. She knew that most security people were permitted to carry concealed weapons.

She'd stall as long as possible.

"We're going to the bank," Norm insisted. "*Your* bank, Lindsay. I know you have more money than your sister. I'll send her in with you but I'll be right behind."

"I wouldn't do that if I were you," Brian called out. He had drawn closer to their trio.

Norm turned slightly, regarding Brian with a hard stare. "Who the fuck are you?"

"Brian Clarkson. Lindsay's boyfriend," he clarified "You can take me instead. I have more money than either of them." He inclined his head towards Lindsay and Jessica.

Brian was offering to take their place! Admiration overwhelmed Lindsay.

"No," she protested, "Brian, no, you don't have to do that!"

"Yes," he declared. He took a step nearer.

Footsteps drew closer behind her.

"Drop the gun." Matt stepped out from behind Lindsay, his own gun aimed steadily at Norm.

"No, I'm taking these two." Norm set his mouth in a hard line. "She told you to come alone!" Norm accused Lindsay. He held his gun against her sister's side.

Parker ran over from the side of the building.

"I did come alone," Lindsay said., "but everyone gets out at this time."

She could see Brian ease closer. At the same time, Parker stepped to Norm's side.

Brian suddenly lunged, grabbing Lindsay and Jessica hard, away from Norm. At the same moment, Parker reached out, getting Norm in a choke hold while pushing his gun arm up.

The gun went off, pointed at the sky.

"Duck!" Brian pulled Lindsay and Jessica to the ground now. Lindsay dropped her purse and covered her head with her arms instinctively.

She crouched there, her heart hammering, Brian's hand on her arm. His other was on Jessica's.

"Are you alright?" Pam asked near them.

"It's okay, everyone." Matt called. "You can get up now."

Lindsay glanced up. Brian still kneeled with his hands and body protecting her and her sister.

Nearby Matt had his gun jammed into Norm's chest while Parker gripped Norm.

Ow!" Norm yelled. "Let go!" He tried to pull away.

"No!" Matt commanded roughly, also restraining Norm.

Brian stood, taking Lindsay upwards with him. Jessica remained on the ground.

"Lindsay." Brian wrapped his arms around her.

From behind her, Evan and Richard—where did he come from?—joined Parker, who still had hold of Norm.

"Call the police," Matt barked.

Norm started swearing.

The fight appeared to drain from Norm. He went limp as Matt continued to press his gun against him. "I don't mind using this," Matt hissed.

"I'm calling 911!" Pam exclaimed.

"He doesn't want me to injure him," Matt said to the others. "You can let go."

The three men let go of Norm. As he continued calling Lindsay and Jessica vile names, Matt told him "Shut up!"

Norm put his hands up. "I was joking. Just putting them on!" he declared. "You didn't think I was serious, did you?" He directed that comment at Matt.

"Sure did."

"We all did." This from Meredith.

Brian held Lindsay close. "Are you alright?"

"Y-yes." She let him hug her so tightly she could barely breathe. "I—I saw you in your car when I came out of the building."

"I was here to tell you how much I love you and to beg you to believe me." He pulled back a little to look into her eyes. "And about a message I got from your Mom."

She stared at him.

"Please, Lindsay," he continued. "I never, ever want to let you go. Especially after witnessing this incident." He crushed her to him again. "I always want to be by your side. I'm never going away. You are the love of my life."

His words were loud enough for everyone to hear, and he sounded totally sincere.

Lindsay believed him. He loved her! Truly and forever! She took his face in her hands and kissed him, long and hard.

"I love you, Brian, and I'm not going anywhere either," she declared when she came up for air.

A cheer went up among her coworkers.

"Shit, what stupid fuckin' drama," Norm cursed..

"If you think this is stupid drama, wait til you see what happens when the police get here," Pam told him.

"I'm innocent! I told you, this was a joke," Norm yelled.

"Some joke," Evan said.

Matt's gun was trained on Norm as he pulled him further away from their group.

Neal had run out from the building. "I thought I heard a gunshot—" concern edged his face. He looked around and his mouth fell open.

"The police are on their way," Meredith told him.

Brian hugged Lindsay hard. She closed her eyes, savoring the moment. This is where she belonged--with Brian. And she trusted him to remain at her side. through thick and thin. Just as he had now.

He'd been willing to risk his own life for her!

"Brian!" She flung her arms around him and hugged him again. "I love you!"

Within five minutes three police cars had pulled into the parking lot. Everyone stood around and told the officers, one by one, what had happened.

When they got to Parker, he said, "I waited until this guy was distracted and then I used a a karate move." Sabrina had also joined them by then.

The police in town were well acquainted with the unusual abilities of TLC's staff and patients, from prior happenings at the Center; and the weird things that sometimes had happened here.

Lindsay and Jessica had told their stories first, but they waited until the police had questioned everyone.

"Okay, we got everyone's statements. We're taking him into custody," the senior officer, a man with graying hair, announced.

Two young-looking officers led Norm away. One was reciting his rights.

"No! It was a joke, I swear!" Norm protested again, as the officers got him into the car. "Well," Parker said, as Matt put his gun in a hidden holster, "Why don't we go inside?"

They trooped into the conference room, where Meredith passed out water bottles. Other staff members who were still in the building, hearing the commotion, joined them.

Lindsay leaned into Brian.

"What happened?" Alicia asked.

Lindsay started, telling the group what had occurred

from the moment of the call from her sister to the police's arrival.

"I was in the lobby," Matt said. "I had a bad feeling that something might happen here today, so I've been hanging around. I decided to approach from outside, until I could assess the danger."

"I got your telepathic message," Parker said simply. "And of course I told Sabrina. She offered to project to where you were, Lindsay, and see if she could be a distraction. But she didn't need to. Brian and Matt had it under control."

"I got your message, too," Meredith chimed in. "You did it, Lindsay! You improved your ESP! Parker and Pam and I 'heard' your cry for help!"

Lindsay looked around the room and saw happiness and admiration from her colleagues' expressions.

"I hoped it would work," she said. "I've never had to try that before." She grinned at them all.

"It did," Pam said. "I grabbed Evan and we pretended to argue as if we didn't know anything, hoping to distract him."

"And I caught *Meredith's* thoughts," Richard said, "and came out to see what I could do."

"And that's—what---what happened," Jessica spoke for the first time. Her voice still shook. "I'm so sorry, Lindsay, and everyone." She glanced around. "For having to--to bring him here. He had the gun, and forced me, and I put you—" she looked at Lindsay—"and everyone else in danger."

They all clamored, trying to ease the guilt they recognized in her expression.

"It wasn't your fault," Parker said. "It was Norm's."

"Don't blame yourself," Pam reiterated.

"Sounds like he kidnapped you," Neal finished.

Jessica nodded. "Yes. Yes he did."

"But it turned out alright," Brian concluded, hugging Lindsay again as he sat beside her. There was a collective sigh.

"I think we should all go out for a drink," Priscilla suggested.

"Absolutely," Meredith agreed.

"Yes, let's," several people added.

Lindsay let Brian lead her outside.

"Let's go in my car. I never want to let you out of my sight again," he said.

Once inside, he briefly told her about the visitation from her mother, on top of his strong urge to see her.

"And as I pulled into the parking lot, I heard you calling out to me as well," he finished.

They had lunch and drinks at a local place. Even Jessica came along. Lindsay indulged in a Midori on the rocks, and Brian, like most of the other guys, had beer. They ordered sandwiches or burgers, and shared appetizers.

There were several toasts to coming through the harrowing incident, including one Meredith proposed to Lindsay.

"…who persevered with hours of practicing until her ESP skills improved," Meredith announced, holding her Chardonnay high. "Brian, Parker, Pam and I are proof that she sent out thoughts and we received them. Congrats on your success, Lindsay."

"Courtney will be sad she missed this excitement," Tanya observed.

"We'll have quite a story to tell her," Madison added.

Lindsay felt her cheeks blush. "Thank you," she said. "I owe my improvement to everyone's encouragement."

Brian squeezed her shoulders. "I'm proud of you."

Since he would be driving, she had a second glass of liquor instead of coffee with the desserts which were shared.

When everyone dispersed, she stumbled a little on the way to Brian's car, although her shoes were low.

He guided her and opened the door for her.

"We have to pick up my car," she said as he slid into the driver's seat.

"We'll get it tomorrow," he said. "The police know it's there and Matt's company does surveillance. You're not used to drinking in the middle of the day like this."

She relaxed in her seat, and within a few minutes they arrived at her apartment.

"I'm happy about seeing your family," she murmured.

He faced her. "It's alright, Linds. We can wait until you're one hundred percent ready if you prefer."

"After today, I know I'm ready," she said, and opened her car door.

He got out, grabbed the duffle from his trunk, and zipped around to take her hand and lead her to her apartment. Once inside, she sighed and led the way up the stairs, plopping down on her couch and leaning back.

"I'm so glad you were there today."

"I meant every word I said," he said, sitting beside her. Grabbing her hand, he shifted closer. "I love you, Lindsay Hughes, and want everyone to know it. I'm not going anywhere. I'm in for the long haul."

"The long…" her voice drifted off.

Brian brought her hands to his lips. "The long haul," he repeated firmly. "I didn't expect to do this today, I wanted to do this over a romantic dinner, but—I can't wait any longer to ask. Will you marry me, Lindsay?"

"Yes, oh yes!"

He scooped her up and whirled her around. "I love you!"

"I love you!"

They kissed, and neither said another word. Instead they showed each other their love.

EPILOGUE

They had their romantic dinner a week later. But this time, when Brian proposed again, he slid a blue satin box out of his pocket. He'd questioned her last weekend, and learned what kind of ring she would prefer.

She gasped at the marquis-shaped diamond he placed on her finger.

"Brian. It's gorgeous!" She held up her hand to admire the sparkling gem.

Several tables around them clapped, and a waiter brought over a bottle of champagne.

"I'm so happy we had the chance to find each other again. And that this time I finally discovered that you are my soulmate. I love you, Lindsay."

"I know how you must have felt when you were struck by lightning," she said in a hushed tone, lifting her eyes from the brilliant diamond ring to meet his loving gaze. "Because love struck me anew when I met you again. I love you, Brian."

They leaned towards each other and kissed, basking in the glow of their renewed love.

THE END

ABOUT THE AUTHOR

Roni Paitchel Denholtz has been writing and publishing for over 40 years. Her short stories, articles and poems have been published in national and regional magazines such as True Romance, Child Life, Modern Romance, For the Bride and Baby Talk. She is the author of nine children's books published by JANUARY PRODUCTIONS, an educational publisher. Her book "Jenny Gets Glasses" was named to the Favorites of First Graders list by the Reading is Fundamental group, which was spearheaded by the late Barbara Bush.

She has published 25 romance novels, beginning with "Lights of Love," published by Avalon Books. Her romance novels have been nominated, and won, many prestigious fiction awards, such as the NJ Golden Leaf award and the National Readers' Choice awards. She is especially known for the award-winning LIGHTNING STRIKES series, a paranormal series with characters who have ESP and other psychic abilities.

In her "everyday life" she was a special eduction teacher in Dover, NJ teaching reading and math to children with learning disabilities and other handicaps while earning her M. A. and writing on the side. She then became a realtor and wrote part time. She has also done volunteer work in PTA, Marching Band parents and

Robotics parents, plus she served on the board of her local animal shelter for 8 years, helping to save and rehome dogs, cats and even guinea pigs. She also taught "Writing for Fun and Profit" in her local adult school and many of her students have gone on to publish articles, poems and books.

Roni and her husband and their dog make their home in beautiful northwest New Jersey. Their daughter and son are grown and married, and she is now a proud grandmother.

You can find Roni often on Facebook, under Roni Denholtz, Author Roni Denholtz and The Lightning Strikes series. She is also on Instagram.

Please visit her webpage at www.ronidenholtz.com and sign up for her newsletter!

BOOKS BY RONI DENHOLTZ

The Lightning Strikes Series
Lightning Strikes
Lightning Strikes Again
Lightning Strikes Twice
Lightning Strikes the Billionaire
Lighting Strikes Anew

Historicals
Marquis in a Minute
One of These Nights
One of These Wylder Nights

"Sweet" Contemporaries
Lights of Love
Somebody to Love
Negotiating Love
Salsa with Mc
A Taste of Romance
Setting the Stage for Love
Room for Love
Forecast for Love
Contemporary Romances
Borrowing the Bride

Contemporary Romance Novellas
Stuck in the Saddle with You
Those Canyon Nights
Return to Forever
Eight Nights to Win Her Heart
Enchanted Vermont Nights
Meet Me at the Inn
Eight Nights of Apricot Cookies
Chocolate Caramel Dreams

www.ingramcontent.com/pod-product-compliance
Lightning Source LLC
Chambersburg PA
CBHW060435310726
48977CB00001B/192